When Edith instigates a new _____
May and Peter, on a warm spring day in 1869, she ignites
sexual awakenings that will influence and shape the rest of
their lives.

Although Edith lusts for Peter, she is aware that May's
desires are directed toward her, and when their triangular
involvement begins to splinter, she leaves her two best
friends to begin a career in Boston.

However, even after choosing what they thought was the
more stable path, they learn that the past is not so easily left
behind.

On their separate, yet connected paths, they find themselves
drawn together, experiencing eroticism, love, confusion,
trust, and grief throughout the course of their lives.

MEMOIRS OF A TRIANGLE

Christine Twigg

A NineStar Press Publication

Published by NineStar Press
P.O. Box 91792,
Albuquerque, New Mexico, 87199 USA.
www.ninestarpress.com

Memoirs of a Triangle

Printed in the USA
First Edition
February, 2019

Print ISBN: 978-1-949909-99-9

Also available in eBook, ISBN: 978-1-949909-94-4

Warning: This book contains sexual content that is only suitable for mature readers, scenes containing infideltity and characters undergoing hypnotherapy, and the death of a main character.

Book One

Chapter One

BOSTON, 1942

Seated in Ella's suite at the Statler Hotel, Jeremy Harris looked at the yellowed papers Ella had put in his hand. A few moments later, he was leaning forward in his chair, completely absorbed. After several minutes, he set the pages down and looked at Ella questioningly.

"Is this what it appears to be?" he asked.

Ella nodded, sliding the remainder of the aged and stained papers over to him.

"I had a phone call from a Mr. Thomas Benson last week. He recently purchased Edie's Fine and Rare Books, my mother's old bookstore?" She paused, looking at him with raised brows to make sure he was following, and then continued, "Mother sold the business to her apprentice long ago, but apparently she retained ownership of the building. The last owner died, and it's been untouched until now. Most of the inventory had been removed, but my mother's office was exactly as it was when she was there. It was like a trip back in time, Jeremy," she almost whispered.

"Mr. Benson tracked me down as the only person with rights to the contents. I came down the day after the call and I've been there all weekend. I found this file in the bottom of a drawer in my mom's old desk. I almost threw it on the pile of trash, but something made me stop and read that first page..."

"I remember the bookstore," Jeremy said wistfully, feeling the tug of something long forgotten. Aunt Edie, as he'd always known her, had taken him and Ella there many times when they were young children. "Just thinking of it now, I can remember the way it smelled: dusty and warm like all those old books, mingled with the scent of beeswax she used to polish the shelves."

He looked into the past as he remembered the pile of large, worn cushions that sat on the floor near the front of the store. He smelled the warmth of books heated by the trapped sun and heard the ping of flies hitting the front windowpane. His eyes began to close as he heard the echo of the soft flutter of turning pages.

Ella had found a rough manuscript, written by her mother, Edith, with a prologue written by May, the woman who had given birth to Jeremy. Never really knowing what to call her, he had simply continued to think of her as Princess Maybelline.

The manuscript appeared to be the beginning chapters of a book about the somewhat shocking love affair Edith had had with Jeremy's parents when they were in their late teens.

Ella had also found a package Jeremy's mother, Eve, had sent to Edith after May died, containing May's journals, a beautiful emerald pendant, and a few small paintings. She pulled two paintings out of a large, dog-eared envelope and gently nudged Jeremy with her bare foot, rousing him somewhat from his pleasant reverie. She used the same foot to slide a box over next to his chair.

Jeremy took the paintings in his hands, studying them. Tentatively, he ran his forefinger across the grooves of colorful, thick, oil paint. Tears began forming in his eyes, causing the colors to blur even more abstractedly. This was his real mother, the woman he'd heard fairy tales about as a small boy, come to life. He saw the worn journals, stacked neatly in the bottom of the box, and he felt the pull of a history that had shadowed him his whole life.

Ella saw he was overcome. She leaned in and put her hand on his shoulder and said, "Oh Jeremy... I'm sorry... She seems to have been a special woman."

He picked up the pages again and continued to read...

MEMOIRS OF A TRIANGLE, BY EDITH TATE

The misty lever, or the incandescent shadow. The goon or the gown; the holy trapdoor. These words came to me as I lay in a state between sleep and awake. These phrases ran, on repeat, before I stopped to look at them. What do they mean? What is their significance? The misty lever pulls open the space to the hinter world. It opens the stage to that beautiful scene of open moors, of vast spaces, of memories from another life. In this place, shadows and omens are shining beacons, messages. Word play, swordplay, words/sword, the knife edge of meaning, the third eye illusion. What is that optical nerve serving the third eye? What is the channel from here to there? The holy trapdoor to the soul. Parallel lines, lives. Strips of stripes. Whispering echoes. Driving down the gangplank. Entering the soulstice. Itching the bookends. Petting the lovers. Are you mad, or are you angry? Check the pulse of your shadow. Whatever enters is downcast. Whatever brings light is sublime. We each run our own shows. We shadow-cast the boxers. Redemption is mute. Righteousness is deadly. Withering decay sinks into fertile soil only to rise as fire for the gut. The alleys are shining as the moon writes its story in their name. The drunk man chokes on his own sputum, his own carriage, his own. Where is the lonely goose who cooks his own plate? These are the flowing talisman. These are the carved hillsides on the horizon. Opening the door and letting the shining light flood in. Taking a bath in the heat of reds and oranges. The strangeness of slippery colors. The pleasant surprise of bright equations.

May Copeland Harris, 1872

ONE—MISTY LEVERS

Running down the drive, hair rippling in her own self-made wind, she runs with joy, creating eddies and turbulence that will change everything. Change being the masterful block of illusion. The year is 1869. The girl is Edith and alongside is her best friend, May. Giggling lovers, they sprint with abandon for the sheer joy of it all. They are drunk on spring air and the newness of tasting the palette of green once again. With the breath of onions shouting their right to dash through space at top speed, and with leeks tucked in their pockets, they fly down the curving pebble drive, racing.

There is a father in this story, but he may just be Father Time. Fathers are teachers of lessons, and time is surely a masterful instructor. Is there a gift time hasn't given, or a need the sands have not carried?

Looking back, through the eyes of centuries hence, it would be easy to describe this scene through a black-and-white lens, but, oh reader, that would be so false, so inaccurate. Edith and May are luminescent with the peaches of youth. Their cheeks are dewy and their eyes are shining with the blues and aquamarines of the sky. These girls are happy, and they wear their happiness inside their perfectly fitting skin. We might think of these girls as old-fashioned, with their long dresses and their antique names, but to them, they were new-fashioned girls and the world was sparkling with possibilities and excitements! We can love these girls and they can love us back. They are our sisters for we share the same father.

Edith ran all the way to the dip in the road, the dip where she'd fallen last spring, in her haste to catch up to Toby, her big brother, and badly twisted her ankle. She'd had to spend two weeks eating frustration while everyone else ate from freedom. Two whole extra weeks of being tethered to the house were enough to make her wary of the hazard. When she slowed her pace, May passed her, laughing, because every good friend knows what's sticking in her friend's veins, but also knows how to unstick it. In this case, laughter and anticipation allowed the blood to fly through Edith's veins again and she picked up her pace. They wouldn't be late. They had a date with fate.

Or at least they had a date with Peter. Peter was the boy they had a mutual crush on and he was so deserving of their every other thought. In truth, for the past week, it was more than half her thoughts Edith spent on Peter. Since she'd seen him washing in the creek on the other side of the woods, Peter was almost all she could think about. She'd spent hours trying to describe every detail of his strange beauty to May, partly because she felt it was only fair to share, but also because she didn't care to think or talk about much else.

They were meeting Peter, or "that Harris boy" as May's mother always called him, for a walk and picnic up on The Meadows. None of the three thought it odd for two girls and only one boy to spend their free afternoon together; they'd done it often enough in the past. They were friends, the sort who grow up together and have an easiness about them. If this spring brought new, edgier feelings for the girls, it only seems natural. They were growing into young women, slowly, with all the sexual flutterings which accompany that age. Naturally, Peter was rowing right along beside them on the river of awakening.

The day was clear and the winds weren't too strong as the threesome made their way into the interiors of The Meadows. The Meadows was a good-sized park on the east edge of town, just over the bridge and past the churchyard. It had a pond and a path and a small wood. Edith, May, and Peter occasionally swam in the pond when the weather was warmest in late summer, but today they were headed to the woods to look for spring flowers and then to the small patch of open space in the woods they'd found as children, where the sun could shine and they would be protected from the breezes. This is where they would lay Peter's blanket for the picnic.

Today, when Edith thought of the spread blanket, her breathing got heavier and she felt a heat between her legs. Later, when Peter would tell a story about his younger sister being missing for two hours, she could only fake her sympathy, lost in her consumption of thoughts about the blanket and Peter and his nearness.

May had hooked arms with Peter and was telling him a story about her mother's butter and bad cream, when Edith had the thought that she would like to be alone with Peter. A strong thought that grew into a strong feeling and then a strong desire. What is a better seed for a plan than desire?

Edith ran through several scenarios in her mind, looking for a way to have Peter to herself, but none provided the outcome she so fiercely desired. So, her mind made the only switch it could. Today's reader may think it is only today's youth who have need for instant gratification, but they would be wrong. The awakening of the carnal has always been accompanied by urgency. It would have to involve the three. The blanket was large enough, and her love for her friends strong enough, to contain the three.

That afternoon no flowers were picked and food wasn't eaten until almost suppertime. Do you remember the feel of wool on damp skin? The smell of new grasses when they are crushed? Can you remember how beauty feels under your fingertips? Mustiness and sweat and the sound of jagged breathing.

These were the background for Edith, May, and Peter, and certainly not what they would think about as they lay alone in their own beds that night, and many after, but they are the very things that decades hence would bring rushing back, unexpectedly, the intense heat of that afternoon. As a father's strongly worded caution about certain dangers comes, unbidden, and so timely, in the face of that danger, so are the visceral memories of youth and lust brought to us, unbidden but so needed, through the cascading years of adulthood by a faint scent in the air, or a melody on the radio, or the glimpse of an incandescent shadow. The misty lever is cranked, and we fall through the holy trapdoor into wonder.

TWO—SHORES OF ENLIGHTENMENT

Peter laid the picnic blanket in the clear spot where the new grass was soft. The sun was shining and aside from a few lazy clouds, the sky was a rich blue. The blanket was an old wool plaid that his mother had discarded to the barn because of some burn holes from the stove. The spot he picked was close to the base of a large elm whose new leaves were a nice contrast to the blue of the sky. Not that Peter noticed, or it played any part in his choosing of the spot. He had simply laid it where he stood. Later, though, he would remember the lacy pattern and favor elm trees over all other trees, even if he couldn't tell you why.

He sat and removed his shoes for the refreshing air. Soon his feet would be calloused enough that he wouldn't need to wear shoes, even on the rocky paths around the garden, but this early on they were pale and soft with winter's recent passing.

While he sat there, he looked at the girls. Edith seemed intent on something behind him and May smiled a new sort of smile at him. On their walk out to The Meadows, he'd been aware of their easy chatter hadn't seemed quite as easy as last fall.

He'd hardly had a chance to see either of his friends over the winter with them living out of town and his chores at the shop. Both girls looked different, in a very pleasing way. He found himself stealing glances at May and receiving shy smiles from Edith. This was interesting to him because he had grown used to looking at certain young women who came into the shop with a young man's appreciation, even thinking about a few of them at night in his bed, but he had never looked at May or Edith with such eyes. They had been playmates, pals, friends, for most of their lives.

They were meant to be picking early flowers, but it seemed there were new plans. The girls stood near to him as he sat on the blanket.

"Come on, I have a game we can play." Edith sat next to him. She couldn't look at him as she said, "Lay on your back, Peter, and close your eyes." She swallowed loudly, trying to find some saliva to coat her dry throat. Let me look at you, let me touch you.

When Peter lay, unsuspecting, on the blanket, Edith said, with a quick glance at May, "May and I will take turns touching you very gently, or not, and you will have to tell us when you think we actually are." Her heart was pounding, but she continued, "We'll try to touch you so lightly you won't be able to feel it."

May's eyes were wide, but a small laugh escaped from her mouth. She dropped to her knees, landing next to Edith and biting her lower lip to control the nervous tremor threatening to erupt.

Peter opened his eyes and looked, questioningly, at both girls. They were up to something, he could tell. They appeared far too nervous for simple, childish games. But when they only returned his gaze, trying for innocence, he laid his head back and closed his eyes. The sun felt good and he smelled the food from the basket.

"Just relax for a minute, Peter, and then I'll take the first turn," Edith said. Her heart was wild. She tried to relax, but the thought of touching his temple was making her all shaky.

She swallowed again. "Okay, I'll start now. Tell me if you can feel me touching you. It could be anywhere," she added. Oh, dear God, it could be anywhere!

May watched Edith, also knowing this was more than an innocent game. She saw heat rolling off Edith, she sensed her fear and lust, although she didn't have a name for it. She closed her eyes because it felt private, what was happening, and when she did, the heat rolled in around her. She heard Peter say, "I feel you touching my hair," and laugh as he said, "Now my left arm." When he said, "My stomach," his voice had changed; it sounded tight.

The heat was lapping at her, and May's cheeks burned. She opened her eyes and looked up into the branches of the tree, trying to suck in some cool air.

She startled when Peter said, "Okay, now it's May's turn." Edith drew her hand back and sucked her fingers absentmindedly while she shifted over so May could get closer to Peter.

He opened his eyes for a moment and noticed May's flush which made his voice catch when he said, "I'm ready, May."

May took Edith's hand in her right hand, for support, while she reached out timidly with her left. With steady fingers she first touched Peter's left cheek, then his left thumb. Even with her light touch, the hardness of his muscles through his shirt was apparent when she touched his shoulder and then his inner knee.

When he didn't say anything, she said, "Peter, you have to say when you feel me."

"I will," he replied and then let out a breath he must have been holding. Suddenly, he flipped onto his stomach and said briskly, "Okay, now you two, it's your turn."

The girls lay side by side on the blanket with their eyes closed. The backs of their hands were lightly touching in the middle. Peter kneeled between them, relieved to have his hardness hidden in the bunches of his trousers. Each girl had on a softly worn blue dress, but May's was a darker blue with green ribbon for trim and Edith's was pale with yellow satin. They had removed their shoes and stockings at his suggestion that the sun was so warm and the grass soft. Looking down on them, with their eyes closed, he experienced new feelings of protectiveness and possession. Edith's hair was a warm brown and May's a few shades darker. Both had pale, winter skin, currently flushed, and their chests rose with their breath. He had to sit on his hands to calm them.

"Ready," said Edith as May swallowed.

Peter reached out to the girl on his left, May. He wasn't sure where was okay to touch, and where was not. He sensed he would be able to do things today, things he wouldn't dare do normally. He settled on her left instep and had to shift again when she made a quick intake of breath and said she could feel him. Edith lay, not patiently, waiting for his touch. To distract himself, Peter turned to Edith and very lightly touched her forearm. She lay still and didn't say anything. So he touched her gently on her outer thigh and allowed his fingers to linger there, something he desperately wanted to do to May. He moved again when Edith didn't respond but deepened her flush.

All three thrilled to the danger of this game. Each, in turn, pushed the limit just a tiny bit further. They mutually sensed a silent agreement to continue.

"My lips are quite soft. See if you can feel them."

'Take off your shirt, Peter, and we can try your shoulders." Peter pushed up skirts to expose strong, lovely calves and then thighs. The lightest of touches grew coarser. The boundaries of three bodies became tangled with exploration and friction.

If you were there, and if you have eyes for heat, you would have seen waves crashing on the shore of enlightenment.

JEREMY FELT THE heat, but he suspected it was the embarrassment of having to read about their parents, enjoying a ménage à trois, and knowing Ella had already read it. He couldn't help but remember their own sexual awakenings, so many years ago.

He cleared his throat.

"Should we order some lunch? Maybe a drink too? A strong whiskey right now would be helpful," he said, taking off his suit coat since it had suddenly become too warm in the room.

Ella gave him a knowing smile. "Don't worry, you've gotten through the worst of it," she said encouragingly.

Jeremy raised his eyebrows, as though asking for reassurance, and then took a deep breath, as if he was preparing to jump off a diving board, picked up the next chapter, and began to read. Ella ordered them some sandwiches and asked for a bottle of scotch to be sent up.

THREE—EDITH

We are all good at seeing what we want to see. It is true that each of our worlds, large or small, revolve around our own person. Edith was a young woman who soaked up experiences, and as she did her world grew larger. As a child, she was the center of a small circle, which grew larger with each passing year. If she were to count the major events to date that lengthened her radius (which she saw in her mind as a sweeping beacon of light, like one emitting from a lighthouse), they would be: meeting May and Peter, always trying to keep up with Toby and his extra five years, realizing death could fracture that which had seemed so solid, learning about love with the two people she loved most, and reading.

May's father had a library full of shelves and shelves of the most extraordinary books. Edith's mother wasn't a small-minded woman, but she would have been shocked by some of the books Edith smuggled to May's room to ingest. May wasn't much of a reader herself, but she enjoyed listening to Edith's commentary on books like A Vindication of the Rights of Woman, or Robinson Crusoe, or, May's favorite, the poetry in Songs of Innocence and Experience. May was often put into a trance, or at least that's what Edith called it, by listening to her soothing voice read aloud. Many afternoons were spent in this way. Edith could literally feel her world expanding and, with it, her lusty desire to live.

So, when her circle had become a triangle, her world had profoundly shifted on its axis. Suddenly there were angles, sharp corners, an edginess to life! It was very exciting, and she explored this new world with the heart of an adventurer. She reveled in her body and the bodies of her friends. She thrilled to the hard peaks of lust and wanting. Edith wasn't one to hold back; she was a girl with a passionate zest for living.

For a while, she had been able to believe they were a perfect triangle. Occasionally it had even been she and Peter who seemed to be the best-matched couple. May had times of keeping to herself, finding reasons to not join them, so that Edith believed Peter was hers. She still believed if Peter had only been fond enough of her, May would have easily conceded him. But Peter was fond of May. She could see it in the ways he favored her; the way he asked her thoughts and opinions, the way he remembered her favorite foods, always, and the way he spoke so often about her even when she wasn't there. It wasn't that Peter didn't treat Edith well; in fact, he seemed most grateful to her. But it wasn't his gratitude she wanted.

The Triangle Inequality Theorem states that the longest side of a triangle must be less than the sum of the other two sides. At some point, Edith began to feel like the long side. She was wonderful in many ways, and she knew her worth, but to her great disappointment, in Peter's eyes, she just didn't add up to the wonderfulness of May and Peter together.

None of them had felt any sort of awkwardness or embarrassment about their affair until it became too obvious to ignore that Peter favored May. They had all tried to pretend it wasn't so, but eventually, they just stopped meeting together.

After a brief spell of despair, when Edith thought Peter and May were secretly meeting without her, she had been relieved to be invited out with Peter. They had headed out, walking toward The Meadows, but Peter had stopped at a bench and sat. He wanted to know if Edith knew why May was refusing his offers.

That is when the embarrassment began. After they had washed off the wet smells of wool and skin and desire; after her need had been quelled, Edith saw she was the second game. And even though her feelings for Peter hadn't diminished, she was too proud to continue. She convinced May she should walk out publicly with Peter while arranging for her to meet him alone in the woods. Edith became the willing accomplice for their secret rendezvous. This decision made her blind to May's own happiness. Only years later, when her feelings and experiences had grown to involve a much bigger world, had she been able to look back and see that Peter was not May's choice, but rather

May's firm decision. The sum of their togetherness was something else altogether. It was a safety net for May.

That is why, when her side of the triangle had fallen away, she spent several weeks feeling lost, tormented, and untethered. She swallowed envy daily, until it began to make her ill, and then she left envy to dry up in a puddle at her feet and swept the dust away with one whisk. Edith became their greatest champion, and with May's help, she realized her beacon had only grown brighter and longer than ever, and it was not so very hard to open again to the fluid and curving allowances of experience. She became, again, the center of a growing world, and with her passions lit and burning brightly, she could see even further into the seas around her.

FOUR—PETER

Peter had known Edith and May since they were little children. He couldn't remember not knowing Edith. When they were around seven, Edith had come to Peter's house for tea, with her mother, and had brought May with her. From that day on, he never saw Edith without May.

When they were ten years old, they'd built a secret fort in the woods behind Edith's house. They'd play house there and Edith would fight with him over who got to be the father. May was happy to be the wife or the child, but Edith wanted to be the boss. She would say, "Fine, I'll be the wife, but the wife gets to be the boss," and then they'd argue about who got to "go to work" until May would gently steer them into another game.

But Edith was fun. She was charged with ideas and energy and always quick to laugh and poke fun at herself and both the others. May was quieter, and he always felt more sure of himself with her. She didn't provoke him or stir up feelings of pride or doubt.

Peter's father owned a cloth shop in town. It was a successful business and he'd been helping out there since he was quite young. When they were little, he would bring leftover scraps to the girls to make dresses for their dollies or ribbons for their hair. He always gave May the green ones because he thought she looked very pretty in green. One Christmas, the girls had come calling and presented him with a gift they'd made. It was a quilt they had pieced together from the best bits he'd given them all year. It was only big enough to cover his legs, but he still kept it on the end of his bed.

As they'd grown older, they didn't see as much of each other because they all had more responsibilities, and he enjoyed chumming around with his other friends, fishing and trapping and building things. Peter was quite handy with tools. When he was twelve, he built his mother an intricate sewing box with moving parts and individual compartments for all her different pins, needles, buttons, and other miscellaneous bits and bobs, topped with a beautifully carved wooden lid. She had proudly placed it on the counter in the shop where customers could admire it, and he quickly began getting orders for similar boxes.

It had turned into a profitable and enjoyable side business that now included tables, chairs, jewelry boxes and specialty orders. With the money he made, he'd been able to purchase a set of quality tools and his father had helped him build a workshop on the north side of their store.

Peter also loved gardening. He'd put in a small garden next to his workshop and had begun to sell his produce along with his other goods. Sometimes May and Edith would come in to admire his work and he would show off a bit. They loved his shop and he felt quite grown up and reveled in telling Edith they had best be on their way because he "had to go to work now." This always got a great laugh out of May, and Edith would grind her teeth playfully, but then he'd feel bad because he knew it wasn't a game anymore and Edith wanted desperately the independence he now had. That was why, when his gardens needed tending and he was busy with an order in the workshop, he would ask the girls if they could help him out and he would pay them good money.

Peter was tall and skilled for his age, and he was proud to have started such a promising business by the age of fourteen. He hadn't expected to be thinking about marriage at the age of seventeen, but he was a man now with a solid business that kept growing...and he wanted May.

How had that happened? The way they had turned his whole world upside down the previous week was astonishing and thrilling and completely unexpected. The last time he'd seen the girls, around Christmas, things had seemed the same as always, and then when they had asked him out for a picnic and flower foray in The Meadows, he had looked forward to spending some time with them, catching up and bragging a bit about business.

He knew he was considered good-looking; girls seemed to appreciate him when they came into his shop with their mothers, sometimes giggling and blushing. But Edith and May had never given any indication that they saw him as anything other than the little boy they had enjoyed ganging up on and getting to do whatever they wanted.

Well, they certainly hadn't had any trouble getting him to do what they wanted last week. Just remembering it made him hard as a rock. How had they even managed it? He was pretty sure he wouldn't have been brave enough to ever try; those two could be quite intimidating when they wanted. And the strangest part was he hadn't ever thought of Edith or May in that way. Now, he couldn't think of anything else. Soft skin, so much soft skin…and lips and breasts. It was an agony to remember. The most surprising part was the wanting. He hadn't known females could have such need and urgency.

Not surprisingly, Edith was the one who had taken charge, and she was a beautiful young woman. She was raw that afternoon and he admired her courage. She wanted him, it was clear. And May? Did she want him? She was more reserved, but her desire seemed just as palpable.

Peter was inexperienced, he hadn't even kissed a girl before last week, but he was pretty sure it wasn't standard for three people to romp together. They hadn't asked him not to tell anyone, but they didn't need to. This would be their secret.

They were meeting again this afternoon and he had already hammered his thumb twice that morning, he was so distracted. He thought about lying alongside May and kissing her sweet lips while Edith nibbled at his neck and ears from behind. Or maybe watching Edith and May kiss while he fondled their curves. He relieved himself with his hand, unable to wait an hour, while remembering the sounds May made, a cross between whimpering and moaning, and then went out to his garden for some fresh air.

FIVE—MAY

A perfect triangle, Peter, Edith, and May. They complimented each other, but unlike math, which is logical, love is variable. A human triangle cannot be easily labeled. They all enjoyed each other's bodies. And surely, they had been enjoying each other's company for years. Perhaps only the social conventions of the day ended their tryst, or maybe Peter's more singular desire.

Whatever the reason, it was hard for all of them, but especially for May. She knew for Edith this was an excitement, an adventure, a passing infatuation. And she knew Peter loved her and wanted her for himself. But her heart, May's beautiful, gentle heart, would yearn, would suffer. She wanted Edith, she had an unexplainable craving for Edith, she just didn't share Edith's stake on freedom and adventure. Sometimes she preferred Peter. He had a beauty and solidness that could pique her sensual appetite, and his own gentleness and desire for a simple life matched her own. If she had to choose, she would choose familiarity over passion, but she would pay a price.

May had been unprepared for the way she had responded to Edith's touches during those times the three of them had been together. Even though they hadn't talked about it, May knew Edith was aware how she felt, and she didn't love her any less for it; if anything, she loved her back in the same way as much as she could.

There had been an easy physical closeness between them from the start, as there often is in young girls. This hadn't changed as they'd grown older, but it had recently come to mean something new to May. Even when Edith had begun to sense a new need from her friend, she hadn't held back her affections. But the truth is, they were growing into women with differing preferences, and Edith was made from a different cloth. Her spirit would take her away from her friends.

Peter was a good person and he would treat her well. He was gentle with her, and if he noticed that she didn't ignite to his touches the way she did to Edith's, he didn't seem to mind. In fact, it almost seemed like he enjoyed the challenge. Once, after a picnic in The Meadows, he'd spent time caressing her back and she'd drifted into her special place and seen visions. When she came back to herself, she found him just gazing lovingly at her. She believed she could have a happy life with this good friend.

When they were younger, Edith was always reading books and coming up with schemes and grand ideas. Sometimes, she read aloud to May while they lay next to each other on May's bed or told her stories she made up in her head, and May would drift into a place that made her feel like she was floating.

It was a place similar to dreaming, except she wasn't quite asleep. Sometimes she would see things in that state, and when she told Edith about them, Edith believed the visions completely. Edith even began to suggest May "trance" on purpose, and she would gently stroke May's forehead while she lay on her back and tell her stories about nature, or specially prepared meals, or small details about her day, in a soothing voice. It didn't matter much what she was saying, it was her voice, and the way she talked, which brought on that drowsy, floating feeling.

Sometimes Edith asked her questions while she was in this state, and May would usually answer, but not remember any of it afterward. The first time was accidental. Edith was reading and didn't realize May had slipped into a trance. The book was about an orphaned girl who had grown up raised by nuns. The girl in the story was always getting into trouble for minor grievances and being told by the nuns that God would punish her, so they didn't need to.

Edith stopped reading and said, "Do you believe God would punish a little girl for ruining her stockings? What a lot of rubbish!"

May answered in a dreamy voice that Edith didn't recognize, "God won't punish you, Edith."

Edith looked at her then, and said, "Of course God won't punish me, that's not what I said," but May appeared to be asleep and didn't answer, so she shook her head with a scowl on her face and went back to reading, but this time silently.

Later that day, Edith couldn't help herself and said in an irritated voice, "I'm not worried about being punished by God, May. I know I'm a good person. Besides, my parents don't leave it to him anyway!"

May had looked at her with a bewildered expression and said, "What are you talking about, Edith?"

After that first time, Edith began to see a pattern and she began asking May questions when she saw her with "the look" and telling her about it later.

May wasn't sure how she felt about all this, but she loved the feeling of being in a "trance," as Edith had begun calling it.

They didn't tell anyone else about it. It was Edith who thought this was a special gift May had and encouraged her to use it.

For a short time, May had tried to take Edith to that liquid place, gently

running her fingers down Edith's forearm
while reciting poetry, but Edith wouldn't
settle; she would become restless or
agitated that it wasn't working. It
wasn't something May could explain or
teach; it was something that just
happened, without effort.

"WELL, YOUR MOTHER certainly had a way with words,"
Jeremy said when he'd finished. "It definitely gives a...ah,
detailed...history of her start in hypnosis."

"Is that what you got out of it?" Ella asked teasingly. "I
guess I was caught up with the fact that my mother was a
vixen and seductress." She laughed, but her tone held a
touch of admiration.

Jeremy smiled and then cleared his throat. "You
couldn't find any more chapters?" he asked, ready to move
to more comfortable ground.

"No. I've been wondering why she didn't finish. It could
be she just gave up on it...or perhaps she thought it would
be too hurtful to my dad if he ever read it."

Jeremy considered this. "Well, he definitely knew
something about their affair. I heard my dad talking to your
mom about it once when he came to visit her. She was trying
to convince him that your dad had never despised him, but
just preferred him to keep his distance, out of jealousy, or
something. I didn't really know what they were talking
about. They used a sort of code, I guess." He realized now
how thankful he was that they did. It was hard to think about
them as young and...well...lustful.

Even though Aunt Edith had shared the outline of this
history with him ten years ago, on her eightieth birthday, in

an attempt to provide information about his real mother, he had conveniently thought of it as an old-fashioned, romanticized story. These colorful details were something else entirely.

He picked up his drink and put the images from his mind. "I'd like to give the paintings to Cate," he said. He gestured at the chapters. "Do you think we can just, ah, put the rest of this away—leave it for the grandkids to discover someday. Maybe they'll be far enough removed to find it all enthralling."

Ella laughed her easy laugh. "Well said, cous. I'll put it up in an attic somewhere... Now, let's eat these sandwiches and then you can take me out on the town tonight."

Book Two

Chapter Two

BLOSSOM

Merry, merry sparrow!
Under leaves so green
A happy blossom
Sees you, swift as arrow,
Seek your cradle narrow,
Near my bosom.

Pretty, pretty robin!
Under leaves so green
A happy blossom
Hears you sobbing, sobbing,
Pretty, pretty robin,
Near my bosom.

William Blake, Songs of Innocence

ONE RAINY SPRING afternoon, when their threesome was still new and they were still full of discovery, they'd had to make a change in plans. They had planned to go to the river, but because the hard rain didn't show signs of letting up, May suggested they go to her house instead. Neither Peter nor Edith could think of a better, more satisfying alternative, so they agreed.

After they'd had some food from their picnic basket, Edith gamely agreed to read aloud, and they went into the library and sprawled themselves comfortably on the furniture.

Edith had a very pleasing voice and Peter settled into his chair to listen. Edith sat next to May, who had draped her arm and head over the back of the sofa, and read a chapter from *Gulliver's Travels*, knowing Peter would enjoy the adventures.

The rain was striking a regular rhythm on the window and the fire was crackling cozily. After a while, Edith could tell May was getting that drowsy trance coming on. May had been watching Edith read, but now her eyes were closed.

Edith noticed Peter, noticing May, with a curious look on his face. Good God, he was handsome. His dark hair had fallen over his left eye while he cocked his head to the right as it rested on the back of his chair. Now he put his feet, which had been propped up on a stool, onto the floor, and sat forward with his elbows on his knees.

The sofa was across from his chair, and a small, red, oriental carpet lay between them. Peter watched May's eyes close and saw the slight flush on her cheeks. He looked up at Edith, questioningly.

"Is she asleep? Maybe she's feeling ill," he whispered, interrupting the story.

Edith thought about this for a moment as she put a marker in the book and closed it and then she answered. "No, she isn't sleeping. Actually, she feels very good right now. She's in a trance." She kept her eyes on Peter to see what his reaction would be. He didn't seem to understand.

"What do you mean?" he said.

"Well, it's something she likes to do. She almost can't help herself sometimes. She isn't sleeping, but she isn't awake either. In fact, if I asked her a question she would answer, but not remember it later."

Peter appeared confused.

"Is something wrong with her?" he asked. He had a look of concern on his face.

"No, she's fine. She'll wake up when I tell her to," Edith answered casually. She tilted her head to the side, thinking. "She always feels really good afterward," she continued. "I tried it a few times, but I couldn't seem to do it."

She knew Peter wouldn't question any of this. Rather than thinking her silly, Peter seemed to think Edith knew everything; she was the wise one of the three. Realizing that made Edith feel a little important and made her want to share with him...and maybe show off a bit.

"Would you like to see? I can ask her something and then you can ask her about it when she wakes up," she said.

Peter looked at Edith with just a hint of apprehension, mixed with curiosity. "Wouldn't she mind? What if she said something private?" he asked.

"I'll just ask her something impersonal," Edith answered. She thought for a minute. "I could ask her what she had for supper last night."

Peter nodded.

Edith sat close to May and took one of her hands, gently, in her own. She spoke directly to her in her pleasant, soothing voice.

"May, can you tell Peter and me what you had for supper last night?"

May nodded yes, but so slightly it was almost imperceptible. In a dreamy voice, she answered, "I had potatoes with fresh butter and radishes from Peter's garden."

Edith looked at Peter. He seemed mesmerized himself. He didn't move his head away from May but shifted his eyes to Edith and gave a slight nod, which she took to mean to ask May something else.

"Do you like to work in Peter's garden?" May nodded just barely again.

"What is your favorite color, May?" she asked.

May replied, "Blue."

Edith paused for a moment, looked at Peter again, and then asked, "May, did you have fun in the woods on Tuesday evening?"

Peter's eyes got wide and he looked at Edith with dismay and fear. She knew she shouldn't have asked that.

She said quickly, "May, you don't need to answer that question. Just keep resting nicely, now, that's good."

May took a deep breath and her head lolled slightly to the side.

Edith looked at Peter and cast her eyes down, embarrassed she had asked such an intimate question. It had felt titillating when it popped into her head, even a little dangerous, but as soon as she'd said it, she knew it was a mistake. She didn't have any right to expose May's private thoughts, at least not without her consent, and she knew May trusted her implicitly. May was her best friend, and she had almost taken advantage of that, by wanting to impress Peter. Or maybe her intentions had been even worse. Maybe she had wanted Peter to hear how May preferred her. Was she jealous of her friend?

"I'm sorry, Peter. I shouldn't have done that. I'll just let her rest peacefully for a few moments before I wake her up," Edith said, flushing herself, but with shame.

Peter looked relieved. She knew he wasn't stupid, he must have some inkling about May's feelings for her. It would be hard for him not to have noticed. Instead of being angry with Edith, he seemed relieved not to have had to hear it. It wasn't that May didn't enjoy Peter's body at all; Edith could tell that in the heat of things, May could be equally excited by both of them. But, whereas Edith would love to be alone with just Peter, she wasn't sure the same would be true for May.

"It's okay," Peter said. "So, she really won't remember any of this?"

"She usually doesn't," Edith answered, relieved that he didn't seem to be angry. She looked at May again and said gently, "May, it's time to come back from your lovely rest now. Whenever you're ready, you can open your eyes... Just take your time...there's no rush."

After a moment or two, May's eyelids fluttered open and she looked around as if she was trying to remember where she was. She stretched and smiled shyly.

"WELL, I'VE ALWAYS enjoyed listening to *Gulliver's Travels*, thank you, Edith. Did you enjoy it, Peter?" May said quietly.

Peter was looking at her with a curious expression on his face and May glanced into her lap. She knew she had gone off to the nice place, and she'd never done that before with anyone other than Edith. Sometimes she could do it when she was alone, by relaxing her body and imagining it growing heavy, like it did when Edith read to her, but now she felt panicky that...that what? That she'd looked foolish? That Peter would think her strange? That her two friends were awake, watching her while she slept? It made her very vulnerable and she tried to swallow down her discomfort.

Edith saw this and reached out to touch her hand. Peter saw it too, and he crossed the small carpet and was kneeling at her feet in an instant. He kissed her knees, through her skirt, and held onto her hips with both of his large hands. His breath was warm through the light fabric, and his hands were firm and protective on her body.

He looked up into her eyes.

"That was amazing, May. Tell me what it's like," he said with true interest and then kissed her knees again.

She squeezed Edith's hand with her right hand and ran the other through Peter's thick, dark, wavy hair while he continued kissing her knees, and then her thighs, through the fabric. When her legs fell apart, his breath caught, and she lifted his head up and leaned down to kiss his lips. He returned the kiss like her lips were the very air he needed to breathe.

Edith looked at the door, to make sure it was closed, and then she leaned over and ran her hand up the back of Peter's thigh, kneading the long, firm muscles while she pulled herself forward. He shivered, and his breath was ragged. He raised his head and leaned in to kiss Edith. She made a sound in the back of her throat and kissed him back.

AFTER A FEW moments, May reached over and guided Peter's mouth to her breasts and then she put her hand along Edith's jaw and kissed her possessively. All three were losing themselves in a frenzy of youthful lust when they heard bells outside.

With great effort, Peter quickly pulled himself away and stood up. His hands were on his knees and he was breathing like he'd just run fast and hard. He returned to his chair while the girls smoothed their skirts and wiped their mouths. There were no locks on doors in this house.

The three sat there, listening to the rain while their breathing returned to normal.

Edith's shame from minutes before was forgotten.

Peter couldn't put together a coherent thought, only knew it was his responsibility to stop, for now.

May's mind was a riot of confusing emotions like splattered colors on a large easel.

Chapter Three

EDITH HADN'T SEEN either of her friends for three days following their afternoon in the library. She had been helping her mother knit and embroider tiny slippers and dressing gowns and swaddling blankets for the niece or nephew who was coming at the end of summer. Toby and his wife, Martha, were expecting their first child and her mother was set on having everything ready early because "you just never know when a baby will decide to make its entrance." Martha reminded Edith, for the hundredth time, about her unexpected entrance on Christmas Day.

"I hadn't planned on you until well after First Night and you caught me completely unprepared," she admonished, teasingly. She liked to imply that it had been a sabotage attack Edith had masterminded from the womb.

Edith used to answer, "Well, I thought if it was a good enough birthday for Jesus, it would be good enough for me," until once when the pastor's wife had heard and scolded her. After that, her mother looked at her as if to dare her to repeat it.

So, there she had sat for three days of quiet handwork, where she'd had nothing to occupy her mind but that rainy afternoon a few days prior. It had frightened them all a little, how caught up they had gotten, so quickly, but Edith enjoyed lingering on these memories while she did her handwork, remembering how Peter's eyes had looked when he'd pulled away—almost as if he was in pain.

She knew they would have to be more careful. For three smart people, they were all more than willing to walk on a pretty dangerous ledge. We know now that the teenage brain is wired to take risks, but Edith only knew it felt thrilling and she wanted more. She was getting warm from too much thinking while she embroidered little lambs onto the corners of a soft, white blanket, when Thomas came into the parlor to announce "a guest."

He looked at Edith's mother while he said, "It is Miss May, and she seems quite distressed, ma'am."

Edith's mother looked at Edith, who was already rising.

"I'll go, Mama. You stay here, and I'll call for you if necessary."

Her mother nodded, saying, "That's fine, dear. I'll be right here if you need me."

Edith hurried into the front receiving room and found May standing at the window, looking out and holding onto the window frame. She turned when she heard Edith come into the room and the frightened look on her pale face made Edith fear for Peter.

"Is it Peter?" she barely managed.

May shook her head and said, "No, it's Daddy. He had an accident this morning with his horse and he's in bed now, unconscious. We think he has a badly broken leg as well. Oh, Edith, he looks awful! Mother is trying to tell me everything will be okay, but I can tell she's very frightened." May's eyes were big, but there were no tears, just fear and uncertainty.

Edith crossed the room and hugged May.

"Your father is a tough man, May. Tougher than most. He'll be all right," she said, sounding as positive as she could. "Is Doctor McAdams with him?"

May replied that he was and he'd said it was too early to tell how things would turn out; the picture would be much clearer by morning. The doctor and his mother would be sitting up with her father all night.

"Would you like to stay with us tonight?" Edith asked. "I'll go back to your house with you first thing in the morning."

May gave a grateful nod and said everything was too frightening at home. It scared her just to look at her father, he was so pale and limp.

When Edith's mother was informed, she called for Annabelle, their maid, to get a bag ready with overnight things and told May that of course she should stay with Edith for the night and she would go herself to sit up with Mrs. Copeland.

She kissed each girl on the cheek, and set off to May's house with Annabelle, to see if they could be of any use. Before they left, she instructed Annabelle to arrange to have a light supper sent up to Edith's room for the girls for later.

Edith took May up to her bedroom and shut the door. Her room was large enough to hold a double bed, a desk, and an armchair next to the fireplace, which was currently empty. It was decorated in browns and yellows, and the window was open, allowing for a slight breeze. She didn't own many books of her own, and none of those she did, seemed like they would be very comforting at the moment. They were mostly Toby's old schoolbooks, for which she had bribed him by offering to do his chores.

May was visibly distressed and clearly having trouble concentrating. She kept repeating, "What will Mother and I do if something happens to him?" while she paced around the room, sitting at the desk, then going to look out the window, and then sitting again.

Edith had tea sent up, but May didn't drink any of hers. Both girls knew horse accidents could end very badly. She tried to reassure May, but May was only becoming more agitated, and it was so unlike her that it began to worry Edith. May was breathing hard and her pupils were big with fear.

She said, "Come here, May," and patted the spot on the bed next to her. May came over and sat. Edith gently guided her back to lay on the pillow, talking calmly and soothingly as she did. May was fidgeting and attempting to sit up, unable to stop the worry from animating her body.

Edith said, with a little bit of sharpness, "May, listen to me. Just take a nice deep breath, hold it and count to five slowly, and then let it out while you count to three."

She realized this was something she did herself whenever she was too excited to be patient. It gave May something to do, so she followed Edith's instructions.

"Good. Now do that two more times." Edith slowed her voice and breathed to match May's, searching her mind, somewhat frantically herself, for something to say or do to help calm May down.

"Slower...count more slowly, May," she ordered, while she began counting out loud herself, and then very gently stroking May from her head, down her shoulders, and down her left arm. She could feel the tension let up just the slightest bit.

"Good May, very, very good," she continued, her voice growing softer and more soothing, "just let go of your shoulders... Good... Feel how heavy your head is...? Just let it sink into the pillow while you keep breathing nice, slow breaths... That's right...that's right... Yes, May, that's very good... Just like a rag doll... Very good, May..."

May wasn't moving a muscle; she had gone into trance. Edith kept talking, wanting to convince May that everything would be okay, but mostly wanting to keep her calm. It had made her very nervous to see her normally calm friend so frightened.

"You're okay, May. You'll be able to handle whatever happens with a clear head and you'll be calm and in control, like you usually are... You're going to be just fine, no matter what happens to your father... You're going to be just fine, May."

Edith continued along in this vein for quite some time. Eventually, she heard the supper tray being set outside the door and realized a fair bit of time must have passed. She needed to wake May because she was starving, and May needed to eat too, so she gently brought her back to wakefulness.

She watched May closely, worried that the pacing and agitation would start up again and she wouldn't have an appetite, but to her amazement and relief, May remained calm. They didn't talk much while they ate their meal, and afterward May said she was sleepy, so they both dressed for bed and climbed under the covers.

In the darkness, May said, "Thank you, Edith," and curled up next to her friend and fell into a deep sleep.

Edith lay awake for a while, thinking. She was thinking about how quickly May had gone into trance from such an agitated state. It didn't seem likely, but that was exactly what had happened. When her eyes grew heavy, she kissed May gently on the cheek and fell asleep.

Chapter Four

THEY WERE WALKING through the woods, following the river. It was cooler and darker here. This wasn't a commonly used path, so it was quite narrow and there were boulders to climb up and downed trees to maneuver around. It was an invigorating hike and the girls were breathing hard. They reached the large boulder that sat in the sun, jutting out over the river, around noon.

They'd been hiking for over an hour and had worked up a good thirst, so before they climbed up onto the boulder, they slid down an even narrower path to the river for a drink. The calm pool here was only shin deep, so they slipped off their shoes and stockings and waded into the river. The water was cool and clear and they gratefully dug their feet into the sandy bottom and massaged them on the small pebbles. They drank from cupped hands and then splashed their faces to cool off.

Edith playfully splashed May, making darker spots on her light green dress. She was trying to lighten May's mood, which seemed very pensive. Edith hiked her skirts and waded in a little deeper. It felt so good. She unfastened the buttons down the front of her dress and slipped it over her head. She waded back to the bank and set her dress and underthings on a small rock near her shoes and swam out to the middle of the pool. Her long hair floated behind her for a few moments before sinking into the green water.

Edith was a decent swimmer and she loved the caress of the water on her naked body. This pool wasn't very deep or large, so she glided around in small circles and floated on her back, letting the sun shine on her breasts.

May watched Edith. Edith didn't try to cajole May to join her, but just let her be quiet with herself. After a short time, May removed her clothes as well and swam out to Edith. The two of them floated and tread water and made fountains of themselves, spouting water out of their mouths into the afternoon sunshine.

When their bodies began to grow cool, they climbed up the bank to the large boulder and spread themselves out on the warm rock to dry. The rock was so large they could lie on their backs head to head. May reached up over her head and ran her fingers through Edith's wet hair. She combed out the tangles and spread the strands out to dry. After a few moments, she turned onto her stomach and pulled herself forward onto her forearms so that her face hovered over Edith's.

Edith smiled up at her as May leaned down to kiss her lower lip. May felt shy with just the two of them. Without Peter being there, she wondered if Edith would enjoy her caresses. Edith lay still; she didn't kiss May back, but she didn't move away either. May moved around to the side of Edith and kissed her neck. She moved her lips down slowly and kissed her right breast. The nipple was hard, but the breast was so soft in May's mouth. May looked up to see that Edith had lifted her head and was watching her. She thought she read something in her eyes and she flipped onto her back and lay next to Edith quietly.

Edith took May's hand in hers and gave it a squeeze. "I'm just not sure, May."

May knew Edith was not someone who would feel frightened or repulsed by her kisses, even if she didn't feel aroused by them either; she was a curious young woman to whom taking chances, and risking failure, was something to be admired and encouraged. And she was willing to try just about anything, at least once. Yes, Edith was the girl who had eaten a worm on a dare and earned a nickel for it, and she was the one who had written a letter to her father at age nine, stating that she should be allowed to go to school like her brother Toby to learn mathematics and history because "I am even smarter than Toby." Unlike the reward of a nickel, this letter had earned her two weeks of extra embroidery lessons with old Ms. Wickham. So, May found her own bravery, and once the sun had warmed her thoroughly, she leaned over a second time and kissed Edith passionately on the mouth. Edith returned her kiss this time, and they tangled their bodies and spent several minutes kissing and touching. May was the first to pull away.

"I want to talk to you about something, Edith," she said while lying on her back again, looking up into the blue sky. "I've been thinking about what happened the day Daddy was thrown from his horse. I mean, what happened when we were in your room."

Her father was alive, and he had all his senses, but it was uncertain whether he would be able to walk again. Dr. McAdams said that, once again, time would tell. He had started coming by the house daily to do exercises with her father's legs, now the other critical healing had taken place.

"Yes, so have I," Edith replied.

She hadn't seen May much in the past three weeks because May had had to stay home and help nurse her father. Edith and her mother had been bringing food and offering assistance, but the girls hadn't been able to spend any real time together. This was the first time May had left the house since the morning after the accident.

When they had awoken that next morning, May had dressed quickly and efficiently, eager to get home, but she hadn't acted panicky or nervous about what they might find when they got there. Instead, she seemed to be enveloped in a state of peacefulness and calm. Edith's mother had met them at the door to deliver the good news that Mr. Copeland had survived the night, but that Mrs. Copeland wasn't faring very well and was suffering from "bad nerves."

May had gone in to see her father, who was sleeping, then to her mother's room where she managed, remarkably quickly, to get her to sleep as well. Edith didn't know what May had said or done to get her mother calmed with so little fuss, but when Edith's mother had expressed surprise, saying she'd been trying herself for hours with no success, she suspected the tranquility now seeming to radiate from May had soothed Mrs. Copeland as well.

Over the next three weeks, Edith had observed May handling almost everything herself because Mrs. Copeland was a nervous wreck. It was May's nature to be gentle, but she seemed now to also have a strength. She very capably handled the running of their home while her mother fretted over her father. There had been a few times when infection had taken hold and things looked uncertain, and even then, May had remained calm and in charge.

May sat up.

"When I went into the trance that time, at first it was like always...just that wonderful floating, and swirling colors...but then something new happened." She looked off into the distance, remembering. "I floated down into the most beautiful garden I've ever seen. I remember lying down on a soft patch of grass."

She looked at Edith and continued, "It's hard to explain this part, Edith, but a shower of lightness...or maybe it was more like a small stream...came flowing from somewhere above me... Or maybe it was all around me..."

May fumbled her words, trying to find the right way to describe what had happened. She continued to tell Edith about how this "light" had washed a certainty of well-being through her whole self.

"Somehow, I knew, in my very bones, that no matter what happened, I would be all right. And even though I was in that garden, which seemed just as real as being on your bed, I also knew you were there with me, and all the other things that had happened... It was like being in two different places at the same time."

Edith didn't say anything but gave May room to continue.

"I've been wanting to talk to you about it." May began plaiting her hair, giving her fingers something to do. She hesitated for a second. "I've been wondering if you noticed anything different."

May didn't want to say it out loud, but she wondered if Edith had been able to see any of the things she had that afternoon. Being in the garden had been real, not like a dream at all. How could she have been there, but at the same time, in Edith's room? Sometimes she wondered if there was something wrong with her; if it hadn't felt so good, it would have frightened her.

"No, May, I didn't notice anything different about you," Edith said.

May, a bit disappointed to hear this, didn't say anything.

After several quiet minutes had passed, Edith said, "When you came to our house that afternoon you were understandably very anxious, but you became increasingly agitated, so much so, I was becoming worried about you. You didn't seem to even be hearing me, really. I'd never seen you like that, May. It scared me." Edith looked at May, seeming to remember her level of concern. "Honestly, I really didn't think I'd even be able to get you to go into a trance, but I couldn't think of anything else to try; it just seemed like the right thing to do...and you did—very easily. I was really surprised, but I just kept telling you that no matter what happened, you'd be okay. I think I was trying to calm myself as much as you."

She shifted suddenly so she was sitting on her heels as if she had begun to feel an excitement building and needed to move. Bouncing slightly on her toes, she said, "I have noticed something different about you *ever since* then, though."

May looked at her with curiosity. Edith jumped to her feet, lifting May with her, so they were standing tall in the sun, with the river flowing its course below them.

The girls looked at each other, May now beginning to realize what had noticeably changed. She was becoming inspired by the thought that her experiences in the trance were what had given her a new-found sense of competence and composure.

Edith said, "May, you've handled everything so well these last few weeks. I'm not the only one to notice. Mother has remarked many times about how well you're coping and how maturely you've handled everything."

She didn't add how her mother had also said, many times, that it was a good thing because Mrs. Copeland had completely fallen apart.

"You really have been okay, May. I think that light... whatever it was, really did give you something, or change you somehow." Edith's eyes shone with excitement and possibility.

May was beginning to share Edith's excitement. Something fundamental took hold of her as she realized these experiences of hers might really be a gift after all. She didn't need to fear for her sanity. Edith was right.

EDITH'S MIND WAS racing; she had never considered giving suggestions to May while she was trancing. But if that was what had brought about this "vision," and the changes in her behavior...what else might be done?

"May," she said, a huge smile starting to form, "I'd like to do some experimenting."

Chapter Five

PETER HAD BEEN bringing vegetables from his garden every other day for May and her family, and he'd also made some tinctures from his herbs for her father's wounds. When he stopped by on this Thursday afternoon, he was greeted, not by their servant, Charles, but by May herself. She had a big smile on her face as she grabbed him by the hand, pulled him quickly into the parlor, and closed the door.

Although he wasn't sure what this meant, he took advantage of the privacy, and of her renewed happy self. He pulled her to him and kissed her with enthusiasm. As he was really beginning to get into it, he heard a sound behind him. He held May away from himself, ready to take full blame and apologize profusely, when he heard Edith's playful, whispered laugh. He spun around with exasperation to find her standing right behind him.

Oh, good lord. He couldn't believe he had been so intent on May that he hadn't heard Edith come right up behind him. He really needed to be more careful. Edith stood on her tiptoes and kissed his rueful expression.

"It's okay, Peter, we have some fun plans for this afternoon. I hope you can spare a few hours for us today?" she said in a low voice.

Oh, yes, Peter could spare as many hours as they wanted. He nodded, grinning. May picked up the blanket from on top of the picnic basket which sat on the floor next to the door. She handed the basket to Peter. Edith opened the door and ushered the other two out into the entryway.

"Mother, we'll be back in a few hours," May called toward the back room where her mother was sitting with Dr. McAdams while her father did his exercises.

"Okay, girls, enjoy your afternoon, you've earned it," her mother called back.

"We were watching for you so that we could get to the door before you knocked," said May once they were outside. "I didn't want to tell my parents you were joining us for the picnic."

"I was watching from the parlor window." Edith smiled. "You certainly seemed happy to see May."

Peter blushed and said diplomatically, "I was very happy to see both of you." To interrupt any further teasing, he added, "So, are you going to tell me what sort of fun you have planned?"

He looked from one girl to the other. He expected Edith to look coy or teasingly provocative, but instead, she seemed to have sobered.

May just gave him her beautiful smile and said, "We're taking you to the rock by the river. I hope the basket won't be too heavy for you to carry all that way."

They'd been having a stretch of clear, warm weather and today was no exception. When they reached the rock, they all went for a swim to cool off. Peter had lost all traces of boyhood. The woodwork in his shop had sculpted him into a broad, muscular young man. He was tanned from the waist up from working in his gardens, which grew larger each spring. His shop orders had also grown to consist mostly of furniture. He especially liked building beds and dressers on which he carved beautifully matching designs, mostly herbs and flowers inspired by his garden beds. He liked to think he was adding a bit of beauty to the world; something that would bring his love of plants right into people's homes. He did wonderful work and was gaining a solid reputation for unique, quality pieces, and his business was expanding accordingly.

Even though these three had been quite intimate several times now, they had never seen each other completely naked. Edith decided to change that today. She removed all her clothes before entering the water.

She didn't hesitate, even though it made her heart pound so hard she was sure they could hear it. She tried to act as though she was perfectly comfortable with it, and, as she had learned in the past, false bravado often becomes true bravado.

She was pretending not to notice their stares while she carefully folded her items, one at a time, setting them on a fallen log, and by the time she had folded her last underthings and was wading into the water, she had lost her self-consciousness.

Peter had always admired Edith, and watching her confident, naked stride toward the water, he experienced a whole new level of admiration. He didn't look at May, in case he lost his nerve, as he stripped off his own shirt and trousers and made a hasty, shallow dive under the water.

May stood at the shore watching her friends. There was so much to appreciate about both of their bodies. Edith had beautiful, soft curves and round breasts. Peter...well, after the shock of seeing his naked self, which was now, thankfully, under the water, she could enjoy the easy smile which lived on his beautifully carved face. Her limbs relaxed as her mind loosened its hold on the physical world, allowing her to experience a wonderful feeling of tenderness.

"May," Edith said softly a few moments later, standing near the shore with her hand outstretched, "join us."

May decided it would be quite easy to become naked with Peter. She enjoyed her own body and realized it would be a pleasure to share it. The slight breeze, and the rays of sun coming through the opening in the tree canopy, caressed her skin while she slowly, almost dreamily, removed her shoes and stockings and then each item of clothing, piece by piece. She hung them from a branch, where they seemed to enjoy their own languid freedom.

Edith and Peter stood in the water, mesmerized, watching May. As she walked toward them, her eyes closing briefly as her feet first entered the water, neither of them could move. Then she opened her eyes and smiled at them provocatively, inclining her head in invitation. When Peter was just a few feet from her, May bent down and scooped an arc of water over him, releasing him from his reverie with a laugh. Edith joined in, soaking May, and they laughed and splashed away any lingering shyness.

They swam around for a bit, enjoying the building buzz of excitement and anticipation, flirting and teasing and fondling until Peter couldn't wait any longer and took each girl by the hand and led them out of the water. The look of wanting was clear on all their faces as the water streamed off their bodies.

That afternoon they satiated their desires on the warmed rock, taking turns pleasuring each other. There were times when it was unclear whose lips and limbs and fingers belonged to whom.

The ways in which Edith, May, and Peter lost their virginity that afternoon were wild and groping, and somewhat reckless. Peter was too inexperienced to know how to be gentle, but they followed desire where it led and were selfish and giving and trusting.

They were lying on the rock, drying themselves after a second dip to cool down, when Peter said with a grin, "Well, this was definitely a more fun afternoon than I had planned. I don't think I'm terribly busy tomorrow afternoon either." The girls laughed, but it reminded them that this really wasn't what they had planned at all.

"Actually, Peter... Edith has some ideas she would like to talk to you about," said May. Peter looked at Edith. Her hair was drying in waves across her breasts. He shifted his gaze to the river in order to focus.

"Oh yes? And what is that?" he asked.

"Do you remember that afternoon in May's library, the day our picnic was rained out?" Edith asked.

"Yes," Peter answered. He remembered everything about that afternoon. He remembered the story and the look on May's face when she had "awoken" from her sleep; when he thought about how he'd kissed her he still smelled the fire in the fireplace and heard the rain hitting the windowpane. He jumped down from the rock to retrieve his pants. It was embarrassing how easily he was aroused.

"Yes," he repeated, from the riverbank. "I remember it well." He took a moment to explore the girls' undergarments since they couldn't see him in the shade of the rock and then he tossed their clothes up to them, and climbed back up himself.

He spread out their picnic while Edith told him about the other afternoon, three days later, the day May's father had had his accident. She told him how May had been so fearful and anxious and how she'd had the idea to put May purposely into a trance, and how easy it had been. She told him how she'd been trying to calm May down, and some of the things she'd been saying.

May continued. She hadn't ever answered his question, that day in the library, about what being in a trance was like. She tried to explain, as best she could, what she usually experienced. She told him about the floating feeling, and the colors, and about losing track of time, and then she recounted how that time had been different. She was able to describe, now, the garden and the shower of light. She realized how comfortable she was telling Peter about all this, and how important it was to her that he understood.

Peter was having trouble concentrating on everything she was saying. May was sitting in the sun, her hair half dry, hanging in clumps and making wet spots on the front of her white slip, allowing a tantalizing glimpse of hard nipples. He took a long drink of his cider and continued trying to listen. Her hands had grown animated and her earnestness touched him.

He hadn't spent too much time thinking about how well May had been coping, but he agreed she had been taking care of everything very handily. He listened while Edith told him her theories about how it was the things she had said that had helped May experience what she did, and how she wanted to do some experimenting to see if that was what really had happened, or if it was just coincidence. If she found out she could really help someone, she was telling him, she couldn't wait to begin trying.

She made sure to acknowledge that she only saw herself as a facilitator and the real possibilities were within the person in trance. Or maybe even, she conceded, from some outer force.

Peter, who attended church most Sundays with his parents, said, "Do you mean God?"

"Well, sure, you could say it is a possibility, I suppose." Edith's extensive reading had taught her there were many beliefs beyond their own Protestant upbringing. Priding herself on her open-mindedness, she added, "I'd rather not try to define it, but just explore what might be possible."

"And how do I fit into this?" Peter wanted to know. He was pretty sure he knew the answer, but he asked anyway.

May said, "Edith would like to start by seeing if she can put you in trance, Peter. It's only ever been me." She went on hastily because she could see the apprehension on his face "You would really enjoy it, honestly. If nothing else, it is pleasantly relaxing, and you could listen to some nice stories."

To further entice him, she added, "I would be there too. In fact, we could see if Edith could put us both in trance at the same time."

She smiled her sweet smile at Peter and raised her eyes as if to question him, or maybe it was more like a challenge.

"Oh fine," he said. "When do you want to do this experiment?" The girls looked at each other and laughed.

"The plan was this afternoon, but I suppose it's gotten quite late already," Edith said. None of them minded needing to reschedule.

"Maybe we'd better pick a less secluded place," Peter suggested after they had finished their lunch and made the most of the late afternoon heat.

Chapter Six

EDITH'S BEAM WAS growing wider and longer. Her horizons were expanding. She was learning about the "arts of love," as she liked to think about it, and she was sure she was learning another sort of art, one she could use to help people.

She knew it would be hard to convince other people what she was discovering about trance; May and Peter were one thing, but everyone else, well, that was something very different. She needed to continue her experimentation in order to be quite sure of herself.

She so craved having a vocation of her own. She envied Peter and his business. Learning how to run a household wasn't enough for her. She liked learning how to keep books and balance a budget, and she was fair with a needle, but it just wasn't enough.

She hadn't told anyone about her plans, not even May. If she was honest with herself, she realized it was because she didn't completely believe it was possible yet, but she found herself daydreaming about an office in the city, with her name lettered on the window of the door. She could see her waiting room, with its comfortable and welcoming chairs. She saw her desk, neatly stacked with files, and her bookcase filled with books. She saw herself greeting potential clients, people who came to her in desperation, hoping for help, and those same people leaving after thanking her profusely. She knew that part was pure indulgence and self-flattery, but she enjoyed fantasizing about it anyway.

PETER HAD TURNED out to be terrific at going into trance, after the first attempt at least. The first time had been a disaster and she had learned some very important lessons from it.

He had set up three chairs in his workshop where they could have privacy but not be distracted—there wasn't one comfortable surface in the entire room! He cleared a space behind his workbench and placed his chair close to May's and across from Edith's, but when the girls arrived, he had moved them a bit further apart, just to be safe.

Edith had begun by telling them to make themselves as comfortable as possible. She felt nervous because this was the first time she had intentionally attempted to put someone in trance other than May.

First of all, she had worked too hard to make her voice soothing, so that she ended up sounding somewhere between dramatic and ridiculous. Second, when it looked as if Peter was having trouble relaxing, she had stroked him like she did with May sometimes, but that had only aroused him. Next, she had misread the signs and assumed he was in trance before he was and had proceeded to ask him a question which he answered in a matter-of-fact voice, with his eyes open, and had returned with a question of his own.

Edith had become so flustered that May had rescued her and said she wasn't feeling very well and would they all mind trying again in a few days. After that, things had gone much better, and she had learned to always take a few minutes to relax first and had even developed a short ritual to make herself focused and calm before beginning.

When she got up the nerve to tell her mother about it, her mother had found it all fascinating and had jumped at the chance to try it out herself. She had even enlisted a few of her friends to come for a "trance party" where she served tea and biscuits. Even though they treated it like a parlor game, she had still been able to get most of them into a trance, and they had all gone home talking about "Edith's sleeping game."

Her father had indulged her because he'd come to respect that she actually had a functioning brain in her head and had accepted that she was bound and determined to use it. He teased her that he preferred whiskey over tea and had poured himself a small glass before he settled into his chair. Edith was certain she had put him in trance even though he claimed to have just fallen asleep.

But most thrillingly, she had helped May's father with the pain in his legs and even Dr. McAdams had taken notice of that.

She had been keeping meticulous notes on her trials and had learned a few things she felt certain enough to be true. These were:

Everyone who did go into trance enjoyed it and found it relaxing.

Anyone who wanted to go into trance could, and anyone who didn't, wouldn't.

Even the people who were convinced they had just been sleeping weren't, though they might look as if they were, and would usually answer questions without remembering later.

Not everyone had visions like May. In fact, she hadn't come across anyone else, yet, who did.

It didn't seem to matter, particularly, what she read, or what story she told; what seemed more important was her intention and the way she spoke. Although she had noticed that most people seemed to be able to relax more easily if she told stories about nature and suggested they imagine themselves in the scene.

Some changes were obvious and instant, and others almost imperceptible, at least at first, but there was almost always some sort of change noticeable for the trancee.

Edith was very inspired by the work she had done with Mr. Copeland following his accident. He had been experiencing constant pain in both legs even though the bones and contusions had healed. Even with the exercises Dr. McAdams had him doing daily, he still barely walked because of this.

Edith had spent an afternoon at their house one day, helping May care for him, while Mrs. Copeland had gone to tea at a friend's house. Mrs. Copeland had fussed and threatened not to leave, worrying about something happening or going wrong while she was away. She had really become a fidgeting, worrying mess, and Mr. Copeland had insisted she go, saying he would refuse Peter's tonics, and all exercise, until she went and had an afternoon off. When she had finally left, he sighed a huge sigh of relief and said it was the first peace he'd had since the accident.

Edith had offered to sit and read to him and he had happily accepted, requesting a new book he had just purchased called *Moby-Dick*. They both enjoyed the exciting seafaring tale and Mr. Copeland told her he loved her soothing voice. After the first chapter, as he lay back on his propped-up pillows and closed his eyes, she began to recognize the signs. His cheeks flushed slightly, he became completely immobile, and his facial muscles went limp. She decided to see if her assumptions were right and to make certain he wasn't simply asleep. She purposefully slowed her voice and began to stray from the story, leading him into a peaceful, pastoral scene.

When he didn't seem to notice the change, she asked, "Can you hear me, Mr. Copeland? If so, just nod your head." She watched for any reaction and was rewarded by the slightest of nods. She smiled to herself because he looked so much like his daughter in trance.

"Mr. Copeland, can you tell me what is the cause of the pain in your legs?" she asked, completely unprepared for what happened next.

He nodded again, almost imperceptibly, and then said in a fearful voice and with a look of dread on his face, "I don't want to ride a horse again."

Her mind started flying in several directions. Could that be possible? Could his pain be caused by an underlying fear? She knew his pain was real because she had seen him wince in agony once when they shifted him during his exercises. Yet, it was true that Dr. McAdams had been unable to find any physical cause for it. Everything had healed well.

How could she help him, she wondered? Should she address his pain, or his fear? Or both?

She was growing very excited about the possibility of really helping someone. She calmed herself and continued with some more soothing banter, instructing Mr. Copeland to relax even more deeply; to sink into his pillows while every muscle in his body loosened up even more. When he looked peaceful again, she let her mind go blank and kept talking. She suggested he imagine himself now on a walk in the country. She described wildflowers and tall, majestic trees and a gurgling stream nearby. Up ahead, she saw a meadow with a fence and she took him there. Inside the fence were some cows, and in the far corner of the field, a horse. She asked Mr. Copeland if he could see the horse. When he nodded, she continued describing the wonderful day and scene, slowly guiding him to the horse, where he fed it an apple he found in his pocket. He stroked its nose.

Edith really wasn't sure whether she should tell him horses were safe; clearly, they sometimes weren't. She decided to leave it as a nice, harmless encounter and see what happened. Then she brought him back to wakefulness. He seemed embarrassed he'd fallen asleep while she was reading, but she just smiled and told him all was well. He remarked that he felt more rested than he had since the accident.

Mr. Copeland sent his wife out of the house again the following week and asked Edith to come and read again.

When she inquired to how he was faring, he answered, "Very well, thank you. I've been up a bit this week. I even managed to get myself dressed and stroll around the gardens yesterday."

Edith continued *Moby-Dick* where she had left off, and after reading one chapter, she slowed her voice and changed the tempo and led him into a trance. She was amazed at how easy it was.

This time she was bolder. May had already told her about the amazing changes at her house, and she'd been thinking about what else she might do. She took him to the same pasture, but this time she had him climb over the fence and walk right up to the horse. When he did, she told him to imagine he was the size of the horse and the horse was the size of himself. She had him cradle the horse in his arms, like a baby. Then she told him that when he was ready, he could just let all the pain go away.

Afterward, he looked like he wanted to ask her a question but ended up just shaking his head slightly and thanking her once again.

She actually cried four days later when May came rushing to her house to tell her how her father had saddled his horse that morning and taken a short ride around the property. He had told Dr. McAdams that Edith was "good medicine," and now the doctor wished to speak with her.

DR. MCADAMS' OFFICE was a perfect reflection of the doctor himself, friendly and comfortable. He didn't like to put on airs and he wanted his patients to feel at ease when they came to him for help. When Edith came at the appointed time, he welcomed her with tea and small talk before he came to the point.

"Edith, my dear, I've been practicing medicine now for over three decades." He was nodding his head as though to confirm for himself what he was saying. "I've seen and learned a lot in that time, and one of the most frustrating parts of my job has been to learn that even when I know how to help someone heal, sometimes they just don't get better."

She'd been trying to decide just what to tell him. Was she ready? She'd discussed it with May and Peter. Peter thought she should tell him everything, but May knew this was very important to Edith. She understood the dangers of being dismissed as foolish at this point, so she had offered to come along and allow Edith to demonstrate with her. Edith considered this but then decided she would take this opportunity to test the waters. She would try to put the doctor into trance. It seemed like a good compromise. She knew Dr. McAdams suffered from arthritis in his hands. If she could make a difference for him, he would know for himself about her "medicine."

Dr. McAdams continued, "That is precisely what was happening with May's father. His injuries had healed nicely, and he hadn't suffered any mental setbacks...but, as you know, he was left with crippling pain." Now he smiled at Edith. "He tells me you have helped him, and I can see for myself that he is markedly improved." He rubbed his fingers across his mustache a few times. "If you have anything to tell me, I am all ears," he said as he put his hands on his knees and leaned forward, ready to listen.

Edith smiled her lovely smile and sat back in her chair, taking a nice deep breath. Without realizing it, Dr. McAdams did the same, copying her posture. She then began to tell him how good it feels to relax, while she visibly let her own body relax into her chair. She began to relate how she had read a story to Mr. Copeland. She retold some of the tales from *Moby-Dick*, and while she did, she changed to her rhythmic cadence and watched Dr. McAdams grow drowsy.

An hour or so later, the doctor stretched his limbs and sat up straight in his chair again. He smiled with curiosity at Edith and remarked on how well rested he felt. After pouring himself another cup of tea, she watched him flex his fingers and look at her with great interest. "I'd like to try that again sometime, Edith."

Of course, she did have success, and Dr. McAdams became another breeze which would help blow Edith away from her friends. He had her start working with him on some of his "difficult" cases. She had about a 50 percent success rate, which elated Dr. McAdams, but frustrated Edith. She was constantly thinking about cases and how she could help more, how she could improve her techniques.

She continued to take careful notes, and Dr. Adams taught her shorthand so she could be more efficient with them. He insisted on paying her and she saved almost every penny. He agreed to keep this as quiet as possible, but people began to hear. She started getting requests for help with pains, pregnancies, sadness, and grief.

It surprised Edith just how much suffering there was. Most people, she learned, kept their suffering close to themselves. If you met this or that person on the street, you wouldn't guess they carried the burdens they did. Peter and May were very proud of her, but they missed their times together. They could see that Edith was going somewhere without them and they contented themselves in spending more time together, just the two of them.

Chapter Seven

THE SICK ROSE

O Rose thou art sick.
The invisible worm,
That flies in the night
In the howling storm:

Has found out thy bed
Of crimson joy:
And his dark secret love
Does thy life destroy

William Blake, Songs of Experience

THE MORNING OF the day the letter arrived had already brought news that would change everything. May had invited Edith for an early morning walk up to The Meadows. It was early December but there still wasn't any snow and they could walk unhindered.

May arrived just after breakfast and the two set off at a leisurely pace, warmly dressed. Edith sensed May had something to tell her. Her mind had been so occupied with thinking about what she had begun to call "trance healing" that she automatically wondered if it was about May's father, or maybe May herself, wanting more therapy. She was glad she had kept her silence, though, when May finally got around to telling her news. She was pregnant.

The wind left Edith. She couldn't get her breath. They were standing on the path, under the pale winter sun, and she hugged May to herself, mostly to keep herself upright, but also trying to reclaim something that had slipped away from her without her notice. She felt, and it was selfish, oh she knew it was selfish, but she felt a gaping loss. How had this happened?

May was telling her how she and Peter would be married in the spring. Edith was vaguely aware it would be one year from their first encounters together. They'd spent the entire spring, and much of the summer, enjoying each other in that way. Then she'd become so engrossed with her study and her work, the weeks had slipped by without her seeing Peter or May much at all. She still thought about Peter in her bed some nights and planned to see him but just hadn't seemed to get around to it. She thought of the times May had tried to get her to join them, but she'd been too busy. It hurt her to realize May and Peter had carried on without her. She loved them both and hadn't thought she might lose them. The thought of Peter's lips and hands on her made her instantly warm, then sick that she wouldn't ever get to feel it again.

May was happy. Edith wanted to be happy for her. Peter and May were going to have a baby! It seemed completely unreal, but totally right at the same time.

The Meadows were empty of people on this brisk December morning. May was talking about wedding plans, and Peter's plans to build a house, but really, she was just talking to fill the gap caused by the recognition that of necessity everything had to change.

They sat on a bench, in a now secluded area, and a tear made its way down May's cheek. Edith shouldn't, but she did. She leaned in and kissed May possessively on the mouth. She knew May well enough to know her one regret was they no longer had a reason to be together in this way. When she finally pulled away, May swallowed and looked down at her hands as if willing them to stay put, but they wouldn't. They reached out and ran themselves up Edith's neck, under her hat and into her hair. She kissed Edith with longing. Edith kissed her back, but she was thinking of Peter. She was already beginning to say her goodbyes.

PETER KNEW MAY and Edith were out walking that morning. He had asked to come along, but May had told him she thought it best to tell Edith herself, alone. It hadn't been hard for him to figure out where they would be, and he wasn't surprised to find them there, on the bench, lost in their passion. He was angry. He realized he had suspected this reaction, which was why he had come spying. He hadn't thought of it as spying when he left the house, but that's what it was nonetheless.

He remained where he was; he wasn't hiding, but he knew they were unaware of his presence. He tried to get a grip on his emotions. He wanted May. He wanted the life they had been planning these past few weeks. He hadn't thought Edith could get in the way of that, so seeing them together now made him uneasy.

When the three of them had been together, it hadn't felt strange for him to witness the girls enjoy each other, but now it did. It hadn't consciously occurred to him that they might have those kinds of feelings for each other without him. Part of him wanted to go and join them, to make things like they used to be, to become a part of what he was witnessing. He had to admit watching them was arousing, but he also wanted to rip them apart. To scream that May was his. To hurt Edith by telling her he didn't want her and never had. He realized this was true. From that very first day in early spring, when they had gone to the Meadows together to look for flowers, it was May he noticed first. It was May who had stirred his blood.

Edith had always been a good friend, and even though she was quite attractive, and had an intense passion which he had very much enjoyed experiencing, she had always had a way of making him feel...unsure, like he always needed to be on his toes. She was always challenging everything, questioning everything, believing nothing was out of her reach. May wasn't like that. Although May was also intelligent, she was more introspective; she liked the order of things as they were.

At least that's what he'd always thought, but seeing her kissing Edith like this, and he had to admit it was May who was taking the lead, a sickness gripped his stomach. Suddenly, he wasn't sure of anything. He felt as if he could lose everything, or maybe he never really had it at all; maybe what he thought he had was just a facade.

Fear gripped Peter now. Gods, he felt sick with arousal and disgust; fear, love, and anger. The knot of emotions formed a hard ball in his gut. He turned to run away from it all before he had a chance to see Edith take May's hands in her own and place them back in her lap and then put her own hands on Edith's still small stomach. Edith kissed May on the cheek then stood and waited, with her arm out, for her friend to take.

May was carrying his child. Edith couldn't change that. The whole way home, Peter frantically turned over plan after plan in his head, searching for a way to make things right. If he'd only known what lay waiting for Edith upon her return that morning, he could have put his mind at ease. But he didn't know that a letter inviting Edith to join a Dr. and Mrs. John Dupre in Boston to work with them at the Dupre Institute for Women was sitting on her desk, ready to whisk her away from them.

As it was, he returned to his shop. He set to some aggressive sanding of a drawer front, the final installment of the dresser he was making for William Cabot to give his wife for Christmas. He had taken extra Christmas orders this year, enough that he would have to give up a lot of sleep to complete, in order to set aside enough money to begin building a home for his bride and child. He planned to start on it with his father in March, as soon as the snows melted. It would be a small home to start with, but he would add on as he could.

The plan was for him and May to tell their parents their news tomorrow at a brunch she'd planned. Apparently, she'd thought it more important to tell Edith first. He cursed loudly when he remembered the way May had run her hands through Edith's hair.

"Damn it all to hell!" he raged, kicking a stack of wood under his workbench, sending pieces scattering.

A few hours later, May came to the shop with some lunch for Peter. Other than a lingering sadness about her, she acted as she always did. She admired his projects and exclaimed how his customers would be so happy this season because of his beautiful work.

"May, I saw you," he said, the muscles in his jaw twitching.

"What do you mean, Peter?" She sat on a clean bench in the corner.

"I saw you this morning...with Edith...in the Meadows." He had a hard edge in his voice.

"Did you follow me?" she asked, challengingly, standing up again.

Suddenly, feeling very nervous, but also a bit enraged that he would not have respected her wishes to tell Edith by herself, she demanded, "Don't you trust me? I told you I wanted to see Edith alone." She had turned very pale and was breathing hard. Peter, reminded of her condition, tried to remain calm.

"Do you love her, May? I need you to tell me the truth."

"Yes," she replied, simply, after a moment. "But Peter, you have to know I love you too. I want our baby, and I want to marry you. I've never hidden my feelings for Edith from you. Honestly, I thought you must be aware of them..."

May fell silent. She remembered how Edith had forcibly pulled herself away and told her they had to put an end to this. She knew losing Peter hurt Edith, not losing her, and it had left a bitter taste.

Of course, everything had to change. She stood and walked to Peter who was making himself busy at the lathe.

"It hurts, Peter. The three of us...we were good together. Don't you miss it?" she asked. She walked up behind him and put her arms around his waist and rested her head on his broad back.

While it had been exciting, and educational, and very pleasurable, Peter could say with confidence, "No, May, I don't miss it. You are all I want. It was fun, but I'm happier now—or at least I was..."

He walked away from her and out into the garden. It had been cleaned up and bedded for the winter. He took a few breaths of the crisp air. What a mess they'd made. And now a baby was coming into this mess. He picked up the maul and took out his anger on the pile of firewood in the corner.

MAY SAT BACK down on the bench in the corner. She took a piece of pie from the lunch box she'd brought him. Even with her emotions tangled like a ball of messy yarn, she couldn't deny her ferocious appetite. It was the most surprising thing about pregnancy: the sudden, gaping hunger that would come over her. She'd never eaten so much in her life. She wasn't sure where it all went because her stomach was still almost as flat as usual. When she finished the pie, she started in on his potatoes.

Peter found her in the corner, with an almost empty lunchbox. He sat next to her, grinning when he saw his supper. "Did you leave anything for me?" She smiled shyly back.

"It'll all be okay, won't it, Peter?" After a short silence, she said, "We have a very hungry baby. I'll get you some more food." She stood.

Peter shook his head. "No, I'm not hungry. Go on home, I have a lot of work to do."

When she looked at him, her eyes were moist, but she wasn't one to beg. She hadn't begged Edith and she wouldn't beg Peter. She hadn't done anything wrong and if anyone should be upset, it should be her. She was losing one of her lovers, not him.

She went home and continued with her plans for tomorrow's brunch. She held her head high and sang lullabies softly to her baby. She determined to put Edith from her mind and from her heart if necessary. She would focus on Peter and the baby and their plans. May had a quiet, strong will and she would move forward without looking back.

EDITH WAS ALL packed. Thomas had taken her things out to the coach. It only remained to say goodbye to her parents. She had hoped May would come to say goodbye, but she had only received a short note from her that morning wishing her all the best.

She knew May well enough to realize this was how she was coping, but it still stung that her best friend hadn't come in person. Her mother had suggested it was probably the bad weather keeping her away and had taken the opportunity to ask her if she wouldn't consider waiting and leaving when the weather was nicer and the roads more easily traveled, one last time.

If things had been different, Edith probably would have agreed with her mother and waited another six weeks, but she knew the sooner she left, the easier it would be for everyone. She needed something else to put her mind to and Peter had made it very clear that he didn't wish to see her.

He had asked her to his shop one week after May had told her their news. She went with the intention of congratulating him and sharing her own amazing news, but when she got there, he was angry. He seemed to believe she must have planted these ideas in May's mind with her dangerous trances. Edith couldn't believe her ears! She had slapped him in the face with all her strength, which was considerable.

This seemed to have at least a little of its desired effect. He had brusquely apologized for making the suggestion but hadn't tried hard to make amends. He asked when she was leaving, and after she told him, he said he thought it for the best, as if she were leaving because of them! He had only expressed cursory congratulations for her in regard to her new venture and had just seemed relieved she was leaving.

Edith learned that day words can be swords. She felt the knife edge of Peter's words and the wound was deep, but not fatal. She didn't draw her sword in defense but left her blood on his. He had aimed for her heart, but he'd missed, and he could clean up the mess himself.

Chapter Eight

BOSTON WAS AN awakening for Edith. Dr. Dupre and his wife were the most enlightened people she had ever met. They had welcomed her into their home, giving her a luxuriously furnished room to use while she stayed with them. Dr. McAdams had made them aware of Edith and her unusual, but highly effective, treatment. They were old acquaintances and he felt she would be more able to grow under their tutelage.

Four years had passed, and Edith had learned and helped much. The Dupre Institute for Women was a home for exhausted and ill-treated women. They were sometimes labeled insane or hysterical by their husbands, or families, but Edith and the Dupres saw the majority of these women had simply been pushed beyond their capacity or abused by their husbands. It wasn't uncommon for women to have seven or more children, sometimes as many as fifteen. They were responsible for feeding, clothing, and caring for their children, their husbands, and sometimes elderly parents or in-laws.

There were state-run hospitals for the truly mentally ill, but the Dupres' home was more of a retreat where women could recuperate and find their physical and mental health again, in order to return to society, and usually their families.

Dr. and Mrs. Dupre believed in some of the more modern treatments of the day. They offered hydrotherapy as a treatment for stress and had baths specially designed for soaking. They believed manual stimulation of the clitoris could give relief to the over-excitability of some of their more distressed patients, and provided it on Tuesday and Thursday afternoons. Mrs. Dupre was organizing a workshop to teach self-stimulation so the women could take this therapy home with them. They had a Chinese man, Mr. Han, who came on Saturdays to work with his special acupuncture needles on the "chi" as he called it, and Mr. Dupre led "talk therapy" sessions, where these women could listen to each other and be heard themselves.

Although their Institute was too costly for the lower classes, the Dupres were also ahead of their time in believing their services should be made available to women whose families could not afford their care. They had consequently secured funding from several wealthy patrons to provide sponsorship for patients in need of financial assistance. They realized it was the women without means who were often the most in need of their services.

The Dupres were excited to add Edith's new healing techniques to their rather unconventional list of offerings and provided her an office in which she could work without interruption or noise. They had expected a professional, and were a little surprised by her young age, but, not being easily daunted, Edith proved herself from the start, and had quickly become an integral part of the team.

Edith was given ample opportunities to practice and perfect her techniques. She threw herself into her work and was completely absorbed in her new career helping these women. She found deep satisfaction when she was able to teach others how to find, and listen to, their own inner wisdom. Although Mrs. Dupre occasionally pressed her to find a suitable young man, she was witnessing, first hand, the downside of marital bliss every day. Even though the Dupres themselves had a very happy marriage, as did her own parents, she saw many women didn't fare nearly so well.

She channeled her sexual energy into her work and satisfactorily released any leftover urges herself. These were the only times she let herself think about Peter and May. Enough time had passed that the wounds Peter's words had caused had healed to leave only a surface scar and she no longer found it painful to think of him. She'd had occasional letters from May, telling about baby Cate and Peter's business. He had expanded his shop to include a small pharmacy from which he sold his tinctures and salves, and May had begun making soaps with his herbs and flowers to sell there as well. Peter had bought May paints for her birthday and she enjoyed dabbling with color. She sounded happy, but sometimes Edith imagined she detected something else between the words.

Boston was an invigorating city. Edith's work kept her busy during the days, but she had ample time in the evenings to wander about and explore. She was earning a respectable income now, and her expenses were minimal, so she was able to furnish her office with fine fabrics and wall art, and to begin filling her shelves with beloved and useful books. She loved to spend her Saturdays wandering from one bookstore to another, browsing for treasures.

One Monday, Edith came to work to find a new patient on her schedule. Her name was Eveline Tate. She was twenty-four years old and had been sent to the Institute by her husband, who had written "frigid" on her intake form as the reason for her stay with them. By this, Edith assumed he meant she didn't fulfill his sexual needs and he wanted to be free of the marriage. Mental illness was a valid reason for divorce, so husbands sometimes admitted their wives for legal reasons. Many of these men were cruel and had abused their wives to the point of making them truly mad. These were fragile women who needed the gentle care and time to heal Edith and the Dupres and their staff offered.

Edith had found that most of these women went into trance easily. She guessed this was because they had already learned to escape mentally from their situations by necessity, and trance work was just one step further. They loved Edith and the strength and peace she could guide them to. For most, this work, along with the healthy diet provided and the opportunity to rest and enjoy the company of other women, was all they needed.

Once the women were healthy enough they were enlisted to help with the cooking and gardening. When they had regained their strength and courage, they were returned to their families or helped to find a new situation when they weren't returning. There were a few women who had mental issues they weren't able to help, and these women they provided for as best they could.

Eveline was a different sort of case. She was reserved when she came to them and didn't speak at all the first week. She did light chores and kept to herself. She didn't appear exhausted or show any visible signs of abuse. She was a slender, well dressed, attractive young woman, and she seemed to be very observant and bright. She didn't have any children and her husband had seen to it that she would be well cared for financially while she was with them, obtaining for her their best suite of rooms.

Edith had approached her on the first afternoon and found her mute. This wasn't wholly uncommon, but usually the mute women seemed frightened or wary; Eveline was poised and calm. Edith explained what she did and asked if

Eveline would be interested, at some point, in trying trance work. Eveline cocked her head to the side as if considering and nodded briefly, with a slight smile.

One week later, she knocked on Edith's office door. Edith's office was a single, large room with two comfortable chairs and a chaise longue on one side with her desk on the other, separated by a bookshelf with her growing collection of stories, poetry, autobiographies, and medical texts. A large window looked down on the gardens. Edith had chosen to decorate the room in calming blues and greens.

Eveline perused the book selection and chose an old book of poetry. She caressed the leather cover and held it to her nose while she inhaled deeply.

She closed her eyes as she exhaled and said with a smile, "I love the smell of books."

These were the first words she had spoken since she arrived.

"Yes," replied Edith, returning the smile. "I know what you mean. Are you a fan of Wordsworth?"

"Not particularly. I chose it for its cover."

Eveline sat in the chaise longue for her first "treatment." She made herself comfortable and watched Edith sit in the chair opposite. Edith sat on the edge of her seat and closed her eyes. She inhaled slowly and deeply and held her breath for a few moments before she exhaled. She repeated this five times and then gave a slight nod of her head. She opened her eyes and found Eveline watching her with a smile. She looked peaceful, serene. Edith began speaking in her soothing voice, taking Eveline on a journey through relaxation and into an imaginary forest.

Before long, Eveline's eyes closed, and Edith detected the small signs of trance. She'd been thinking about Eveline all week and had decided to be direct with her. She already sensed an inner strength and calm within this woman, unlike so many of the women who ended up in the Dupre Institute.

She deepened the trance to a suitable level for questions then asked, "Can you tell me why you're here with us, Eveline?"

Eveline nodded, almost imperceptibly, but didn't speak.

"If you would like to talk about it, just raise one of your fingers into the air...any finger is fine."

Eveline's slim hands were resting in her lap and Edith didn't detect any movement.

"That's fine then, Eveline...just continue to relax even further...allowing your own inner wisdom to work on resolving any problems you might be having..." she continued.

She gave Eveline suggestions that she would be able to face any difficulties she might experience with ease. Her own inner intelligence would work things out in the right time, and at the right pace, for her. She then brought her out of trance and sat quietly, waiting for Eveline to speak.

"I visited my childhood home," Eveline said after several minutes. She had taken her time returning to the room and normal wakefulness. She smiled. "Just now, while I was sitting here. Isn't that remarkable?" She looked as if it had been a pleasant visit.

Edith asked, "Were you a child again, or were you your adult self?"

"I was somewhere in between, I think," Eveline answered.

"Would you like to talk about it, Eveline?"

"I saw my friend there." The smile had left Eveline's face and she looked sad. "Her name was Margaret, but I called her Magpie. When she died, I agreed to marry John. My parents didn't want a girl 'like me' so I had nowhere to go. John offered me a home," she finished.

Edith sensed she didn't wish to talk anymore, for now, and suggested they have lunch and work together again the next day.

Edith lay in bed that night, thinking about what Eveline had said. She guessed Margaret had been Eveline's lover. She thought of May. The last letter she had received from May had been three months ago. Baby Cate, as Edith still thought of her, even though she was hardly a baby anymore, was a happy child and the apple of her mother's eye. Most of the letter was a recitation of the love of a mother for her child.

May didn't often mention Peter directly in her letters. Edith didn't know if this was because May thought Edith still loved him and didn't want to rub salt in an old wound, or if there was another, less pleasant reason. She wondered what their love life was like. She had expected news of a second pregnancy by now. May had gotten pregnant so easily the first time, and she obviously loved motherhood.

Thinking of May and Peter always made Edith restless, and she needed her sleep. She allowed her limbs to grow heavy, and her mind to quiet, and her last conscious thought before she fell into sleep was of a small patch of open space in a familiar wood.

EDITH CONTINUED TO work with Eveline and learned that Margaret had died from a simple fever; she hadn't been a strong woman. The two had had an affair when Eveline was eighteen, which they tried to keep quiet, but Eveline's parents learned of it and said she was unnatural, a sinner who needed to repent or live her eternity burning in hell.

Eveline had spent a year conflicted about her strong love for God and her unnatural desires. For a short time, she had believed her parents and had prayed for an end to her sinful lusts, but her prayers hadn't been answered. She had stopped going to church and her parents had told her not to dirty their doorstep again. She'd moved in with Margaret who was a few years older and owned a small home of her own. They had twenty months together before Margaret died.

Margaret hadn't been strong in body, but, according to Eveline, she was fiercely intelligent, independent and strong-willed. She helped Eveline understand that God didn't create souls he didn't love; she was as loved as any and all in his eyes. She gave Eveline an education in love, but more importantly to Eveline, she opened her eyes to a just world, a loving God, and books. It seemed Eveline and Edith shared a love of books. Edith opened her small library to Eveline and they spent some pleasant evenings discussing the likes of Van Goethe and Mary Wollstonecraft.

Eveline had met her husband, John, when she had applied for a job as his secretary. He was an investor in the city and he had hired her after a short interview, saying she had impressed him with her quick wit and intelligent questions. She sensed that he might have also found her attractive, but he had always behaved in a gentlemanly and professional fashion. When Margaret had died, he had asked her to marry him and she had accepted.

She told Edith she was a practical woman and knew she would have a much easier life as the wife of Mr. Tate. She spoke fondly of her husband, telling Edith that John was a good man, and he loved her, but over time, he had figured out her secret. He hadn't called her hateful names or shamed her or thrown her out. He'd thought maybe he would be able to change her; she'd just been led astray by Margaret and his love would be enough to "straighten her out." Then he'd begun to hear things about the Dupre Institute and about Edith, in particular, and thought his wife might benefit from a short stay there. She had agreed, and three weeks later had been admitted.

One evening when Edith and Eveline were sitting in her office, reading silently, Eveline put down her book and said, "Edith, can you fix me?"

She was looking at Edith with hope and courage in her eyes. Edith put a page marker in her book and folded it closed. Although she had guessed this was why John Tate had sent his wife to them, neither of them had voiced it precisely.

She looked directly into Eveline's eyes and answered, "No, Eveline, I can't. I can't fix you because I don't believe you're broken."

Eveline's eyes teared up and she looked sad.

Edith continued, "I can help you to help yourself, though, Eveline. Do you believe there is something wrong with you? Do you believe your God has made a mistake?"

Eveline sat up straight and answered simply enough, "No." She dried her eyes and nodded to Edith. "No, of course, you're right. I don't believe that, though it would be much easier if he had."

Edith leaned forward. "I can help you, Eveline. I can help you find the strength to manage whatever life brings you. That is enough for anyone. If we can flow, like a river, around our obstacles, then life can be joyful. Our journeys are not meant to be arduous. Do you believe me?" she asked. This was her purpose in life: to help others on their life's path. She desperately cared about these women life brought to her.

Eveline whispered, "I don't really want to change. I want to be myself. I've been trying to be someone else, I've been trying so hard...but the truth is..." She looked up at Edith. "I don't want to change."

Edith nodded and smiled at Eveline.

"Being ourselves is the only route to real happiness I've seen."

She put her book aside and leaned forward to take her friend's hands. "Would you like me to help you talk to your husband? At least to explain why I can't help 'fix' you?"

She wasn't sure how Dr. Dupre would feel about that, but she felt compelled to offer.

"No," replied Eveline. "I'll tell him." Then she added, "but I would like for you to meet him. He truly is a good man. I'll finish out my month here and then I'll talk to John. I'm not afraid to be on my own anymore." She smiled bravely at Edith. "At least, I hope not to be by the end of the month."

Chapter Nine

PETER WAS WEEPING in the garden. He blamed himself for May's inability to carry another pregnancy to term. She'd just had her fifth miscarriage in four years. She was weak from the loss of blood and he feared for her. He had come out to the garden to make her another tincture of raspberry leaf and nettles, but he'd found he couldn't see through the tears that had started flowing. He gave in to his grief and guilt and sat against the side of his shop and wept hard.

This is how he had come to understand things. May had conceived Cate when Edith was still here. He believed, now, that May's love for Edith was what had allowed her to carry their first child; he thought of her love as incomplete without Edith. He had selfishly wanted her only for himself, but that wasn't what was good for May. Peter had begun to think of May's womb as a triangle. With the love of the three they formed a healthy whole, the symbolic chalice, but without Edith, the triangle was open, broken, and couldn't support a baby.

May tried to tell him she was perfectly content with Cate; she didn't need more than her husband and daughter, but Peter didn't believe it.

After her third miscarriage, Dr. McAdams had advised Peter to stay out of May's bed for a while. She was weak, and her body needed time to heal. Another pregnancy too soon could be dangerous, he'd said. That's when Peter had begun to believe he was the cause of the losses. He twisted things around in his mind, as we all sometimes do.

Peter's knowledge of herbs was very useful, but he believed another kind of healing was even more powerful; in his mind, Edith's trance healing was May's only cure.

He had begun to say odd things to her. The other day, just before this latest miscarriage, he'd said, "May, I want you to go into trance like you used to, and I want you to imagine Edith holding up this baby." Another time he'd said, "Maybe God is punishing me for getting between you and Edith."

May tried to reassure him that she didn't need Edith, she didn't love Edith, it had been a girlish infatuation. And it was almost true. May didn't have many of those feelings or thoughts about Edith anymore; she had put that part of herself away, somewhere in a safe place where it didn't continue to haunt her. She was a mother and a wife, and she was happy. She loved helping Peter in his shop and gardens. She loved making soaps from his flowers and herbs and packaging them specially. She loved making a home for her family. If she never had another child, she would still be happy enough for a lifetime.

Peter made the tinctures and picked some vegetables to add to their soup and went back to May's bedside. She could see he'd been crying, which alarmed her more than anything. He was a sensitive man, but he usually expressed his emotions through his beautiful wood carvings, or through singing; he couldn't carry a tune, but she loved his singing. When they were particularly strong emotions, he took out his ax.

Before this last miscarriage, she had talked to Dr. McAdams, secretly, about Peter. She was worried about him. Recently she had found him talking to himself, chastising himself for being blind or selfish or evil. His workload was backing up because he was spending too much time trying to care for her and Cate. Dr. McAdams had promised to talk to Peter soon.

That afternoon she sent a note with her mother to the doctor asking him to see Peter right away. Dr. McAdams went into the shop the next afternoon to casually talk with Peter and had found a man under much stress. He had a very busy business and a wife he adored who was having too many miscarriages. Without realizing Peter was suffering from torturous guilt, Dr. McAdams unknowingly played right into it.

He suggested a small break from things might help May. He was in touch with Edith out in Boston. Since May hadn't seen her good friend in years, perhaps she could take the train to the city and have a nice visit? May's mother would love to have Cate to herself for a while, he was sure.

Edith had been working hard at the Dupre Institute and the doctor and his wife were very happy with her efforts. He was sure if he wrote to them, and explained things, they would happily give Edith some time off to spend with her old friend.

This confirmed for Peter what he had spent the past year convincing himself of: May needed Edith to get better.

Dr. McAdams thought all this was a perfect solution for everyone. May could have a break from childcare and running the house; Peter would have a chance to catch up on his work and get rest in the evenings, and May's mother could spoil her granddaughter as all grandmothers enjoyed doing.

When May heard what the doctor had planned, she refused.

"Peter, are you mad? I don't have any interest in going to Boston. What I need is you and Cate. My mother can come every day, if you like, to help out, but I'm not going anywhere."

Peter needed May to go; he felt like it was his penance. If he were to let May see Edith he could be purged from his jealous selfishness and the world would be right again.

"It's for the best, May. I want you to go. I want you and Edith to be friends again." He said this last part pointedly.

"Peter, please listen, we are not being punished," May pleaded with her husband. "We have a beautiful daughter. One child is enough." She could see he wasn't listening. "We were almost still children ourselves when we...well, when we messed around, the three of us. It was harmless exploration. I'm sorry it hurt you, but it didn't mean anything." If she was also trying to convince herself, it didn't make her pleas any less fervent. He knew May didn't want to leave. She seemed afraid.

Peter begged, his voice ragged, "May, please go. I can't go on like this anymore." His voice broke. "I feel like I'm going mad sometimes. I can't take the pain my jealousy has brought upon you."

With May's heart breaking to watch her beautiful, talented, kind husband fall apart, she said, "Okay, Peter, I'll go. It's okay, I'll go, and I'll make everything all right." She hugged him to her tightly.

FOUR WEEKS LATER, May was on a train, heading to Boston. It was a sunny early September morning and her spirits rose. Ever since she had agreed to go, Peter had seemed more himself. As her departure neared, he had begun to tackle his projects with renewed vigor. She'd even heard him singing while he was working again lately. Her strength was slowly returning.

She had called Peter to her bed one morning before she left. That night she had dreamed about picnics and rivers and flesh and had awoken feeling more aroused than she had in years. Peter was nervous of loving her, the doctor had warned against it, but her enticements were too much for him to resist. He couldn't remember the last time she had seemed aroused. He was as tender as he could be. May kept her eyes open, cherishing her good husband.

She really was looking forward to this break. Maybe Dr. McAdams knew what he was talking about after all. Edith had written to express her delight at the prospects of May's visit; she would see to it that May had every chance to recuperate. She would meet May's train that evening and bring her back to the house.

Chapter Ten

EDITH HAD BEEN surprised to receive Dr. McAdams' letter and then May's. They had arrived at a very interesting time. Eveline had finished her month's stay at the Institute and gone home to talk with John, as she had said she would. The following week Edith had received an invitation to dinner at the Tates' and accepted.

When she arrived, she was somewhat taken aback at the splendor of their home. It was more a mansion than a house, sitting on a hill and overlooking the city. The well-appointed circular drive promised a lavish home, which is what she found. She'd known they had money but had not guessed an investor would be quite so well off. Mr. Tate must be one of those rare monied men who feel the need of an occupation. She was shown into the drawing room where Eveline was waiting for her.

"Hello, Edith," Eveline greeted her warmly with a hug. "I waited here for you because I know this place can be intimidating. You look lovely tonight." She leaned in and whispered in her ear, "Thank you for coming."

Edith marveled at how easily Eveline played the role of matron of such a grand home, knowing what she did about her almost-poor upbringing. She looked lovely, poised, and completely comfortable.

"Have you talked to John about things?" Edith enquired while she removed her coat, making a note that she really needed to acquire something more in fashion. She was wearing the same coat she had brought with her from Colfork.

"Yes, my very first evening home. It wasn't easy, but he listened respectfully," Eveline answered. "I'll let you know he was quite disappointed, Edith. His face fell when I told him you hadn't been able to fix me, but then he just nodded when I told him I didn't want to be fixed." She continued quietly, "We haven't come to any decision as to what to do about our situation, but he says, for now, I am welcome to stay and share his title."

Edith raised her eyes with surprise. This John must be quite the unusual man; she'd seen many men throw away wives for much smaller "offenses." She looked forward to meeting him.

She was not disappointed. When he joined them in the drawing room for a drink before dinner, he took her hand and raised it to his lips. She felt a tingle of excitement and a heat she hadn't experienced in what she now thought was far too long. She was sure she flushed on the spot and tried to hide it behind her chatter.

She was placed across from John at dinner. He was dressed in evening wear, making her glad she had worn her best dress. She kept finding herself staring at him. He wasn't handsome in the traditional way. He didn't have Peter's height and breadth and chiseled face, but he certainly had something.

She saw Eveline watching her and trying to hide a smile. Oh gods, was she so transparent? It must be because she'd hardly gotten out in the last four years.

They had a delicious meal with lively conversation. John shared her and Eveline's interest in books, though his taste was more along the lines of detective stories, and he was very interested in her work. Without faltering, he made a simple announcement. Eveline had informed him of Edith's declaration that she didn't feel Eveline was broken, thereby negating the need to be fixed with her trance treatments. He didn't argue with this or try to persuade anyone of anything. He and Eveline obviously continued to have a nice relationship and laughed easily with each other. Oh, Edith liked this man.

He wanted to hear about her cases and was intrigued with the few anecdotal stories she shared. He didn't ask her to perform "parlor tricks" as had happened a few times in social settings, and she was grateful for it. She took her work seriously and would have been disappointed if he'd trivialized it.

Eveline watched John and Edith intently. She'd guessed they might suit each other, and she had been absolutely correct. They were smitten. She was so pleased. She loved John for the wonderful man he was, and she had come to love Edith as well. They were a perfect match for each other.

That evening, when Edith arrived home late, she had found Dr. McAdams' and May's letters on the hall table. She would write a reply first thing in the morning, but for now, she wanted to remain in the dreamy state she had been in since meeting John Tate.

IN THE THREE weeks from receiving May's letter, to the day she arrived, much had changed in Edith's life. To put it simply, she had fallen in love. It was a complicated situation, but John had declared the same feelings for her. It was ridiculously simple, he'd said, but at the same time ridiculously complicated.

"I thought I loved Eveline," he told Edith on their third outing to the park. "But now I've met you, I feel like it was just practice for the real thing." Edith couldn't believe this was happening. He continued, "The funny thing is, I now have a marriage of convenience to Eveline, the very woman who brought us together, and thanks to you, somehow it all works!" He laughed. He had a contagious laugh and Edith joined in. It was a strange situation, to say the least. The best part was none of them were trying to hide anything, and they were all very happy with the current change in the situation.

It was not lost on Edith that she was, once again, part of a triangular affair. This time, though, it didn't seem doomed at all. None of them knew how they would handle this affair from the outside, but for now, it didn't matter. Perhaps the unusualness of their situation allowed them to move forward more quickly than they would have otherwise thought appropriate, or maybe they were just two people who were very much attracted to each other, and couldn't keep their hands off each other, or their lips.

Edith had grown up since her last love affair and though she would always find a tryst in a secluded place out of doors thrilling, it was wonderful to be loved in a bed. She still had to hide her love from society, and she did spend time thinking about that as well, but she didn't dwell on it. She was smart enough to enjoy what she was given.

She spent most evenings with John and Eveline now. They would have dinner together and then Eveline would excuse herself and go to her rooms. Their love was new, so John would take Edith by the hand and lead her to his own masculine rooms. She loved the way he smelled, and she loved undressing him. He had experience as a lover and knew how to take his time with her. He loved to watch her come apart under his fingers, and she almost couldn't stand the ecstasy when she discovered his tongue worked even better.

She told him about her sexual awakenings with Peter and May. He was intrigued and a little shocked and seemed relieved that the two of them had married. She painted it as a youthful exploration, but he sensed something a bit deeper and said so.

"Well, I was rather devastated when I first found out about their pregnancy, I'll admit, but I really did leave it all behind me quite quickly when I moved to Boston," she said. "I think it might have been hardest for May," she added reflectively.

"I'm glad I'll have the opportunity to meet her." John smiled at her with obvious intrigue.

When she looked at him with a questioning expression, he said, "I seem to be blessed with 'unique' women in my life. My mother was a strong woman; my father practically cowered before her." He laughed. "And my sister left for Europe at the ripe age of sixteen, governess in tow, whom she managed to sneak past with ease, apparently, and married herself a duke without telling any of us!"

He continued, now counting off on his fingers. "Let's see, my first 'love' was an older woman, seventeen to my fifteen, but it turned out she loved her violin more than she loved me, which is no easy thing for a young man in love to take I can tell you. She is currently unmarried and first violinist for the New York Philharmonic, though, so that does make it a bit easier to stomach, I suppose. My next romance was to a younger girl. She dumped me for an older man, a handsome sailor of the high seas...who could compete?"

He turned more serious. "After that, I stuck with casual relationships...until I met Evie. I hired her because I enjoyed her spirit and intelligence, and yes, her obvious beauty, and I fell pretty hard for her. I guess I suspected Margaret was her lover early on, but maybe I didn't take it seriously enough. When Margaret died, I'm embarrassed to admit I thought she would just forget all that and fall for me."

Edith saw he'd had real feelings for Eveline, and the fact he'd eventually accepted her as she was, and remained her friend anyway, despite his own heartache, moved her. They were lying in his bed having this confessional conversation, and she snuggled in close to him, putting her hand on his heart.

"I think this might be made of gold." She smiled into his eyes.

"Gold is not the strongest of metals, you know? Please be gentle with it," he said with a sincerity that made him so vulnerable it staggered her.

She exposed her own vulnerabilities to him then, not breaking eye contact, as she made love to him in the adventurous ways she'd been fantasizing about but hadn't been brave enough to try.

He'd told her of his inheritance. He was wealthy and neither apologetic nor proud about the fact. He had money to spend on her, and he did. Eveline took Edith to her dressmaker and the milliner. John told her he loved her and would treat her as he would treat an adored wife. They didn't discuss the possibilities, or the impossibilities, of this. For now, this was enough.

Chapter Eleven

IT WOULD BE understandable if May's arrival wasn't as eagerly anticipated by Edith as it had been when first planned. It's hard to find room for another person, no matter how beloved, when you are in the midst of a new love affair. But that wasn't the case. Edith was beyond excited looking forward to being with May. It had been over four years since she'd seen her friend, which is enough time for any thorns to wither and fall; any sort of bad water to flow under any bridge; any bitter taste to be mellowed.

And besides, Edith had realized it was time to get her head out of the clouds and back to her work. Even if May wasn't arriving tomorrow, Edith would have reaffirmed, for herself at least, her dedication to her patients. She hadn't stopped working these past few weeks, but she definitely hadn't been doing her best work. You would forgive her that, and she forgave herself, but maybe her patients would have a different perspective, and we couldn't blame them. Many of them were at the Institute for help they needed because their own romances had failed them or had crossed the fine line between love and hate.

Edith put away her fancy new dresses, cleaned up her desk and her rooms, and sat down to look at her patient files. Mrs. Audrey Johnsson was ready to be discharged. She had come a long way and, through daily practice, had learned to take herself into trance. She was able to calm herself in a matter of minutes whenever she started to feel anxious. She claimed to be looking forward to seeing her eight children and husband again soon. She had stopped the obsessive behaviors that had landed her at the door of the Institute and was looking much fitter and heartier, and happier too, than she had when she'd arrived.

Mrs. Mary O'Reilly was another story. Edith spent time looking over her history again. She had arrived nine weeks ago; her husband claiming she was "stark, raving mad." She did seem to have mental issues, it was true. She had a habit of lifting her skirts and relieving herself at the most unusual and, by most standards, inappropriate places.

Dr. Dupre had figured out that she was suffering from severe bladder prolapse, poor thing, and had fitted her with a device to help, but this didn't explain why she would think it okay to use the dining room as a toilet. Edith had worked with her twice a week and had managed to get her into trance by the fourth time. Going deeper each successive time, Edith had been able to learn how Mary had been badly treated as a child. She'd been forced to hold herself from urinating by both a horror of a father and, coincidentally, by a cruel teacher for the two years she had attended school until she wet herself. This had been relatively easy to straighten out once she'd found the root cause, but there was something else unusual about Mary. She said her name was Paulo and she was a man.

It didn't seem to matter that she had all the typical female parts, she still insisted she was Paulo. Her husband had informed them she had started doing this, two months prior to her arrival at the Institute, for no clear reason. Mary had just woken one morning referring to herself as Paulo.

Edith had witnessed people in trance believing they remembered another life. Interestingly, most of these women were devoutly religious and most adamantly did not believe in reincarnation. She didn't press them on this in their waking state, but after experiencing what they believed to be a past life, they didn't seem to have any problem incorporating this new information into their regular view of things.

This was still an area she was studying; she found it fascinating. Whether they actually remembered other incarnations, or their minds were just making up elaborate stories, didn't seem to matter to their healing. She was planning to talk to Mr. Han about reincarnation as he was a practicing Chinese Buddhist.

Mary believed, at least part of the time, that she was this Paulo in her waking state, something Edith found especially interesting. When Edith had taken her into trance a few weeks ago, she had gone very deeply. She began speaking in another language. If Edith had to guess, she would say it was Italian, but she had no way of knowing for sure. She sounded angry, or indignant, whatever she was saying. Edith asked her if she could speak in English and Mary/Paulo had answered, "Yes, of course, I can. Do you think I'm an idiot?" She/he had related, with convincing detail, that Paulo was from a small village outside of Roma. None of this was anything Edith hadn't seen before, but what really shocked her was what happened when Paulo asked for drawing paper. Edith found a sheet of blank paper in her desk and Paulo had used her pen to draw a self-portrait. A strikingly good one too. He was a middle-aged man, with a head of full, dark hair and a mustache. He said he was an *artiste*.

When Edith had later asked Mary to draw a simple picture of a vase on her bookcase, in her waking state, she had drawn something vaguely resembling the vase, but with the talent of a small child. Mary/Paulo was one of the stories she had entertained John with the first night at dinner, changing the names and circumstances, naturally.

After looking over a few more cases, she did her own trance work. It usually helped her to focus and many times she had gained some insight into a case on which she was stuck. She allowed her limbs to grow heavy and focused on her inhalation and exhalation. The warmth began to flow through her body and soon her conscious mind drifted away, allowing room for deeper currents to ignite.

Edith usually allowed herself only fifteen to thirty minutes to trance. That was enough. She didn't time herself, but prior to each session, she simply told herself she had up to thirty minutes after which she would come back to ordinary wakefulness, and she always did, feeling as refreshed as if she'd had a nice nap. Today she spent the whole half hour in trance.

She journeyed through the Lexington Gardens where she and John had spent time recently, but in trance, she saw it through a reddish glow. The glow was coming from somewhere up ahead, so she followed it. It became brighter and brighter until she found the source emitting from a statue. She had come upon the back of the statue, so she circled around to the front and was shocked to see it was a representation of Peter. He had a grimace on his face, as though he was suffering greatly. Medusa and her curse sprang to Edith's mind. She put her hands up and tenderly cupped Peter's face and the statue melted into a liquid, red puddle at her feet. The puddle grew until it was so large she couldn't see across it, like an ocean, and she removed her clothes and swam out into the warmth, naked.

Edith slowly came back to her room. Keeping her eyes closed she tried to recall what she had seen. She had trained herself to recall much of what came to her in her meditations because she believed they were messages or lessons for her. She remembered bathing nude in the heat of red, and she remembered something about Medusa. She opened her eyes and picked up her notebook. She wrote "warm, red, nude bathing, and Medusa," and just as she was setting her notebook down, she added "statue of Peter." *Hmmm.*

She looked at the clock and saw she still had some time before she needed to leave for the train station to pick up May. She went to her bookcase and located her book on Greek mythology. She thumbed through to the section on Medusa. She picked up her notebook again and wrote "ravishingly beautiful woman, raped by Poseidon in Athena's temple, Athena casts spell to curse her." Interesting. Edith already knew that red symbolizes life force, fertility, passion, but also anger and uncontrolled emotions. For her, nude always signified that she was open and exposed, not hiding anything.

She sat, lost in thought. Statues are beautiful in form, but dead in spirit...but melting could signify the opening of emotions or an awakening to new understandings...and Peter. She pictured the look of anguish on his face.

MAY SAW EDITH before Edith saw May. She watched Edith scanning the crowd for her. She was even more radiant and beautiful than before. May felt an old longing that had lain dormant stir. She took a deep breath, raised her hand up above the crowd, and called to her friend.

Edith heard May before she saw her. Just the sound of her familiar voice made her feel glad in her heart. She spotted May ahead and pushed her way through the hordes of travelers to greet her. They were hugging and laughing. They kept holding the other away for a better look and then hugging fiercely again.

Edith saw that May had been unwell, but she also saw a hint of color in her cheeks and the life in her eyes. She felt too thin; Edith would need to fatten her up a bit and told her so. May laughed and said Peter had been trying without much success with all his tonics and herbal cures.

"No more tonics for you. Butter, pastries, beef, and eggs from now on," promised Edith. "Starting now; I have a lovely roast with potatoes and onion ready." She bit her lip to hold back the tears and smiled. "I'm so happy to see you May, genuinely." Tears welled in her eyes as she kissed May gently on each cheek.

EDITH ARRANGED TO have a porter bring May's bags to the house and then put May into their waiting carriage. May was very tired from the traveling, but it was a pleasant drowsiness, now she knew she was in good hands. She fell asleep, leaning on Edith's shoulder, before they had made it two blocks.

She woke in the darkness of pulled curtains in the most comfortable bed she had ever slept in. She lay there, reveling in the silence and comfort of it. Eventually her eyes adjusted to the dim light. She saw her things had been stacked near the foot of the bed and someone had opened the bags and hung her dressing gown on a hook to her right. She got out of bed and put it on. Whoever it was had also thoughtfully laid her slippers on the floor next to the bed.

She pulled back the curtains and looked out of the window. The house sat on a curving street lined with trees and other large stately homes. She imagined herself and Edith, strolling arm in arm down the brick walk as the colors turned, and her heart opened a bit more. She must write Dr. McAdams soon to tell him his medicine was already working. When she turned around, an elegant room met her gaze. Edith really had landed on her feet.

May went to the basin and freshened up and then dressed in a comfortable gown and went out to find Edith. She didn't have any idea what time it was, but she was ravenously hungry.

May had arrived on the 7:30 p.m. train. By the time they'd reached the Dupres' home and made short introductions, May was too tired to eat. The roast had been put away for storage and Mrs. Dupre had taken May to the room they had set up for her. It was down the hall from Edith's and had a beautiful view of the front garden.

May was almost stumbling as she climbed the wide staircase, and when Mrs. Dupre pulled back the eiderdown she had collapsed gratefully onto the bed.

Having had plenty of experience with exhausted women, Mrs. Dupre made quick work of undressing this one, having the same thought that Peter, May's mother, and Edith had had. *We need to fatten this one up!* When her things arrived, Mrs. Dupre had them sent up to May's room and Edith had seen to the unpacking. May hadn't stirred through any of it.

It was almost noon when she made her way downstairs. Edith was sitting at the dining table working on some papers. She smiled and stood to pull back a chair for May.

"Well, you certainly slept like the dead. I hope you're hungry because Mrs. McCray has gone all out for our guest," she said.

May sat and said, "Oh Edith, this home is so lovely. I want to thank you for having me."

"I couldn't be happier to have you here. You need a break and I am going to pamper you and spoil you," Edith replied with sincerity.

"I wanted to ask you something, Edith," May continued. "I know you're so busy here with your work..." She faltered and tried again. "I know you have a very important job now, and I don't want to get in the way...". She felt suddenly old and shabby next to her friend. Edith seemed to shine with confidence and ability and competence. She had charged ahead with her life just as she'd always planned. She was sitting here, next to May, in the most stylish of clothes, with a modern hairstyle, and important looking papers, which all made May feel a little bit embarrassed of herself, a little bit left behind even.

"May, ask anything you like! The Dupres have given me a week off to devote just to you. Really, anything." She paused and waited for May to continue. When, flustered, she could not find the words, Edith said kindly, "May, I'd like things to be like they used to between us, before everything got confusing. Do you think we could just start out being our comfortable old selves?" She reached out and took May's hands. "It's so, so good to see you." This was the genuine, earnest Edith that May had always known.

Edith dropped May's hands and jumped up. "I almost forgot!" she exclaimed. "I have a welcoming gift for you." She ran from the room clapping her hands with delight.

May smiled. *Okay then,* she told herself, sitting up straighter and pulling herself together, *this is Edith, you goose, your best friend in the world and she's very happy to see you. So what if your dress isn't the height of fashion?* Her spirits rose again, and she smiled widely in anticipation of her gift.

Edith came back into the room with a small package tied with light blue satin ribbon.

"Open it now, before you have your breakfast," Edith demanded and placed it in May's lap. May untied the ribbon and set it on her plate. She took the lid off the box and lifted out a gold necklace with a large, oval, emerald pendant, set in a simple but elegant setting. It was the most beautiful and exquisite thing May had ever owned.

"Turn it over," Edith said quietly. On the back, "To May, Love, Edith," was engraved in a delicate script.

"Oh Edith," May said. "I don't know what to say. Thank you, it's absolutely lovely."

"Let me put it on you." Edith took the necklace and placed it around May's neck. May lifted her hair and Edith did the clasp. Edith came around to the front of May to look at her gift.

"It's perfect!" she said. "I knew it would look gorgeous with your hair and eyes." She clapped her hands again. "I remember what it felt like to come to Boston at first. Everything is so fashionable and modern here." She smiled. "I wanted you to have something to make you feel sparkly. Now, let's fill that plate of yours." As she spoke, she began to load it with cakes and meats.

While they were eating, Edith remembered that May had been trying to ask her a question, so she said, "May, what was it you were going to ask me?"

May set down her fork and looked Edith in the eyes. "I wondered if you might have time to do some trance work with me. Maybe we can get to the bottom of why I keep miscarrying. Dr. McAdams says he can't see any reason why my body won't hold on to a baby again." She hesitated and gathered her courage before continuing, "Peter has developed some odd ideas, and I promised him I would talk to you about it." She said this last part with resignation, but also determination.

Chapter Twelve

THE LITTLE BOY FOUND

The little boy lost in the lonely fen.
Led by the wand'ring light,
Began to cry; but God, ever nigh.
Appear'd like his father, in white.

He kissed the child, & by the hand led.
And to his mother brought,
Who in sorrow pale, thro' the lonely dale.
Her little boy weeping sought.

William Blake, Songs of Innocence

MAY SAT IN the chair in Edith's office. She might have felt nervous, but she didn't. She closed her eyes and let herself drift off to the sound of Edith's familiar voice.

She listened for a while and then she wasn't listening anymore. She was floating in a rainbow of colors; blues and greens, turning to indigos and soft violets. She wasn't aware of a body, just a mind. She wasn't aware of time or space. She could have been floating there for years, or maybe just for a minute. It didn't matter. Eventually, she sank down, down, down, into warmer colors; she was the colors, or the colors were her. She was a swirling, changing liquid flow of oranges and yellows.

Some part of her consciousness heard Edith guiding her into ever-deepening places and she went willingly, relishing the empty and peaceful spaces.

"May, I want you to think about when you were pregnant with Cate. I want you to imagine you are in that time again…when you're there, just give me a nod of your head…" came Edith's guidance from somewhere distant.

After a few moments, May smiled slightly and nodded.

"Very good, May. How do you feel?" asked Edith.

May said, in a sleepy voice, "I feel good. I like it when she kicks."

Edith continued, "May, can you see inside your womb? Can you see baby Cate growing inside you?"

Again, May nodded.

"And how does your womb look?" Edith asked.

"It looks healthy and round and soft."

"That's very good May, very good." Edith's voice was soothing. "I want you to remember your second pregnancy now… Let me know when you're there."

May paused for longer this time. Finally, she nodded her head.

"And how does your womb look now?"

May began breathing like she was trying to catch her breath. "It's cold here, not good...nothing to hold on to..." She tried not to panic.

May began to feel colder. It wasn't at all pleasant. She looked for the warm liquid, but now she was swimming, not floating. The water was cold. A large wave came over her head. She sunk down below the waves and breathed in the liquid cold.

Edith said, "Okay, that's very good work, May, you can just move back to a pleasant memory *now*." She was silent for a few minutes, and May relaxed.

She saw a door and peeked in its window. Inside looked cozy. There was a fire burning in a hearth, and a warm animal skin rug lay on the floor in front of it. She opened the door and went inside and laid down on the soft rug and curled up. She watched the flames dancing and then the flames became music and she fell into a dream.

"May, can you tell me anything about your last five pregnancies? Is there anything important to know?" Edith asked.

"He keeps trying to come, but there's nothing to hold on to. He says it's too cold and slippery."

"Who tries to come? Who is he?".

May answered matter-of-factly, "Cate's brother."

In the dream, May is walking along a path by a river. It's a nice, sunny day. She sees a little boy on a rock in the middle of the river. She waves to him and he waves back, calling to her, but she can't hear what he's saying because the river is too loud. Then dark clouds come and the river rises and she watches the little boy wave goodbye and go floating down the river. Then the sun comes back out and she goes down to the river and takes a drink in cupped hands. She swallows his words. When she tastes them, she understands that he said to wait for him by the riverbank. He'll be back. She sits down to wait.

Edith asked May to visit her womb one more time, now, in the present.

"I'm there," May said with a small nod.

"And how does it look now?"

May answered in a hushed, reverent voice, "He's here again."

Edith took a few deep breaths. "May, is Cate's brother comfortable this time?" Edith asked, her tone suggesting she was considering the possibility that May was pregnant again already.

May has been waiting on the shore for eons. She opens her eyes from sleep and looks out to the river. The little boy is back on the rock. He smiles at her and she smiles back. She beckons to him with her arm. He reaches out his hand and the river disappears. She is holding his hand and leading him through a deep valley. The sun is setting and the sky glows brilliantly with oranges, reds, and violets. She is back to the liquid golden colors. The boy is telling her he has been waiting for her to come find him. She answers that she's been looking in the wrong places. It's warm here and she finds a shallow dip in the earth, which is also liquid color. She realizes she is now carrying the boy and he has fallen asleep. She gently lays him in the cradle of all and kisses his brow. She speaks into the sunset two words and they meld and melt into the fire. "You're home."

Finally, with the faintest of smiles on her lips, she whispers her answer to Edith's question. "Yes, he is."

"JOHN, SHE'S PREGNANT." Edith and John were having an early walk in the park while May slept late. They hadn't seen each other since May's arrival. Edith was walking slowly, as though still trying to digest everything.

"Do you think you should send her back to Peter?" John asked with obvious hesitance. Edith had already told him about the run of miscarriages and must be considering what might happen if she stayed.

"No. From what she's been telling me, Peter is taking all of this much harder than she is. She doesn't want to tell him about this pregnancy yet, John." Edith had already argued with May, until she'd run out of reasons, telling her she couldn't keep this information from Peter, but May had won. She was absolutely serene, but Edith could tell under the serenity was an iron will.

"Her plan is to stay here until the baby is born," Edith continued. "She says no place is more ideal. Honestly, John, when she told me what Peter had convinced himself of—that I was the 'missing link,' I could tell May thought he'd lost his mind. But now? Now she seems to believe the same!" Edith repeated what May had told her about her trance. "She's convinced that without me, she never would have found him—the baby, that is—and now she has, she's not leaving until he arrives."

John listened silently. When Edith finished speaking, he said, "Well, it seems to me you should both move in with me for the duration. I have plenty of room, as you know. Eveline can help care for May and keep her company while you work." He grinned wickedly. "And I finally have an excuse to move you into my home." He stopped and took her hands firmly in his. "And don't think I will ever let you move back out." Then he bent down and kissed her on the mouth to stop her from any arguments.

Chapter Thirteen

MAY AND EDITH were having supper with the Dupres. Mrs. Dupre couldn't contain her glee that Edith was moving out.

"Don't think for a minute that I won't miss you like the dickens, even though I'll see you daily at the Institute, but Edith! Well done!" She was treating the news that Edith was moving in with John as though it were a marriage proposal. "Well, just as good as!" she'd said when Edith corrected her. She said he was the prize of the century, and here, Edith had to agree. The Dupres had been made aware of the unusual circumstances John Tate found himself in but were not fazed by the "minor" complications.

When Edith had relayed John's offer to May, May had expressed an unexpected sense of adventure about it. The fact John was married to Eveline, and she not only still shared his home, and his name, with ease and friendliness, but was also a good friend of Edith's, didn't seem to bother May at all. She said she couldn't wait to meet the man who had swept her friend off her feet and the woman who had brought them together. It seemed May was experiencing an awakening. The ease and enjoyment with which she had taken to city life surprised Edith.

May ate a hearty supper. Even though she was again with child, before having fully recovered her good health from the last time, she wasn't experiencing any morning sickness, and her appetite was superb. She kept exclaiming, with a contented smile, that she hadn't felt this good in ages.

After supper, when May was helping Edith finish up her packing, Edith brought up a subject which had been traveling around in her mind for the last few days, specifically, since May had made the announcement that she would stay in Boston to deliver this baby.

"Ah...May..." she began, a little unsure of how to best say what was on her mind, "what are your plans for Cate while you're here?" Deciding the best tack was a direct one, she added, "Won't she be missing her mother, and won't *your* mother have a lot of questions?"

May had already written to Peter to tell him she was having such a good rest here, she had decided to stay on for a while to make a full recovery.

"And, more to the point, May...aren't you missing your daughter?" Edith finished.

May slowly nodded. "Yes, of course, I miss Cate," she said, considering, "but Edith, you have to understand that this baby is also my child. I have to do what is best for him right now. Cate is of an age where she thinks she's having a grand adventure with her grandparents, and my parents have assured me they are happy to have her for as long as necessary. They were really good parents, Edith, and I sometimes think Cate spending this time with them might also be best for her right now."

She went on to explain, "Peter has been under a lot of stress these past eighteen months, and his behavior isn't always what's best for a child. He vacillates between spoiling her rotten and putting up with very bad behavior, as though she can do no wrong, and then treating her like she is an adult, expecting her to behave like a young lady instead of a little girl." May paused, as though reflecting, and then continued. "It really has been hard on Cate, and her behavior has been, well, difficult at times." She took a deep breath and released it. "Her misbehaving was really wearing me down, if I'm honest." She looked up at Edith. "I need this break," she said simply.

Edith nodded her understanding, and they finished the packing in silence.

Edith was thinking of her dream about Peter, the statue. His grimace made her sad. Poor Peter. She sat quietly, lost in thought. If looking at Medusa had turned him to stone, with such an awful grimace on his face...who was Medusa? If it was herself, as she guessed, what was her responsibility to him now? The love affair the three of them had conducted that warm spring and summer had hurt Peter.

Chapter Fourteen

PETER SET THE letter down on his workbench. It smelled like fancy perfume, not like May. He picked up a sanding block and began rhythmically working on a long plank while he muttered to himself. "Well, that's nice for May, but what about me and Cate? Has she thought about that? I thought Dr. McAdams recommended one month...two at the most... He didn't say it would take any longer." He turned the plank over and began again.

Yes, he had wanted her to spend time with Edith... In fact, she hadn't wanted to go, and he had begged her. Maybe he'd made a mistake. Maybe Edith was a bad influence. Before May left, he had convinced himself it was all his fault; his jealousy of May's feelings for Edith had caused the loss of all those babies. May said Cate was enough, but with each loss she became a little more distant from him. She blamed him too.

He was noticeably thinner. Even though his mother or May's brought food for him, he didn't always remember to eat. Without May and Cate in the house he didn't have any sort of schedule; he ate at odd times and slept at odd times. When Dr. McAdams had stopped in to check on Peter, he'd noticed he didn't seem very focused. His gardens, which were usually so neat, were becoming weedy and messy, and all the backed-up orders he was supposed to be catching up on were in incomplete piles around his shop.

May's mother had brought Cate over to spend the evening with her father two nights ago, but after observing the state of things, had made an excuse to stay there with them, and had taken Cate home early.

Peter began imagining May and Edith together, in the ways they had been four years ago. He worried the images around in his mind like they were being played on repeat. He made up new stories about those days that weren't true. Stories making Edith out to be an evil enchantress. He forgot, or ignored, the fact he had grown up admiring her and she had always been a good and loyal friend. He didn't remember anymore that Edith had wanted him all along; that it was May who desired Edith, not the other way around.

He picked up the letter, looking for hidden meanings, and then set it down again in a state of agitation. He went into the house and began gathering things for a journey. He had to see May. He had to get her away from Edith; convince her that he and Cate needed her at home.

He realized he was sweating, and a feeling of nausea came over him in a wave. He threw up into a bucket that sat in the corner of the bedroom and then he slumped to the ground. The cool floor felt good against his hot cheek.

PETER LAY IN a haze of fever for several days. He managed to pull a quilt off the bed to cover himself when the chills took over his body.

He dreamed he was swimming in the river, naked, with Edith. She pressed her body against his erection and just when he was about to find his release, five dead babies came floating up to them, bobbing in the water and glaring at him accusingly. Nausea rose again and he vomited into the river.

Later, he imagined he saw May aborting a smaller version of herself. The blood was everywhere, and she was screaming.

He was walking through the forest, the ground soft under his feet. New green shoots carpeted the forest floor. Sun shone through an opening in the canopy up ahead and as he looked up to it, the largest, most majestic hawk he'd ever seen came swooping low out of the waterfall of sunshine. It came toward him, arcing up as it drew close. He grabbed its wings and was lifted into the sunshine.

A cool hand was on his forehead. Someone was lifting him to the bed. Much later he half awoke as someone sponged his body with a cool cloth that set him shivering violently. He was covered with fresh blankets and sung to. More time passed, and he found himself swallowing a few drops of what must be some kind of magical water. He had never tasted water so good. He could feel it slide all the way down his parched throat. He vomited it up again.

EDITH LOOKED AROUND the familiar wood shop. Shavings covered the floor and a disordered scattering of piles of half-started projects filled the space. She picked up Peter's broom and began to tidy up. There wasn't much else she could do. She had helped Mrs. Harris get him cleaned up and as comfortable as possible before his mother had gone home. Edith promised she would stay through the night in case he needed anything. Mrs. Harris had been with him for the last two days and she needed rest. Dr. McAdams thought he was probably through the worst of it now.

While she worked, she considered how she felt about leaving Boston the way she had. Near the end of the fifth week after moving into John's house, Mrs. Dupre had come to her office with an envelope that had arrived at their home the day before. It was addressed to May. She studied the envelope because it was on Peter's stationery but was addressed with a woman's hand. The postmark showed it had been posted four days earlier. She tried to consider what this might mean and could only come up with bad news. She couldn't get the image of Peter grimacing out of her mind.

She closed the door to her office and opened the letter. If it was bad news, she would need to be very careful how she handled telling May. Even though May was feeling good and eating well, Edith was very aware that this was a critical time for her with this pregnancy.

The letter was from Peter's mother, telling of how she had found Peter feverish and hallucinatory when she'd brought his supper over. She didn't know how long he had lain on the floor in that condition because the last time she had stopped by the house had been three days prior. She was extremely worried about him and thought May should hurry home.

On her way back to John's, to tell May the news, Edith decided she would go herself. It was a sudden decision she didn't really remember making. She was trying to decide how best to approach May when she realized she would make an excuse and go herself. She told herself it was to spare May in her delicate condition. But if that were true, why hadn't she confided the truth to John? She had lied to them both.

Then she had lied to herself. She told herself she was a healer, and she was going back to help Peter. But she wasn't a doctor, and fevers were hardly her specialty. She set the broom down and sat on a low bench, leaning her head back against the wall.

John had been curious at the suddenness of her decision but hadn't questioned her or tried to stop her. She'd told him she'd received a letter from her own mother, asking for a visit because her father wasn't well. She told him she would go right away; it had been too long since she'd been home, and besides, she could check in on Peter and Cate while she was there.

Good God! She now realized what a large lie she'd gotten herself into. It gave her a sick feeling in her stomach when she thought about it. She loved John. What was she doing? It wasn't like her to sabotage herself. She considered herself lucky to have such a good man love her. Why was she here? She should put herself on the next train back and go confess everything and ask for his understanding. He would probably give it to her.

May should be here with her husband. No, no, she shouldn't. That wouldn't be good for her or the baby, and maybe not even for Peter when he learned the truth. For now, she would stay put and do her best to smooth things over when she returned to Boston. She picked up the broom again and began to energetically tidy up.

PETER OPENED HIS eyes and tried to focus them. Edith sat on his bed, singing to him.

She saw his eyes open and brought a sip of water to his cracked lips. "Just a tiny bit," she said gently, supporting his head with her other hand, "you need to keep this down."

After he'd swallowed, he croaked, "What are you doing here? Where is May?"

She saw panic rise in his eyes, as the thought that something must have happened to May made its way through the fog in his brain.

"May is fine, Peter. She's still in Boston. I thought it best to come myself." She had already thought about how she would explain herself to Peter. "I wanted to make sure May didn't catch your fever since she's still recovering her strength," she half lied.

He watched her through his droopy eyes for a moment longer, then they closed, and he fell back into a deep sleep.

Edith continued sitting on his bed, singing softly. It soothed her. Even in this feverish state, he was handsome. Over the past few years, she had begun to believe she had exaggerated his good looks in her mind. She hadn't been prepared for the instant wave she felt low in her belly when she first saw him, lying in bed, with a flush she could almost have believed was from spending time in the outdoors; rugged good looks.

She didn't even try to stop herself from leaning forward and softly kissing his forehead. Anyone witnessing the scene would have believed it was just the kiss of worried affection, but it warmed her lips with a pleasant zing. She brushed his hair off his forehead with her fingertips and then allowed them to continue down his temple, cheek, and along his jaw. She knew this face so well. There were definitely some lines, though, that hadn't been there the last time she saw it. Worry lines, some people called them. He had been under stress, poor Peter.

EACH DAY PETER was improving. He had regained enough strength to sit up in bed most of the day. He was able to eat bland foods and was starting to complain about his restricted diet, which they all knew was a good sign. But it also made it harder for Edith to keep up her lie. With Peter fully conscious, he had been drilling her with questions about May, and she had begun to spend more time taking Cate out to play or going to visit her parents.

Cate was an engaging little girl. She had the looks of both parents, which made for a very pretty child. She didn't seem to miss her mother. Edith guessed she was still young enough to adjust to her change in circumstances without problems. She had introduced herself as Aunt Edith when they met, and they'd found themselves in an easy relationship. May's mother was grateful to have Edith take Cate off her hands for a few hours each afternoon. It's difficult to get things done when you have an inquisitive youngster following you around.

Cate enjoyed helping Edith clean up the garden. It was time to get it ready for winter, and even though Edith didn't have a lot of gardening experience, they were able to get quite a lot accomplished. This afternoon, Peter came outside for a visit, while they were working. Cate had taken her hat off and was happily getting dirty and Edith had taken her coat off to cool down. They were chummy together, telling jokes and laughing easily. They hadn't seen Peter come down the porch steps or along the path. He stood watching them, unobserved.

He didn't know if he had been dreaming more of his feverish dreams, or if Edith had really been kissing and fondling his face rather frequently, but either way, the man hadn't been in May's bed for months, and couldn't be blamed for the effect watching Edith had on him.

"Well, isn't this a sight," he said to announce himself. Cate jumped up and ran to hug his legs.

"Daddy! We're putting your garden to sleep. Aunt Edith says it wants to hibernate like the bears do."

Peter chuckled. "I guess you could say it like that," he answered his daughter, ruffling her hair.

He looked at Edith. She was even more beautiful than when she left. She didn't look intimidating like he had come to think of her over the preceding four years. Her clothes were of a fashion he hadn't seen, very slim fitting, with a low-cut bosom. He blew out his breath.

"You're looking very well, Edith," he said. He sat on a garden bench because having all the blood rush to his erection, while he was already weak, was making it difficult to stand and breathe at the same time. She came over and sat next to him. She put her hand on his knee with a familiarity that neither of them objected to.

"I'm so glad to see you up, Peter," she said. "You had us all scared for a bit there."

He should ask about May now; he knew Edith wasn't telling him the whole truth, but he decided to just let it lie for the moment. He was feeling good and he didn't want to ruin it. Edith leaned in closer than she would have if other adults had been present. He was too fatigued to care if it was improper.

LATER THAT NIGHT, after Cate had gone back to her grandma's, and after Peter and Edith had had supper together, Edith suggested he should retire early; he'd had a long day.

This had to have been a tiring day for him, but he appeared invigorated by getting up and out.

"No, not yet," he answered. "I'm not sleepy."

An uneasy quiet grew between them as they sat at the uncleared table.

"Why are you here, Edith?" Peter finally asked. He sounded like the old friend she'd grown up with, not accusatory or suspicious, just curious. Maybe even a little glad. She looked at him and saw a small smile on his lips.

His eyes were looking directly at her. She flushed. It wasn't nervousness about lying that brought the heat; it was that old familiar lust. She looked down, but not for long. The temptation to meet this challenge was too much for her.

"Are you glad I came?" she asked suggestively.

Her hand was resting on the table and he put his over it, continuing to watch her. It was large enough to completely cover hers, and it was warm. He turned her hand over and rubbed his thumb up and down her palm and the inside tender part of her small wrist. Her heart was hammering, and she saw his breathing was shallow and rapid.

Suddenly, he slid his chair back and put both hands around her waist. He lifted her onto his lap, so she was straddling him. Even in his weakened state, he was a strong man. His arousal was starkly evident, and it awakened in her a memory of innocent lust. He kissed her neck, sucking and murmuring about how he'd missed her and her fire.

When she tasted his mouth, it was too easy to yield to the frenzied passion that had been stirred up. They slept together in his bed that night and satiated each other's needs, but they were both aware of the shadows and whispers of regret lurking in the corners of the room.

She would curse herself for being so reckless, but not until it was too late.

EDITH ALMOST PUSHED Peter off her. The daylight streaming in the windows had brought clarity and sanity back to her. She couldn't get dressed and out of his bedroom quickly enough. Peter didn't try to stop her. He would have been happy to keep her in his bed all day, but he could see there was no sense in trying.

"What were we thinking?" she kept repeating while she gathered her clothing and dressed. She talked about John and how she loved him. Peter could hear the fear in her voice which was not something he was used to. Edith had always been fearless, and he realized, with a little bit of happiness for her, and maybe a little bit of sadness for himself, that she had found something she was afraid of losing.

He pulled on his own pants and made them some coffee. While they sat on the porch to drink it, he said, "It's okay, Edith. This will be our secret. No one else will ever know."

Her expression told him she believed him. He laughed, sadly.

"What?" she asked, staring at him.

"I miss May," he answered simply.

Chapter Fifteen

MAY AND EVELINE were having tea in their cozy drawing room. A fire had been built to take the edge off the cold day. It wasn't winter yet, but the November days had grown chilly. May had thought the Dupres' home was grand, but John's was grand on a whole different level. The house wore long manicured lawns, gardens with paths, and statues by a pond on its exterior, while its interior showed understated opulence, comfort, and good taste in every one of its many rooms. May and Eveline had an entire wing they shared. They had their own sitting rooms, dressing rooms, and even their own small dining room. This gave Edith and John a respectable amount of privacy.

"May, you look really splendid today. I believe pregnancy suits you very well," said Eveline and looked away, as if she felt silly for saying it when she thought of all the difficult miscarriages May had suffered.

But May just smiled at her new friend and said, "I feel splendid." May wondered if Edith had ever told Eveline about their "interludes." The fact that Eveline preferred women was certainly no secret among the four of them. It was accepted as a matter of fact, which was a marvel to May.

May was looking good and she knew it. Her figure had filled back out and her complexion was creamy with good health again. All the fine food, sleep, and daily exercise had been of benefit to her, but she knew the happiness she was feeling here made the biggest difference.

When Edith had suddenly left for her parents', May had experienced fleeting guilt that she didn't offer to go with her. She knew she should have. She really didn't have any reason for staying here. Her excuse for staying had been Edith and now Edith was gone. She worried that Peter would be angry, but then conveniently put it out of her mind. She didn't want to think about Peter right now.

Eveline did know about May. John had told her the things Edith had shared with him about their juvenile love triangle. Edith had been a bit vague, but he understood what she wasn't saying. He'd shared this with Eveline one evening when it was just the two of them at home. They'd been spending a nice evening alone, playing cards and enjoying each other's company for the first time since May and Edith had moved in. John was drinking scotch and had told Eveline that maybe they would both get lucky in love. He wouldn't have said such a thing if he'd been sober, but scotch tended to make him a bit loose-tongued and irreverent.

There was no denying there was an appealing sensuality about May. Eve doubted if she was even aware of the effect she had on other people. She had watched both men and women stare at her with appreciation, even John. But it wasn't just May's physical beauty, which was appreciable; something else pulled people toward her. Something quiet and strong, untamed, not wild, but raw.

Under different circumstances, things might have been different, but circumstances were what they were. May was pregnant and had a husband. Eve sensed a struggling undercurrent and knew that May needed some time and space to determine her direction. She wanted to be a friend to her, not a distraction.

Eveline was too polite to ever disclose her thoughts, but in her eyes at least, May looked plenty fit to travel. She was still early in her pregnancy, not really even showing yet. Each day, the two of them went for long walks and May's stamina was as good as Eveline's. The fact she was still here, while Edith had gone back, was evidence enough that she had some hard decisions to make.

May had taken to sitting close to Eveline, making excuses to touch her, looking in her eyes for just a moment longer than normal. If Eve wasn't as perceptive as she was, she might have taken advantage of this. May was definitely opening a door. But Eve knew that, for now anyway, she was opening the door to have a look inside. Sometimes we open doors and choose not to enter. Eveline was a woman who had experienced a lot of pain in the process of learning to love herself and she knew this decision needed to be made by May without her influence.

She was thinking these thoughts while they drank their tea, remembering the very real suffering May had also endured. It wasn't surprising that some of the doors she was opening, or having opened for her, were enticing. Life in the city was new and exciting for her. Being a guest in John's home introduced her to a life of ease and comfort that must be quite different from what she was accustomed to. Peter sounded like a good man. She hoped for all their sakes that if May did choose a new course, the damage left in her wake would be minimal.

She softened and really looked at May. They were sitting next to each other on the divan. She turned her body so they were facing each other. "Would you like to go out with me tonight?" she asked. She was supposed to go to the opera with John, but she knew he wouldn't mind one bit if he was excused for the evening. "*The Snow Maiden* is being performed at The Castle Square Theatre."

THEY WERE DRESSED in evening wear and waiting for the driver to come around to the front with the carriage. Eve had lent May a dress and some jewelry to wear to the opera. Even though May looked the part, she was feeling unsure of herself, out of her league. She'd been having a great time, imagining herself a sophisticated city girl, living the life of high fashion and leisure. But this was different. She realized she had no idea how to fit in with the wealthy Bostonians who would be out tonight. Eveline looked gorgeous and completely comfortable with the prospects of the evening. May took a deep breath and raised her head to try to gain control of her confidence.

It worked until Eveline said, "We'll be sitting with the Rockfords tonight. Will is the son of Mr. William Rockford Sr. and Elsa is the daughter of the Weston-Meiers." She raised her eyes as if this was impressive information. May searched her mind for some reference. She found none.

Eve continued, "After the performance, we'll have drinks and supper with Amelia Tudor and her son, Ivan. You may have read about them in the papers?"

May suspected Eve was filling her in on the events planned and the people who would be there so she would feel more comfortable. Still, panic began to rise in her chest. She didn't know how to speak to these friends of John and Eve. Obviously, they were important people she was expected to know something about. She'd been fooling herself and making a fool of herself. She looked at Eveline, half expecting her to be laughing at her, mocking her. Instead, she saw only a look of concern.

There was no delicate landing; she crashed hard.

Eveline rushed into the house, yelling for John. The driver followed, carrying May. When John saw what was happening, he ushered them into the nearest sitting room where the driver gently placed May on a chaise lounge. She was pale as a sheet. John sent the driver for the doctor. "Get him here now!" he instructed. "I don't care if you need to make a scene, just get him in that carriage post haste!"

Eveline had loosened May's dress and was speaking to her in gentle, hushed tones. She had learned a thing or two from Edith about calming language and she was using it now. "It's going to be all right, May...just take some nice deep breaths."

May was breathing too fast and hard. Eve continued, smoothing her hand slowly through May's hair even though her own heart was racing. "Look into my eyes, May... that's right, just continue to focus on me... Very good, May...nice, slow breaths..." She forced her own breathing to slow so that May would have something to follow and continued talking to her in a soothing voice. She sent for some chamomile tea and fed small sips to May while she continued her soothing instructions with efficient effect.

When the doctor arrived, May had already gotten some of her color back and was resting comfortably. Eveline had done a good job in calming her down. The doctor examined her and said what she needed was some quiet rest. He ordered her to bed for three days and recommended "no exciting activities" for a fortnight.

John wondered why he'd bothered fetching the doctor. Eveline had skillfully handled the situation. He'd never seen her so masterfully in charge. He was impressed with this unusual wife of his, but he would have to think about that later. Right now, he had an important guest in his home who needed his attention.

"I'll have her taken upstairs now, Eve. I could have one of the servants stay with her tonight..." he began, but Eveline interrupted him, as he'd suspected she would.

"Of course not, I'll stay with her myself."

While she was being carried to her rooms, John asked Eve to stay behind for a moment.

"What do you think happened? Should we send word to Edith?" he asked when they were alone.

"Honestly, John, I don't know what happened. She seemed so well today and then out in the foyer tonight, as we were preparing to leave, she began to grow pale and shaky, then she fell into my arms. Luckily the driver had just pulled around," Eve answered. "She seems well enough now. I'll have a talk with her in the morning and then we'll decide what to do."

"Very good." John liked that Eveline was in control of the situation. He felt out of his depths. "You handled her with impressive skill, Eve, the way you soothed her with your voice," he added with admiration in his voice as she turned to go out of the room.

Eveline turned back around and laughed. "You make her sound like a horse I was gentling. Good night, John."

She gave him a kiss on the cheek and went up to May's room.

MAY WAS FEELING better in the morning, but she'd had a very real scare the previous night. She thought of this baby growing inside her, her little boy. She remembered cradling him in her arms in the dream. Last night had brought her back to herself, had grounded her. She wanted desperately to hold him in her arms, for real. A few tears ran down her cheeks at the thought that she could have lost him again. She thought of Peter and her heart began the process of melting.

When Eveline woke up on the cot that had been brought in for her, May was already sitting up in bed and writing a letter to Peter. Eve smiled to herself. She recognized a woman who had temporarily lost herself, only to find herself again, and this time even stronger than before. Eve had been that woman herself, more than once.

"Good morning, May, how are you feeling today?" she asked.

May set down her pen and looked over. "Much better..." She looked down into her lap for a moment and then back up at Eveline. "I'm sorry for ruining last night. I feel quite embarrassed today actually."

"Embarrassed?" asked Eve. "Whatever for?"

"I don't know, Eve... I feel very confused, I guess."

In her letter, she was telling Peter about the grand homes and different pace to life in the city. She wanted to try to make him understand it wasn't just rest she needed, but a change in the patterns they had fallen into. She needed a life that extended beyond just her and Peter. What that could look like she wasn't sure.

Eveline had awakened some dormant feelings of arousal in her, and she enjoyed the closeness they were sharing. If she wasn't pregnant she might let herself explore where it could lead, but, for now at least, her main preoccupation was carrying this pregnancy through and she wouldn't do anything to jeopardize that.

"When I was young, I was certain what kind of life I wanted. I wanted to live in the same place I grew up, surrounded by the same people I had always known." She tried to explain her confusion. "I didn't crave new experiences like Edith did. I liked familiar things... I guess new things made me feel...edgy and a bit, I don't know...nervous?" She was rooting around looking for a way to explain what she didn't even understand well herself yet.

Then it hit her...yes, she liked to keep things simple and familiar because that edgy feeling was, quite literally, like being on the edge of a precipice. It gave her the same feeling of vertigo some people experience with heights. She didn't trust herself to not leap into the abyss. What had she told the little boy in her dreams? She had been looking for him in the wrong places.

May had mistakenly thought playing things safe could protect her. Well, it obviously hadn't worked. She had taken some leaps lately and she had enjoyed herself. She felt good venturing outside her limits. Maybe last night was just a lesson in taking things more slowly, or, hell, maybe the breathlessness that had overtaken her was just the wind rushing up under her sails.

"Eve, what would you think about meeting my Peter? What would you think about my inviting him and Cate here?" If she was going to change her life, she couldn't leave her family behind. She patted the bed next to her and invited Eve to come sit by her.

JOHN STAYED HOME from his office in case he was needed at home. Besides, there were a few things he wanted to look into today. He was working in his study, sitting behind his mahogany desk, when Eve knocked at the door. "Come in, Eve, I was just thinking about you," he said.

"Oh yes?" she replied.

He smiled his beautiful smile at her, with a hint of suggestion.

"Yes," he said and left it at that. He looked at her with raised brows, waiting for her to say what was clearly on her mind.

"It's May," she began.

John's face turned more serious. "Is she all right?" he asked.

Eve came into the room and stood across the desk from him.

"Yes, in fact I think her health is perfect. As good as ever. This is more concerning some things she talked to me about this morning. You already know that she would like to stay here, with us, until her baby is born." John nodded. Eve went on, "Well, she thinks she might want to stay on in Boston permanently."

She stopped speaking for a moment, still a bit surprised by May's quick change in plans. "She asked if she could invite her husband and daughter to come stay as well."

Eveline explained May's plan, which had developed while she sat with her that morning. May had the idea that perhaps they could use the guest cottage and Peter could do some projects for them, maybe even work on the grounds, in lieu of a rental payment. She wanted Peter to experience the city the way she was, in the hopes that he might want to settle here.

"You seem unsure as to the soundness of this plan, Eve," John remarked.

"I guess it's just so sudden," Eve explained. "I do wonder if May is being a bit impulsive. She hasn't confided this to me, but I suspect that as recently as yesterday, she wasn't sure she even wanted to keep her life with Peter. And now, all of a sudden, she wants to bring him here to live. I'll be honest, John, she has spent the last week flirting with...well, flirting with me. I don't think she knows what she wants."

John raised his eyebrows. "Flirting, eh?" He was quiet for a moment and then he said, "Let me tell you what I've been flirting with." He came around to the front of his desk and leaned against the edge, tapping a rhythm with his fingers on the wood.

"I've been thinking about opening a retreat center. I want to give Edith a place of her own. She's always talking about new ideas of how to help these women, and I know for a fact the Dupres have to turn down every other woman who is brought to them because they simply don't have the space. I've been reading about spas where people can go for a rest—not just women, but anyone in need of a rest."

John stopped. He picked up a large, colored, glass marble and began turning it around in his hands. Eveline waited for him to continue. She was intrigued by his idea and knew from experience that he would get around to how this might relate to what she had said.

"After watching you with May last night, I had an epiphany. I'm truly a brilliant man," he said with a wide grin.

She smiled demurely back and waited for him to continue.

"I want you and Edith to run it together, as co-owners," he finished with a look of sincere interest that was touching.

Eve stood mutely where she was for a moment trying to fathom what he had just said. John rushed on to explain how it was perfect in so many ways. As an investor, he believed it would be a wise venture. Edith was interested in the healing aspects of the business, and after seeing Eve with May last night, he knew it was a venture she was also suited to. However, he thought she would be most useful in running the business side. She had shown a real acumen for working with numbers and the administrative side of things while working for him and he would be available to consult with at any time.

They would own it together, and he would loan them the capital to get it started. She would have her own financial independence, as well as a very generous alimony settlement, and would therefore be free to divorce him—so he could then marry Edith, naturally. He was so excited about the brilliance of his idea, he was out of breath when he finally stopped.

"John," she faltered, "I don't know what to say... You certainly seem to have thought about this in detail, and I know you have a keen eye for investment... Do you really think we could do this?"

She was getting more excited with every passing second. A business with Edith; she couldn't think of anything more perfect. Eve had to sit down and catch her own breath.

Something nagged at the back of her mind. Oh yes, May! "John, what about May and her ideas?" she reminded him.

"Ah yes, May," he said. "Well, what if, after the baby is born, you were to hire her in some capacity. She is an interesting young woman who, no doubt, could bring something to this venture...and this Peter, if he's as good a craftsman as May says, I'm sure he wouldn't have trouble finding work in the city." He looked sideways at Eve. "And if things don't work out with him, I'm sure you could help her find her feet." He winked at her. Eve shook her head, grinning. "In the meantime, if Peter wishes to come, they are welcome to the guest house."

Eveline hugged him hard. "You really are a one-of-a-kind gem, you know that? Thank you for being so bloody good," she said earnestly. Before she got to the door, John was already seated and ruffling through his papers again.

Eveline needed some time to think alone. She went to her room to sit quietly. Edith had shown her how to take herself to trance, but she hadn't practiced lately with so much commotion in the house. Now, with Edith away and May in bed, per doctor's orders, this was a perfect time.

She made herself comfortable, allowing her body to grow heavy, focusing her mind on her breath. In this way, she was able to calm her mind which had been racing with thoughts, questions, and ideas that had begun forming the moment John had presented his remarkable plan. When she opened her eyes, she realized it was nearly time for lunch. While her mind was still clear, she got up and started on a few lists of things to begin with, things she would run by John at dinner. She'd worked for him long enough to have learned some research skills which would be very helpful in getting this off the ground. After a bit, she grew restless with ideas again and went to check on May.

When she entered May's room, May exclaimed excitedly, "I felt him! I felt him move, Eve! Come here and sit by me." She patted the bed. Eve sat next to her. The excitement was contagious. May took Eve's hands and spread them on her stomach. "Just hold them there for a minute and maybe he'll move again," she said. Eve held still, concentrating, and was rewarded with a small blip under her hands.

"I felt it! May, that was amazing!" She leaned forward and kissed May. It was meant to be a friendly gesture, but May leaned into it and kissed her back. For a few moments, they got lost in the sensations. Eve's hands moved from May's stomach to her hips as she held on. When she pulled back, she was on fire. Oh good lord, this day had had too much excitement already. May's eyes looked smoky with desire, her lips bruised with the intensity of the kissing.

Eve shook her head slowly back and forth. "No, May, no, we can't do this." She backed away from the bed. "As much as I would enjoy loving you, I can't. You need to figure some things out first." And she turned and walked into the hall and closed the door.

Chapter Sixteen

EDITH HAD BEEN staying with her parents for the last week. The first few days, she had stayed at Peter's. It had not seemed at all untoward since he needed nursing, but when Peter's mother had come by with supper and pulled Edith aside to tactfully remind her that Peter had a wife and child, she had moved back into her old house, chastising herself for being so careless.

It was really nice to see her parents. They both had aged a bit but were doing quite well and loved to listen to her stories about work. She told them about John but had to be careful because they wouldn't understand the unusual circumstances. As she talked about him, she realized just how foolish she'd been. She loved her life in Boston, and she loved John. When her mother asked when the wedding would be, Edith had been vague and said they hadn't really progressed their courtship to that point yet, and her focus was her work for now, desperately hoping she hadn't ruined things.

She was still taking Cate each afternoon. Most days they went to visit Peter for a while, bringing him lunch, and eating it with him. The first visit back to his house, after their brief affair, had been awkward and she was grateful to have Cate there. She went back, alone, that same evening to tell him she regretted what they had done. She loved John and had a good life with him. He agreed they couldn't carry on. He loved May and needed to try to work things out with her.

They managed to find an easiness between them again. On the nice days, she and Cate worked in the garden, finishing its hibernation, and when the sky had turned dark and rained, they had played games with Peter at the table.

Peter was almost ready to get back to work. Edith knew it was time for her to go back too. She missed John. Edith felt as though she had put something to rest, closed a chapter so to speak, and was ready to get on with her life in Boston. Peter was the past, John was her future.

For Peter, it was a little different. He had enjoyed it when Edith had sat in his lap that night and kissed him. He was feeling clear minded again, like the high fever had somehow burned off the madness that had been plaguing him for some time now.

After they'd made love, he hadn't felt guilty, only sad. May had been pulling away from him almost from the start and he was ready to face that now. They'd kept up a facade, even between themselves, which was probably what had made him crazy. May behaved as she thought she was supposed to, but it was as if she was playing a role. He knew she had tried hard, and he didn't blame her. They had made a beautiful baby girl together, and there had been good times, but they needed to have a real conversation; they needed to figure out what was true and what was not.

Edith planned to leave on the Friday morning train. It was hard to say goodbye to Cate. She had contemplated asking Peter if she could bring her back to Boston but then wondered if May would want that. She understood May had needed rest, but now, she couldn't understand how she wouldn't want to be with her sweet daughter. Anyway, she could see Cate and Peter were very fond of each other, so she left it alone.

When she arrived at the station early on Friday, she was very surprised to find Peter there with a bag. "What on earth are you doing here?" she asked.

"I'm going to see my wife. We have a lot to talk about, Edith."

More than you know, she thought. Out loud she said, "I'm glad, Peter, and I'm glad you'll have a chance to meet John."

She had the entire trip back to decide if she should tell him about the pregnancy.

JOHN WAITED FOR Edith at the station. He couldn't wait to take her in his arms and kiss her breathless, but he was even more excited to tell her about his idea. He hoped she would be as happy as he and Eve were; she'd be able to run things exactly how she wanted.

When she stepped off the train, he waved to her and she ran to him. He did take her in his arms and kiss her breathless, but when he let her up for air, instead of being able to tell her he had news, she cleared her throat, looked behind her, and beckoned to a gentleman who was standing, somewhat awkwardly, behind her.

"John, I would like you to meet May's husband, Peter." She turned to the man. "Peter, this is my John." John extended his hand, while in his mind he was noticing how ridiculously handsome, and well built, this Peter was.

"It's a pleasure to meet you, Peter," he said and then turned to Edith with a question in his eyes.

"Peter surprised me at the station this morning. He has decided it's time to see May," she answered, trying to tell him with her eyes that he didn't know about the baby. She wasn't sure he got the message, but in any case, the two men shook hands, and John, all business now, had them and their bags loaded into the carriage.

Edith had worked out a plan on the train, and on the ride home she put it into action. "John, I'm sure Peter would enjoy going to your club for drinks before dinner. It will give May and me time to freshen up." John never went to his club, so she was sure he would understand this meant she needed time to prepare May for the surprise visit.

"Of course," replied John nonchalantly. "We'll drop you at the house and head right over. You can tell Mrs. Leeds to hold dinner."

Peter leaned forward. "If you don't mind, John, I'd rather go to see May first." He paused for a moment then added quietly, "It's been quite some time."

"Of course," John answered, not seeming to notice that Edith was silently prodding him to try to persuade Peter otherwise. Frustrated in her attempts, she sat back into her seat waiting for another opportunity.

When they had disembarked from the carriage, Edith hurried out first, saying she would go let May know Peter was here. He told her he would go himself, and Edith tried to argue. John took her by the arm, pointed Peter in the right direction, and guided Edith toward their rooms.

"But..." she began.

John cut her off. "Peter is May's husband, Edith. He can go to her room if he wants, it's really not our business." He stopped and turned to her. "Besides, I have something to tell you—" he raised his eyebrow "—in private."

"Oh." She smiled in anticipation and followed him willingly, forgetting about Peter and May. She was glad to be back.

PETER MET EVELINE when he passed through the sitting room. He guessed who she was based on Edith's descriptions and introduced himself. He hadn't known what to think when Edith had told him about John and his wife Eveline and their unusual situation, and of how Edith and May had moved into their home. She had left out what had instigated the move, of course, but described the living situation in detail. It had surprised him to hear May was so comfortable there, but the information had only further confirmed for him that she wasn't the person she had been trying hard to be.

"Good evening, you must be Eveline." He bowed as he introduced himself. Eveline seemed startled but kept her composure.

She tilted her head up to look him in the eyes, "It's a pleasure to meet you, Peter, I have heard so very much about you. I'm sure May will be thrilled to see you. She was just writing to you this morning, in fact, to ask you to join her here. Shall I take you to her room?" She was surprised when this handsome man refused, saying if she would just point out the door he would prefer to go alone.

Peter knocked briefly and opened the door. He was very anxious to see May and he wanted to see her alone. Whatever unknown things lay between them, he loved his wife and always had. He stepped into the room and paused in his tracks. She was sitting up in bed, looking lovelier than he remembered. She had a look of shock on her face, and time stopped for a few moments while they just stared at each other.

"Peter?" she whispered finally. "Peter, what...how...how did you know?" Then she jumped out of bed in a panic. "Is it Cate? Oh God, is she okay?" He took the three steps to her bed and held her, reassuring her that Cate was fine.

"You look lovely, May," he murmured into her hair. She hugged his familiar frame hard.

"I'm so glad you're here."

"We have a lot to talk about," they both said at the same time.

"First things first," he said, "why are you in bed?"

She sat back down and swung her legs up onto the bed and then scooted over to make room for him. She was a little shy, which was odd because she'd never felt that way with him before. She was also nervous because she had no idea how he would take everything she had to tell him.

It felt good to have his solid presence next to her. Peter was one of those large, quiet men who radiate calm. She noticed the difference in him. He hadn't been that calming presence for some time before she left, but she sensed now it had returned. He really was good looking. Strangeness and confusion gripped her when she remembered kissing Eve in this same spot only a few hours earlier.

Peter sat on the bed and closed his eyes for a moment. He took her hand in his, but before he could say anything, she said, "Peter, I'm pregnant again." He took his hand away and looked at her.

"Pregnant?" It didn't make sense. He turned a deep red but said in a controlled tone, "Who is the father, May?"

May looked confused. "What do you mean, who is the father? You are of course! What are you suggesting!" She was growing indignant.

He looked at her. "How could I be?" He wanted to believe her, but...and then he remembered the morning before she left. They had found a space of peace together in the midst of all the unrest. "How far along are you?"

May told him how she'd found out shortly after arriving. Interestingly, no one had questioned her vision. She must have only been weeks along at that point, far too early for any other indicator.

Peter listened to her story. He believed her. He knew May had a gift of visions, and regretted his attempts to squelch it. With his mind clear now, he could see his jealousies had done them both great damage. Sadly, his fear of losing her might be the very thing that had caused it. If he had instead encouraged May's gifts and trusted her enough to explore her heart; if he had been willing to set her free, things might have been so different these last few years. He felt a sadness that by holding on too tightly, he had robbed her of her happiness. She took his hand again and squeezed it. He smiled at her. Maybe it wasn't too late.

"So, we're going to have a son?" he said. May watched Peter's face. Hope began to bloom, replacing the sadness, only to be reined in again. He'd seen her lose too many babies.

"Peter," she said softly, "I felt him move this morning, and again this afternoon."

It was reason enough for hope, so they both hung on to it.

Chapter Seventeen

AS SOON AS John had Edith in his arms again, he didn't let go. He wrapped his hands in her long hair and kissed her possessively. He had gotten used to having her often after she moved in with him, and he'd missed her. John was a very passionate lover. Edith was almost glad she'd had her brief encounter with Peter; John's lovemaking was free from doubts, guilts, and ghosts. She felt at home with John in a way she had never experienced before. Any doubts that may have lingered for her were gone. She kissed him back with equal fervor.

He laid her on the bed and undid every one of her torturous buttons. When he finally had her out of her dress, he stood back to appreciate her soft, pale skin and her round curves and mounds. Edith moaned in the back of her throat when he kneeled between her legs and pressed his hot breath through her last piece of undergarment, which he then hastily removed.

After a few moments, she pulled him up to her and kissed him deeply and then climbed over him so that she was straddling him. His breathing became ragged as she lowered herself onto him. They held each other's gaze until John groaned and closed his eyes.

Later, they snacked on the supper John had thoughtfully prearranged to have sent to their rooms, and then he turned to Edith. She looked so beautiful leaning onto the curve of the divan wearing only the silk nightdress he'd bought her as a gift when she moved in. The sheer, teal blue played with the color of her eyes, making them shine brightly.

"I have something very important to talk to you about, Edie."

She loved her new nickname. She had never been called anything but Edith and she thought this modern version suited her well. She looked at him expectantly.

"I want to invest in you," he said. "Well, more precisely, I want to invest in you and Eve."

She wasn't sure what he meant, but she could tell the subject was very exciting to him. She sat up and he proceeded to tell her all his plans for the retreat center. He jumped from one aspect of the plan to another in chaotic fashion. He was gesticulating and pacing animatedly, but she listened to everything with rapt attention, and soon had all the pieces together.

He told her the operational ideas that Eve was already working on and gave a brief accounting of the potential properties he had looked at. He told her how he'd already spoken with the Dupres and had their blessings and their help. Then he stopped in front of her and knelt between her knees once again. This time he took her hands in his and said, "So many of the details are falling into place...but the real heart and soul of the project—the life of the center, and the care and healing of its residents—needs to be created by you. What do you think?"

Then he stopped and became quiet and still. He was waiting to see her reaction. She had been listening so intently she'd hardly moved a muscle. He didn't breathe as she sat there motionless, staring at him, and he couldn't tell what she was thinking. Every doubt he'd had, every fear that he had overstepped himself, swam around him—but then the sun broke through. She threw herself at him. She launched into his arms, which he barely had time to put up to catch her, before they both fell backward, laughing, onto the floor.

After they had managed to disentangle themselves and put their nightclothes on *again*, John said, "Edie, there's one more aspect of this plan I didn't mention before." He grew serious now as he continued. "I didn't want to bring up this part until I was certain you wanted to take on the running of your own Center. I wanted to make sure the two parts weren't a package deal for you." He looked keenly at Edith, letting her know he wanted her to understand what he was saying. "No matter what you think of this next part, I want you to know that I am 100 percent committed to helping you with this business."

She sat next to him on the love seat, her body turned toward him.

"Edith, for me, the best part of this would be that Eve will have something of her own, a place to call home so to speak... She has agreed to a divorce... In fact, she's the one who suggested it." He paused and looked into her eyes and then got on his knees before her again. "Edith, when that happens, will you make me the happiest man alive by becoming my wife?" he asked.

This time there was no launching, no tumbling to the ground, and no laughter. There was tenderness, reverence, and simple joy as Edith agreed to marry the man she adored.

EVELINE SAT AT her desk, engrossed. She was working on figures for the costs of meal preparations for their new center. There was so much more to be done than she had initially realized, but she loved this sort of work. She liked figures, and calculations and variables. She had come back from a meeting with Mrs. Dupre yesterday with a large file of valuable, time-saving information. She wasn't aware that Peter had knocked at her open door.

Peter stood in the doorway, unsure of whether he should knock again. She looked busy and he didn't want to disturb her concentration. On the other hand, he hadn't had many opportunities to speak with her alone, and he might not get another soon. May and Edith had gone for tea at the Dupres, but he expected them back within the hour.

It was the movement he made as he turned away from the door, then back again, as he wavered, that caught her attention in the corner of her eye. She looked up, startled.

"Peter," she said. "I'm sorry, I didn't see you there."

He still looked unsure about entering, but maybe this was because it wasn't an easy topic he wished to discuss with Eve.

"I'm sorry, I didn't mean to disturb you... I could come back another time..." he offered.

"Nonsense. Please come in. I could use a break anyway," she said.

"Can I pour you some?" They had gone into the sitting room together and sat facing each other over the tea table. Eve poured them each a cup and put out some biscuits on a small serving tray. She indicated for Peter to help himself. She was curious as to what had brought him to seek her out. He seemed a bit uncomfortable, so she busied herself with tidying up the tea tray, giving him time to find his words.

Peter was a tall, well-built man. He moved slowly, with a calming deliberateness. His question was simple, but the answer was important.

"Eveline, has May been happy here?"

Ah. She cradled her teacup and leaned back into the cushion, exhaling. She looked directly at Peter. His own gaze did not waver, but he wasn't going to rush her. She liked that he was a direct, but patient, man.

"Yes, I think she has," she began. "I'm sure you can see for yourself how much better she's looking from when you last saw her." She took a sip of tea, thinking. "Obviously, I don't know her like you and Edith do," she continued, "but perhaps that makes it easier for me to notice certain things." She stopped and looked across at Peter. He nodded his head slightly, encouraging her to go on. "While we were waiting for her to arrive, Edith told me that May might not take to the city very easily. She said May was a girl who likes quiet and familiar surroundings. But I must say this is not how I see her." She smiled. "I see a woman who is blossoming here. It's true that maybe, at times, she needs to take small steps, but she loves the bustle of the city."

Eve stood and walked to the window. She looked down on the avenue below. "We've walked miles together every day since she came here. May never wants to take the same route twice. She loves to chat with the shopkeepers and neighbors out strolling. She tells me about her ideas and dreams. She seems happy." She turned around and looked at Peter again. "She talks about you a lot, Peter, and Cate."

Peter nodded again. He understood that Eveline was May's friend and she would want to be careful about what she said, but he sensed there was more she might share if he gave her time.

Eve took another deep breath and let it out, considering. "I suppose it would be all right for me to say that I believe all the new experiences she's having have made her feel a bit confused inside. She's a special person...she has a sensitivity to things most of us don't..."

Eve was trying to find the right words. "I get the sense that May is feeling her way around...trying to find her path." She stopped. This really was a conversation Peter should be having with May.

Peter stood and walked over to Eve. "Thank you, Eveline. I appreciate your honesty. May has spoken highly of your friendship to her and I would like to thank you for that."

He turned to look out the window and was quiet again for a while. Finally, he said, "She's asked me to stay here. She wants to bring Cate here and make this our home."

The way he said this was telling.

"I don't like the city," he said simply. "I need the forests and the open spaces. I like the simplicity of rural life, I guess." He continued in a sad voice, "I thought that was what May liked as well, and I do wonder if this is just a passing fancy; an exciting interlude...but if it's not..." He didn't finish his thought. This wasn't Eveline's concern and he shouldn't burden her with his doubts and questions.

When he turned back to her, Eve saw his sadness. She knew he wanted May to be happy, and she felt for him. She didn't believe it helped anyone to sacrifice their own happiness for someone else's, though, and she said so. "Maybe she should work with Edith again," Eve suggested. "I believe she has her answers within her. Perhaps it's time for her to find them."

"WHY? WHY CAN'T you give it a try?" May was reasoning with Peter. "You can do your work here just as easily as back home. You would have even more clients here."

Peter answered calmly, "May, I don't need more clients. I have my hands full as it is." He turned her to face him. They had taken a stroll in the garden and they both were bundled against the cold. Peter's breath showed as he breathed out a sigh. "Look, I've already told you I'm not cut out for the city." He shrugged with his hands. "I understand that you find it invigorating and exciting, but I find it stifling. I couldn't work here. My inspiration comes from nature."

He stopped. They had gone over all of this, multiple times. He sat down on a bench and stretched out his long legs. May remained standing. She walked over to the fountain, emptied for the winter, and slowly circled it. When she came back, she tried one more time.

"We could get a place just outside the city. A place with some land..."

He took her hand and pulled her down beside him.

"May, I don't have money like John does. This is a fantasy." He held her gaze, trying to make her understand this part. "If we lived here, it would be in a small house on a street crowded with other small houses. This—" he gestured at John's home and estate. "I can't give you this," he ended with a hint of exasperation.

He was sorry he couldn't give all this grandeur to May if that's what she wanted, but it wasn't at all what he wanted. He was happy in the home he'd built with his father, using their own hands. He'd thought it was a home fit for a queen. It was comfortable and beautiful. His best woodworking skills had gone into it, along with a layout that could easily be added onto in order to accommodate a growing family. He trailed down the thought for just a moment and then turned back. Even with two children, their home had plenty of room. In truth, he probably wouldn't ever need to add anything.

But it wasn't this. He couldn't give her this.

How could May be so foolish? Of course, Peter was right. Every time she pictured them here, it was living in the same style she had been enjoying since coming to Boston. She wasn't being realistic. Edith and Eve could have this, but not her, she thought with some bitterness. She was the same old May she'd always been; married to Peter, who was the same old Peter he'd always been. If she'd been honest with herself, she would have realized this was all just a dream.

She did sit down now. She could feel herself deflating. As she shrunk, her anger grew. Peter watched her face turn angry. Although her expression didn't change much, her eyes grew stony; this look made him sad. What he had to offer his wife was no longer enough, if it ever had been.

"I need to get back. My shop is a mess and I need to get to work," Peter said quietly. "I'll stay through the end of the week, which will give us a few days to work out details, but I'll leave on Friday." Today was Tuesday. He felt empty.

Hearing that he was leaving, that he was willing to go without forcing her to follow, melted her heart again. What was wrong with her? she wondered. She had a perfect husband, a nice home, a daughter and a child on the way. How could she be considering staying here? He was absolutely right; he always saw things as they were, never romanticized... She couldn't have Edith's or Eve's lives. She didn't have a husband with wealth and she didn't have a profession, but she did have a beautiful daughter and a considerate, talented husband who loved her. She inwardly chided herself for being so silly.

"I'll go with you," she said.

"No," Peter replied. This time, she sensed a little of the stone in him. She'd taken this too far and angered him. "Don't play games, May. You're a grown woman and it doesn't suit you. You can't have it both ways. You can't just pick me because you can't see a way to having everything else you want."

He struggled to sound kinder; he didn't want to risk upsetting May too much while his son was doing such a good job hanging on this time. "We don't need to take any drastic measures right now. I want you to stay here until the baby is born. It's best to do things this way, for now at least. I will have time to get caught up with my work, and you will have the support of Edith and Eve through the pregnancy."

Making the effort to be kind had softened him and he took May in his arms. Despite her confusions, which were confounding, she was a good woman. She just needed some time. Maybe this really would be for the best.

"I want you to figure out what it is you want," he whispered into the top of her head. "Do you understand what I'm saying? I'm giving you this time and space to answer that question." He couldn't look in her eyes, because he didn't want her to see his tears. He knew what he wanted, and he was holding it tightly.

AFTER SUPPER ON Thursday evening, John invited Peter into his library for a drink and cigar. Neither of them was the cigar smoking type, but John enjoyed the idea of the custom. His library was comfortable, with large, worn leather chairs and handcrafted bookcases. When they each had a drink in hand, and Peter had had a chance to examine and admire the woodworking, they both took a seat. John took his time getting to the point. It wasn't customary for him to get involved in others' affairs unless they were close to him; but, Edith had asked a favor.

He liked Peter, at least what he'd seen of him. He seemed to be the sort of person John liked doing business with. He was honest and clear about who he was and what his intentions were, which was somewhat rare, at least in the world of business.

"I understand you're quite a fine craftsman yourself, Peter."

Peter nodded yes. "I've been at it since I was a young boy," he answered.

"I've always leaned more toward numbers myself," John responded thoughtfully. "My father tried to prime me to take over his business. He owned a shipping company. I worked for him for a few years, but I soon learned that I had a knack for spotting opportunities. I needed to diversify." He took a sip of his scotch and raised his glass to admire the color. "This is one of my new projects. What do you think of it?"

"You're distilling spirits?" Peter asked with raised eyebrows, his tone skeptical.

"No," John laughed, "imports." He became serious again. "You have a knack with wood and I have a knack for turning a profit."

"Ah," Peter replied. "I think perhaps Edith has been talking to you?"

John smiled. He appreciated a man with quick perception. He could do business with Peter. "Yes, she has." He stood and walked around behind his chair. He thought better when he was moving.

"I have a proposal. I imagine you've heard something about the retreat center Edie and Eve will be opening?" He paused, giving Peter a chance to answer.

Peter responded in the affirmative.

"Edie has asked me to speak with you." He purposefully called Edith by his pet name. Peter was a very handsome man and, with their history, he wanted to lay some claim. It made him feel a bit childish, but also safer.

"She would like to offer May a position. It could be short term..." Here he stopped pacing and looked at Peter before continuing. "Or long term," he said pointedly. "Edie tells me May is considering staying in Boston and she...*we*, want you to know that if she decides to stay, she will have a place here, with Eve."

John wasn't sure about this offer. While he was in no real position to criticize, he believed a woman belonged with her husband and children... Still, he had to admit that circumstances sometimes led people outside society's conventions. He found himself in the slightly uncomfortable position of offering to aid in the heartbreak of this man sitting across from himself. If he refused, May would have no real options but to go home with her husband. He swallowed and looked into his glass. He and Peter shared something, he realized. Both men were acquainted with life outside the boundaries of convention, both were intelligent enough to see the grace an open mind can offer, but still, he guessed that Peter was not happy with his offer.

Peter seemed to be thinking about what John had said, but when he spoke his reply wasn't what John expected.

"I'm glad Edith found you." He chuckled. "Since we were children that girl has been intimidating to me. She was always sprouting ideas and schemes; always challenging... everything!" He went on, "I'd think I'd caught up with things, only to find out she was already moving on to the next." He smiled fondly. "She's a rare woman, fiercely loyal and determined." To himself, he added, *fiercely passionate as well.* "I'm glad she's found a man who can keep up with her; a man who can breathe some wind under her wings." Peter paused and sobered. "I wasn't a good friend to her in the end. My jealousy got in the way."

John didn't understand. Edith hadn't told him that was a problem. Peter could see the confusion on his face.

He said, "She never even told you, did she? That's what I mean by loyal." He explained, "When May got pregnant, I was so happy. I wanted May to myself." He looked at John. Peter assumed that John knew at least something about their tryst and he was looking for confirmation of this before continuing.

John nodded. "Yes, Edie mentioned it was a bit of a blow for her," he said carefully.

"Yes, well, I'm afraid May's feelings weren't quite so clear. I became jealous of her feelings for Edith. When I heard the news about her offer in Boston, I'm embarrassed to say I was glad. Even though the news was hard on May... I wanted her gone. I wasn't nice about it either." He looked directly at John. "Edith doesn't know it, but I blamed her for all of May's miscarriages." He looked down. "I suppose not right away, but I let my anger find a target, and she was convenient. I hadn't seen her in a few years and I had built her into some sort of sorceress, with her trances and all." He laughed ruefully and returned his gaze to John. "She hadn't done anything to deserve my anger...all she ever did was love us."

John was silent. He didn't like the idea of his fiancée loving this man. He would be a hard competitor.

Peter continued, unaware that he was about to drop a bomb. "And even with all that, she came to me when I was deathly ill and helped nurse me back to health."

John remained silent as Peter went on. "Like I said, I'm glad she found a man with an intelligence to match her own and an appreciation for her skills. The two of you are well matched."

Peter seemed to remember what John had brought him in here to say. "I appreciate what you and Edith are offering May. It is a comfort, but I want to be honest with you, John, I hope she doesn't accept it..."

John heard what Peter was saying, but he was also doing what he was very good at. He was filling in a spreadsheet in his mind. Usually it was numbers he moved around, analyzing and making decisions about them, before anyone thought he could have even begun. He was good at taking people by surprise, making or rejecting offers or plans before they were ready; this ability gave him a leg up in business. But now he was doing this with dates, facts, information shared and withheld.

John was a good person, but a shrewd businessman, and he didn't like to show his hand.

"Yes, well, the offer also extends to yourself, Peter. Edith thought you would be the perfect choice to help design her Institute. Based on her recommendations, the job is yours if you want it. It would keep you here in Boston for a while, but the salary would be substantial. You have at least a month to decide." He turned back to Peter. "Can I give you a refill?"

THERE WERE CERTAIN things John knew. Although making assumptions based on partial information was often a mistake, he had learned that when it came to his intuition, he could often get away with it. On the other hand, he hadn't been very well tuned in about Eveline. How he'd managed to miss the fact that Margaret had been her lover still baffled him. But, then again, if he hadn't married Eve, he wouldn't have met Edith...so maybe it was all in the cards. However, he now had reason to doubt Edith; maybe she also wasn't who he thought she was. He wished he could take this circular line of thinking and pull one end to straighten it.

These were some of the facts shifting around in his head, along with the certainty that Edith must have lied about her father being ill, not only to him, but also to May. Which also meant she had lied to both of them about Peter. Peter said Edith had "nursed" him, and the thought didn't sit well with him. Peter had arrived, with Edith, in Boston. Edith had asked John to offer him a job that would keep him here for an extended time while working closely with her. She had been back in the city for four days and hadn't gotten around to telling him the truth—this despite their unofficial engagement.

But other facts needed placing on his spreadsheet. He didn't pick up on any undercurrents of desire between Edith and Peter.

Along those same lines, Edith very obviously had plenty of lustfulness for himself, and Peter clearly loved his wife and had chosen her over Edith years ago. Edith also loved May and had helped her with this pregnancy. If the pregnancy didn't go to term, the chances that Peter and May would stay together would be much slimmer. Despite this potential opportunity, if indeed she wanted Peter to become available, she had done what she could to help May get healthy. Also, Peter wished to return home. He had no interest in Boston.

If you can imagine a spreadsheet, or a large game board, if you will, that would be the backdrop on which all these pieces of information were moving around, and John wasn't a man to make a move until he had strategized and analyzed everything. He wasn't foolish enough to dismiss her without a proper weighing of all these facts, and more.

All this was going on in John's head as he poured another few fingers of scotch for Peter, who seemed content to sit back in his chair and enjoy this rare treat. It didn't take long for him to work out what to do.

"If you'll excuse me, Peter, I think I need to talk to Edith. Please feel free to enjoy the library and the scotch as you like. I'll wish you a pleasant journey now since I won't be seeing you off tomorrow." Even though he didn't need to, he added, "I'm sure you know how to be in touch with Edith so you can give her your decision about her offer."

He left, closing the library door behind him, and headed to the sitting room where he knew the ladies would be talking shop.

"I AGREE, EVE, the baths are a must. I've been reading about Turkish baths where special salts are used with good results. I think we can improve upon what they offer at the Institute..." Edith was interrupted by John entering the room without announcing himself. They were in Edith's sitting room, which used to be Eve's.

Eveline looked at John's face and made an excuse to take her leave. "I think I'll go check on May now. We'll talk later, Edie. Hello, John," she said as she passed him on the way out.

Edith glanced at John and had the irrational thought that she'd like to follow Eve. "And how was your meeting with Peter?" she asked.

"It wasn't a meeting, Edith," he answered a little coolly. She noticed he didn't use Edie, which she had grown used to hearing from his lips. She cocked her head to the side and squinted at him. She couldn't imagine how things could have gone poorly with Peter; all John was doing was offering some options and maybe some peace of mind to him.

Then it hit her. She sucked in her breath. Of course! How could she have been so careless, so forgetful? Peter must have mentioned his being ill and her coming to him.

Edith didn't often feel afraid or even nervous, but she did now. There was way too much at stake here. She let her breath out slowly, trying to steady her nerves. She couldn't read his expression. John had sat down across from her, in the place Eve had just vacated. He was staring at her. She flushed. Better to take the offensive she decided.

"I'm guessing from your demeanor that Peter told you about his illness," she said. John didn't say anything or change his expression at all. This had the effect of flustering her. She bit her lip and tried again.

"I was planning to tell you when I got back..." she faltered, realizing how feeble this sounded. "It's just that...well..." She tried again. "It's just that you made me so happy that first night, and gave me so much to think about, I put it out of my mind," she ended with a lame shrug and weak smile. She hadn't been trying for manipulation when she mentioned how happy he had made her; it was true!

When he still didn't respond, she continued, "I'm sorry, John. Mrs. Dupre gave me the letter that had been sent for May..." She recounted how she'd thought it best not to upset May in her condition so had decided to go herself and make up a reason. She left the obvious, glaring fact that she had also lied to him unspoken.

"I see," was all he said. John had learned the less said, the better in business negotiations. If he stayed quiet, the other party felt the need to talk and usually ended up saying much more than they had planned to. He was unconsciously using this tactic on Edith now.

"John, he's an old friend. That's all. I love you. I only wanted to help him and spare May from worry and the hardships of travel. I only stayed at their place the first two nights to give his mother a rest." She thought about the way she had touched Peter but put it from her mind.

She was becoming very unsettled and rattled by his calm silence and unwavering stare. It probably made her say what she would immediately regret.

"Honestly, John. I'll admit that I kissed him one night...but it was almost a relief because it made me realize I really don't have any feelings left for him." She was pleading with him and her insides turned sick when she saw the look on his face; it went from calm to ice in seconds. He rose and walked from the room without saying a word.

"John," Edith cried. "Please come back, we need to talk..." But he was already gone. She crumpled into the chair, breathing shallowly, with a knot of anxiety in her stomach.

JOHN BURST BACK into the library. Peter was still sitting where he'd left him. "You bastard," he said as he took a swing at Peter's face before Peter had even had a chance to rise. Peter may have been considerably larger and more muscular than John, but he was caught completely unawares. Besides which he was a peaceful man, even a pacifist, and wouldn't have considered defending himself against his host.

He held his nose, which was bleeding. John took a handkerchief from his breast pocket and handed it to Peter.

"How dare you enjoy a dalliance with Edith and then come to my home as a guest," he spat out. "Both of you have deceived May and me." He was becoming tired of his anger already. He wasn't good at holding a grudge, but he was good at cutting a deal short as soon as he saw it wasn't in his best interest. Cut your losses to save your gains, was his general policy. He wanted this man out of his house immediately. He wanted to create a scene. He wouldn't give up Edith without a fight. The image of two men, dueling at dawn in a mist, came to his mind. Yes, he would enjoy the opportunity to publicly win Edith, and shame Peter at the same time. He was on the verge of cutting when he thought of May. Damn it! He could not live with himself if he were to cause her to lose another baby.

"You will leave in the morning as planned." He was back in charge. "Nothing will be said to May for the time being. As for the proposals I offered earlier, May's still stands." He didn't need to say that Peter was no longer welcome here.

Peter cursed himself. Then he cursed Edith. She had told him about her lie to May, with the intention of saving her the worry, but she hadn't told him she had also lied to John. He thought about how much he had enjoyed Edith's flirtations and kisses. If she hadn't stopped things, he was pretty sure, if he was honest with himself, that he wouldn't have. What was wrong with him? He didn't deserve May. He was guilty of the very thing he had been angry with her for.

He really wanted to curse Edith again, but he was an honest man, even when it hurt. He had already spent too much time blaming Edith for their troubles. He had to shoulder his share of the blame. Back when they were teenagers, he hadn't turned Edith away, even though he wanted to have May to himself. And when May was refusing him during that period of time, he had gone to Edith willingly and enjoyed it. He hadn't even minded sharing May with Edith as long as he was part of it... What a mess.

John watched Peter. He could read a lot on his open face, even with the bloody nose. He could tell Peter hadn't known Edith had lied to him about going home. He could also tell Peter was blaming himself for some things. Bloody right! But it takes two people to transgress... He turned and left the room, leaving Peter to take whatever action he saw fit, and he went looking for Eve.

He saw that May was alone when he passed her room, so he continued down the hall to Eve's rooms. She had a very nice suite, and he found her reading next to the fire in her sitting room. It was cozy and comfortable here and John knocked quietly on the doorframe.

He hadn't needed to because Eve had heard him coming and was looking up at him. "Come in, John," she said kindly. Eve could tell something had happened. When she'd seen his face earlier, she hadn't been able to read it well, but she knew something was very wrong.

John sat in the seat across from Eve, leaned back, and closed his eyes as he blew out his breath. Eve gave him a few moments' peace before she gently prodded, "What's happened?" She was aware of a slight uneasiness in herself, a fear that whatever had happened might mean the end of the dream of the retreat.

It had become much more than a dream in all their minds. They had already gotten a fair bit of concrete work done. She was counting on this more than she would have admitted to John, especially at the moment, but this business venture offered her the chance to stand alone, to be on her own, with a purpose and a future.

John heard the worry in her voice but didn't connect it to their plans. He was a businessman, and this was a solid investment, not something he would drop for emotional or personal reasons. He had initially come up with the idea while having lunch with a colleague whose client had recently returned from a spa in the Adirondack Mountains. He had praised it so much that his lunch companion was seriously considering sending his wife there for a rest. That planted the seed and he had followed up with some inquiries and then drinks with Dr. Dupre. At first, he simply thought it would be an ideal business for Edith and Eve, but the more he learned about the market, the more convinced he had become about it being a worthwhile investment as well. He didn't stop to consider why Eve might be worried because he was too caught up in his anger, and his jealousy.

Eve listened calmly to his tirade. He had stood again and was pacing while he recounted the events of the evening. She was surprised that Edith would have lied to John; it was clear to her that she was very much in love with him, and it was equally clear to her, as it had been from the start of her friendship with Edith, that the two suited each other very well. She waited until he was finished and then told him so.

He had stopped pacing and was beginning to calm down.

Eve was smart enough to not try to falsely pacify him. She went right to the heart of the matter. "So she kissed him... Is that what has you so angry and upset?" He winced.

"I was upset about the lie and went to Edith straight off. Sure, I was unhappy about it, but I reasoned there might be, if not a perfectly good explanation, at least one I could stomach... But, damn it! Yes! How could she have kissed him?" He was getting worked up again, and he tried to breathe deeply to calm himself down. The way his nostrils were flaring and the breath was rushing out of them in short spurts was almost endearing to Eve.

"John, it was just a kiss. I can guarantee you it meant very little. Try to remember that Edith, May, and Peter have a very interesting past. Things have been more tangled for them than you can imagine." She continued because he was listening to her. "I know Edith didn't spend any time thinking about Peter until May came here. Naturally, a lot of old feelings, hurts, and...yes, I'm going to say it...sexual feelings were brought back to her consciousness. The human mind is complicated, and we know this better than many because of all the stories Edith has shared with us about her patients... And because of our own unusual circumstances," she added quietly.

John had taken his seat again.

"I'm sure it was hard to hear, but at least she admitted it. Try to hear what she said after that...about it being a relief... It makes a lot of sense. If I were you, I would recognize what you have and not go looking for problems that don't exist." She got a faraway look in her eyes as she finished. "You and Edie have the real thing... That doesn't come around every day, and believe me, you never know how long you'll have together. Don't waste time fighting over nonexistent problems."

Eve stood up and walked behind John's chair. She rubbed his shoulders until they began to relax and lower.

He let out an audible moan and reached up to put his hand over hers. "You are a wise woman, Eve, thank you."

She leaned forward and kissed him on the cheek, whispering, "It was just a kiss, you can afford to let her have that," and she left him to figure things out.

Chapter Eighteen

"WHAT HAPPENED?" MAY was already pulling her gown around her to get out of bed, but Peter held up his hand to stop her.

"It's nothing, just a bloody nose, don't bother getting up," he said.

"And a black eye starting, I would say," May replied, but she leaned back into the pillows. Her back had been bothering her that afternoon and had gotten quite painful during supper so she'd come up to bed to try for some relief. She winced a little as she adjusted the pillows to be more supportive and Peter saw it.

"Are you all right? Is it the baby?" he asked with concern.

"I'm fine, just a bit of a twinge in my lower back. I'm better than you anyway, from the look of things." Peter came and sat next to her on the bed. He had her lean forward so he could knead his knuckles into the flesh along the base of her spine. "Ahhh," she almost purred. "That feels so wonderful, Peter..."

He remembered doing this for her when she was pregnant with Cate. It felt good.

"Are you all packed?" May asked. She was sorry he was leaving in the morning, but also a little relieved. Having him around, after they'd made the decision to be apart for now, was a little uncomfortable. "And are you going to tell me what happened to your nose?"

"No, no I don't think I am," Peter answered slowly. "Going to tell you what happened, that is. I am packed and will be leaving early, so I wanted to say goodbye now." He continued, "Listen, May, I know things are a bit unclear for you right now. I want to say that I understand. I don't really like it, but I do understand. You may have feelings...for Edith...you need to work out. I don't want her between us anymore." He was determined to say everything he needed to. "Edith is a very good person. I'm glad I can see that again. I wish her only the best, honestly. I realize she has been a good friend to both of us, and I'm grateful for that... I know her feelings for me are gone. The only uncertainty is your feelings..." He glanced down at the floor.

May interrupted him. "How do you know her feelings for you are gone?"

He looked up at her and answered honestly. If there were questions, and certainly questions were going to be asked over the next few days, he didn't want to be part of any lies. "She had a chance to test them...we both did...and I can tell you without a doubt, I love you. I want you." The look of urgency in his eyes when he said this made her warm. "And I can also tell you that Edith loves John."

May had been getting ready to tell Peter he didn't need to worry about her feelings for Edith, that her indecision came from other places, but now she wondered what he meant when he said they'd had a chance to test their feelings. "What do you mean, Peter? What are you talking about?" she asked warily. Her mind traveled over the past week since he'd been here, and she didn't understand what he was referring to. Peter wasn't answering right away. He appeared to be trying to figure out what he wanted to say. Then May thought about her surprise when he'd arrived. He'd come back with Edith. Edith had been in Colfork for two weeks.

"I see," she said in a voice that made Peter sick in his stomach. He wasn't good with complications. He knew solidly what his own feelings were; he knew what he wanted, but apparently, that wasn't going to be enough. He had made a mistake, yes, but that wasn't the beginning of their problems. May had changed. Maybe she'd been changing all along and he just hadn't seen it. He hadn't wanted to see it. He realized now how crazy he must have seemed, ranting about Edith being the cause of the miscarriages. He'd been busy ignoring the fact that May wasn't as devastated as he was. She'd been growing more distant from him from the start.

"Don't do that, Peter," she said, the warning tone clear. "Don't start making things up in your head about me." When he looked at her with confusion, she continued with heat. "Everything shows on your face. Whatever you and Edith did together stands alone. I had nothing to do with it. Don't even try to convince yourself it was somehow my fault." She sat up straighter and raised her voice. "I have done nothing but be a loving wife to you. I stood by you this past eighteen months when you struggled with your demons." She was building up to something, finding a power she didn't know she had. "You begged me to come here. I didn't want to leave you and Cate, but you begged me... I worried about your sanity. I agreed to go because you were falling apart. I was afraid for you," she paused. This felt good. She needed to vocalize these things. "And then I came, and I'll admit, it was a good idea. I did need a break."

"I learned there is more to me than just being a good wife and mother. I love the bustle of the city. I love the grand life I've been enjoying here." She stopped and looked at Peter. Somehow, hearing he had been unfaithful made her bold. "And I've been having some feelings I haven't felt since before we were married, but not because of Edith...because of Eve."

Peter laid his head back on the pillows. His head was splitting with pain all of a sudden, and his black eye and bloodied nose was only a part of it. She was right; when he'd kissed Edith, it hadn't had anything to do with May. He'd been lonely, and Edith was a beautiful, sensual enticement in the familiar and comfortable form of his old friend. And now May was confirming his fears for him, but apparently, they were not directed at their old friend, but a new one, and he didn't know what that meant. He couldn't think anymore and let himself escape into sleep.

May closed her eyes. She was aware of a swirling mix of emotions which began to form into a swirl of colors. Anger, sadness, fear, strength, joy, acceptance.

She let herself sink down into the welcome, comforting stillness; the familiar, quiet depths. Her conscious mind drifted off and she recognized an inner voice. It was speaking in gently pulsing vibrations. Let it be. She saw the hillsides far away on the horizon...then closer...then she was above them, sinking down toward the crest of a hillside covered in pine. She saw the deer and smaller animals moving with purpose along their well-worn paths. She smelled the freshness of the cool air emanating from the shadows of the pines. A woman wearing robes that flowed and blended with the earth itself was beckoning to her with one hand, while in the other she had a golden lantern which she set down on a bed of pine needles. As she did, her robes fell back, and it was Eve. The needles caught the flame and the world became a brilliant light. So bright that there was nothing else, just the light. Time disappeared while she bathed in the knowledge of all. She became aware of a blueness emerging from the center of the light, growing infinitely larger as it moved toward her. As it stretched out, it became an inviting path which she entered and began to ride, like a leaf on a river, moving effortlessly, occasionally circling in an eddy and then moving farther along, bobbing and floating, ducking under the surface of the light, and then reemerging with clearness of spirit. She saw through her own spirit as the murkiness was washed away. She sparkled with the dewiness of a clear palette. She became the deer, following its path, without the need for decisions, just moving with awareness and alertness, by instinct, until she came to a beautiful garden with fountains and flowers. Peter was there, carving a delicate red rose. He turned and smiled at her, offering his rose. Cate smiled up at her from the center of the petals. She took the rose in her cupped hands and it began to grow roots and the roots became her fingers which grew back up over the rose and the rose became a womb.

Peter's head was resting against her shoulder. She slowly opened her eyes. The candles had burned down, and the room had grown dark, and May could only make out the silhouette of his hair. When she shifted into a lying position, he moaned and brought his hand up to his face as his head shifted. A peacefulness had filled her. Tomorrow Peter would go home. She cradled her stomach with her hands. She made a decision without giving it any thought. She would go home herself, at least for a visit. She needed to see her daughter. She felt a longing for the woods.

Chapter Nineteen

THE CRATES, FILLED with books and files, had been tucked under blankets and tied down. The Dupres had gifted Edith the chaise longue, which so many women had lain on to receive their "trance therapy," and the workmen had carried it out to the sledge as well. Edith would miss this place. She had learned so much here and her office felt like an extension of herself. She knew she was moving forward to even greater opportunities, but she would always love the place. Dr. Dupre had asked her if she would be willing to do some work for them on a case by case basis and she had readily agreed.

She should be filled with excitement at the prospects lying before her, but everything had been dulled by John's continuing coolness. He had listened to her explanations, but she didn't have any good excuses. The fact she'd kissed Peter hung between them like a fog bank, cool and dense.

Everyone was very polite to each other at the house, but the underlying discomfort was getting to her. She sat down in her chair. Her office had been emptied and everything was being taken to the home John had purchased for them. He and Eve had found it last week and John had moved quickly. It was a large estate with two extra workers' cottages, and a stable they would convert to another cottage, on the property. The main house was in good shape, and the necessary renovations to the cottages could be completed after they opened for business. The original owners had been horse people, but their heirs weren't and had run the place down a bit, making for a very attractive price. Edith would be taking a few months off work in order to concentrate on their new venture.

The strained conversations that had had to take place between her and John had taken a toll on her. John went out of his way to discuss all the details with her and make sure she was in agreement, but she deferred most decisions to him and Eve; business was their expertise, not hers. Two weeks ago, she would have shown more interest in it all, but now she just couldn't summon the strength. They were still sharing the same bed, but John hadn't touched her since the evening before Peter left. The tension was exhausting her.

May knew about her and Peter. Edith didn't know how much she knew, but May was the one who had told her about Peter's bloodied nose. When she had told her, Edith's eyes had widened with shock. Neither woman knew the details, but both were bright enough to make accurate deductions. May hadn't asked any questions but had said, "Maybe it's a good idea to test your feelings. Perhaps I should follow your lead, Edith," as though she were accepting a challenge. Edith didn't know exactly what she meant and wasn't sure she wanted to, and then May had announced her plans for a trip home and invited Eve to go with her.

They planned to be gone for three weeks. Eve had happily accepted the invitation, saying she'd never been very far outside Boston and was excited to see the land Peter had talked so lovingly about. Edith hoped May wasn't going to make the same mistake she'd made but knew it was not her place to give advice. They were leaving in five days. May appeared fit and confident about traveling, and Eve would be there to help and to watch out for her.

Because Eve would be gone for three weeks, they had spent quite a bit of time together, going over details for the property, and even being with Eve was a bit awkward. Edith knew Eve thought very highly of John and she felt ashamed, even though Eve never broached the topic. Why did everyone have to know? When it had happened, she'd seemed so far away from Boston and John; she never dreamed the news would travel.

She closed her eyes and allowed her body to grow heavy, quickly descending to a very deep level.

She found herself on a beach with softly lapping waves. Walking along the water line, she noticed small waves washing away her footprints—as though she hadn't been there at all. There were some trees giving shade higher up the beach so she went up and sat under one of them. As she looked up at it, she saw it was actually a large hourglass, larger than herself. The sands were falling in a mesmerizing flow that never depleted. She watched the flow as time passed, but never ran out. At some point, she realized the grains of sand were white flower petals. As she watched, they began to float down more and more slowly, until time was standing still. With the petals suspended within the glass, she saw all the space between time. She stood up to have a closer look, and all that space began to vibrate. She became aware of the vibrations in her body. They grew stronger until she began to separate into pieces and become mostly space herself. She vibrated like that, suspended in space and time. She was space and time...eternal...

Edith became aware of tapping on the doorframe. She came back to herself in a rush.

Dr. Dupre was standing in the doorway. "I'm sorry, Edith, I could see you were resting, but I don't have much time today, and I really hoped to talk to you before you left," he apologized.

"Of course, please come in, Doctor." Edith assured him it was all right.

Since the other seat had been packed and moved, he leaned against the window frame. "I won't beat around the bush, you know that's not my style," he continued without preamble. "John spoke with me yesterday. He asked my advice about a certain situation. He framed the question as though he were inquiring for a friend, so I answered in kind—but I suspect he was asking for personal reasons?" He raised his brows in question and Edith gave a small shrug and nod. "Yes, well, it really is no concern of mine, but I am fond of you both, so I want to tell you what I told him... Women are not given the same 'allowances' that men are in a marriage. If a man strays, it is considered his business only and women are expected to bear it silently. We've seen plenty of patients here, as you know, who have shown us this double standard often causes problems for the woman's state of mental health, while their husbands carry on blissfully ignorant of the damage they have caused. If you turn this double standard around, you are bound to cause mental anguish in the man, are you not?" He lifted his chin and looked sternly, like a reprimanding but loving father, at Edith. "It is my belief that neither sex can be expected to bear the weight of infidelity without repercussions."

Edith did know exactly what he was talking about. She had personally worked with many of these women. She understood what Dr. Dupre was telling her and it hurt, but also helped, to know what kind of suffering she had subjected John to. He continued, "I told John that open communication and mutual expectations of fidelity would make for happier unions. I also told him that sometimes we find opportunities for growth where we least expect them.

I've witnessed many hurts healed through simple forgiveness...including forgiving oneself." He gave her a genuine smile. "Go talk to him, Edith. Surface wounds are quick to heal when tended to promptly. When we don't tend to them, they can fester and get ugly."

She thanked the doctor for his wisdom. She would miss working with this wise man. Feeling rested and restored with the faith that time would heal, she closed the door to the office and headed home.

"IT ISN'T LIKE you to hold a grudge, John, what's going on?" Eve asked. "I don't believe this is all about a kiss..."

They were in John's study. She had come in to go over some confusing numbers with him and found him trying but failing to get some work done. He needed to catch up with some business from the office, and with all the doings of the retreat center taking up his time lately, he had neglected some of the work for his regular clients. This is what he was doing when Eve came in and found him on his third attempt at a cordial letter of inquiry to an investor that kept coming across as contempt.

John growled at her in his frustration, so rather than continuing to confront him, she pulled up a chair and asked to see the letter. Before she had become his wife, she had been a very good secretary. After a quick read, she took a fresh piece of stationery and composed the letter he had been trying to write all morning.

"There," she said, "now what else can I help you with?"

Having her here helped John with his concentration and the two of them worked companionably and efficiently for three hours. When they had finished with two large piles of work, John smiled appreciatively at Eve. "Let's have our tea, Eve, we've earned it."

"It's something Peter said. I can't get it out of my head." They had finished their tea and now Eve had helped him get caught up, he could focus again. "He said that Edith was fiercely loyal." He shook his head as though trying to dislodge something. "She wasn't loyal to me. I trusted her completely, but apparently, she didn't think enough of me to consider how much this would hurt us. I don't think she thought of me at all." He added, "She always wanted Peter. I can understand why. No man could compete with him in looks, and he has an undeniably easy and assured disposition." He was unable to hide his grudging admiration. "What I can't get out of my head is what if she was just having one last try for him? What if I'm second choice?" he finished sadly.

Eve sat quietly, lost in thought. When she spoke, she said, "I don't believe you are second choice, John...but what if you were? Does it change the love you feel for Edith or the love she gives you? I think it might be to our own detriment that we always think we need to be first. If instead, we just go fully into our endeavors, whether love, friendship or business...if we give ourselves wholly, we will be happy." She smiled with encouragement at him. "You love her, and she loves you. Margaret used to remind me what the Lord's Prayer says when I hated my parents for not being able to accept me. 'Forgive us our trespasses.' And do you know what? I didn't forget, but when I forgave them, the hate and anger left, and I was happy again."

Eve didn't voice all her thoughts, but she decided she should have a conversation with Edith. There were some questions whose answers might help her as well. She encouraged John to take his mare for a ride. It was something he didn't make time to do often enough, but he loved it. She believed it helped clear his head and bring him back to his center. She was surprised when he readily agreed and went to change for riding.

It didn't take long to find Edith. She was helping May pack for her trip. They were talking, easily, about May's excitement to see Cate again. May had gone shopping that morning to get some special gifts for her and was showing them to Edith. Eve watched them from the doorway for a few moments before interrupting. It was nice to see them comfortable with each other again and she wondered what had made the difference. Eve knew May was aware something had happened between her husband and her friend, but she seemed ready to forget it more quickly than most women would, and she wondered how much of that was because of their shared history and how much of it was because it really didn't bother her. May saw Eve out of the corner of her eye and smiled privately at her. Eve returned her smile.

"Eve, come in," Edith said a moment later when she saw her standing there. "I was just going to go look for John." She seemed lighter on her feet, happier than she had since the night before Peter left.

"I just left him, Edith. We spent the morning catching him up on some work. I actually enjoyed it; it reminded me of the days when I used to work for him in his office in the city."

Neither May nor Edith had known John or Eve in those days. They'd never met Eve's Maggie. It seemed odd that they had all known each other for as short a time as they had. They'd become such good friends.

Eve came into the room to tell her John had, amazingly, taken her suggestion and gone riding.

"Oh, how wonderful!" Edith said happily. "Well, never mind, I'll talk with him tonight."

Eve led Edith over to the window. The ground was white with snow, and they could hear sleigh bells in the distance. It was almost Christmas. "Edith, John talked about you today. Maybe I shouldn't tell you what he said, but I just feel that if you knew his deepest worry, and could reassure him, then you two could move beyond whatever difficulties you've been having." She looked questioningly at Edith to ascertain whether she should continue. Edith was a little nervous to hear what John had been saying about her, and truthfully, a little annoyed that he had been talking to Eve about her, but bravely asked to hear what it was.

"He's afraid he's only second choice... The man loves you so much, and he's afraid you've only come back to him because Peter wouldn't have you."

This isn't what Edith would have guessed he'd been feeling. She expected anger, distrust, even disgust, but not this. She shook her head sadly, "I feel so bad that I've put John through such doubts..." she faltered. "He's such a good man." Taking a deep breath, she squared her shoulders and said, "I really don't deserve his forgiveness, Eve, but I will beg for it if necessary...as soon as he gets back from riding." She was determined to make him understand he was the only man she wanted.

Eve remained looking out the window and without looking at Edith she said quietly, "Edie, could I come see you in your room in a little while? I have something I'd like to speak with you about privately."

Edith looked at her and nodded. "Yes, of course, I'm going there now."

EDITH SPENT SOME time working on her Christmas gift for John. She was copying out his favorite poem in calligraphic style and when she was done, she would have it framed to hang in his office. She enjoyed the concentration and the crisp beauty her hand created on the clean sheet.

She was working on the third stanza when Eve appeared in her door. "Come in." She smiled at her friend.

Eve came over to admire her work. "That's lovely, Edie! I had no idea you had such talent," she exclaimed. "What a perfect gift for John."

Edith set the paper and pen aside. "I'm glad you showed up when you did. My hand was just starting to cramp." She shook her right hand to loosen it. "The tea should arrive shortly," she said as she rose to put another log on the fire.

Eve sat next to her on the footstool in front of the hearth and tucked her feet under her. She watched the flames, allowing her mind to clear. "You don't need to tell me what happened between you and Peter. I'm sure you have your reasons for going to him...but—" she drew a breath "—but I'm wondering if you might have an opinion on his relationship with May. I wouldn't want to cause any problems between them. May has...well, she's shown interest in me, and I'm wondering if it might be problematic for me to go home with her. I do not wish to be the cause of marital discord or be a distraction when they need to be working things out."

Edith continued to poke idly at the fire. Many thoughts were working through her mind and she was trying to sort them out. It was several minutes before she spoke.

"When I went to help Peter get well, I told myself it was to protect May and her fragile pregnancy. I suppose, though, that was only part of the truth. I wanted to see Peter. We used to be such good friends..." She put the poker down and sat back on her heels with her elbows propped on her knees. "Eve, it wasn't Peter who stopped things, it was me. I realized quickly that I'm not the same person I was back then, back in Colfork...but Peter wasn't interested in stopping. He said he and May hadn't shared any real passion for years." She looked sadly at Eve and continued, "I know he loves May—he always has—but I'm not sure she ever really felt the same for him...and I think he's finally realizing that. Poor Peter."

"Would you like my opinion?" Edith asked. Eve nodded her head.

"I don't think May should make this trip without you. In her condition, she shouldn't be traveling alone. Whatever problems she and Peter might have between them, they will have to work them out whether you're there or not... They have to... May is pregnant with his child. I know May cares deeply for Peter, and I know her family is very important to her..."

She took a sip of tea and added, "I think it's a good sign that she has finally decided to go back. I suspect once she's back in her home, with her daughter, and her parents close by, she'll realize what a huge thing she'd be giving up...but I asked John to let Peter know that whatever happens, if May decides not to go home, she'll have a place here, with us. I think Peter is resolving himself to the possibility."

Eve scooted off the stool and stretched out on her back in front of the warmth. She looked so comfortable and relaxed that Edith decided to join her and laid next to her on the soft carpet. The heat and comfort felt wonderful. She began thinking about laying here with John later, after his ride. She was very eager to make things right with him again. She thought about Eve and how she had tried to love John, and realized, for the first time, how hard this might be for Eve.

"Do you have feelings for May?" she asked casually, looking at the ceiling.

Eve turned her head to look at Edith. "I suppose I do," she admitted. "I don't want to get in the way of their family, though. I honestly hope she stays with Peter and they raise their children together...it's what I'm encouraging her to do..." She turned on her side then, so her whole body was facing Edith. "Don't you think that's for the best?"

Edith nodded. She was thinking about the little boy on the rock in the river. The little boy who would want Peter for his father. Yes, Peter was a good father. She thought of him and Cate together and smiled.

"Yes, yes, Eve, I think you're right." Then she added, "But we never really know where love will take us... You deserve your happiness as well, and so does May." She made a silent prayer that Eve wouldn't get hurt.

They stayed there, enjoying the fire and each other's company until it grew dark outside.

Chapter Twenty

TEN DAYS LATER, upon the very same carpet, John and Edith exchanged their Christmas gifts. John admired his favorite poem, written with loving endeavor by his fiancée, who now wore a beautiful ruby ring on her left hand. Edith kept holding her hand up to the light from the fire to enjoy the reflections dancing on the stone. She was as full of happiness as is possible to be. They had the house to themselves, with May and Eve in Colfork, and although they would be hosting Christmas dinner for sixteen guests later, they were keeping Christmas morning just for themselves.

"Thank you, John," Edith said again. "I will make the best, and most devout," she added pointedly, "partner for you, my love." She leaned over to kiss him. "To whatever mysteries of fate that brought us together, I am eternally grateful." She smiled and kissed him again.

John sat up and took hold of his teacup and raised it toward Edith to make a toast. She laughed and picked up hers as well.

"To the fates," he said.

"To the fates," she echoed.

When he set his cup down, he had a serious look on his face. "When I was out riding that afternoon, I was thinking about some things Eve said to me. She's quite wise, you know? Basically, she said in order to be truly happy, we have to jump into things with our entire selves."

John picked up her left hand and absentmindedly played with the ring. "That's why I rode directly to the jeweler's and bought you this ring. I didn't want to wait, I wanted to give it to you that night, but when I found you waiting for me... Well, when you jumped me—" and he chuckled at the memory "—I knew we'd already given ourselves to each other, completely, and no ring would make any difference. I've always been a pretty happy man, Edie— I've been lucky, I guess—but when I feared you might not love me...well, I don't want to feel that way again. Thank you for loving me." He reached out with his right arm. "Come here."

Edith snuggled into the curve of his arm and chest. She fit perfectly.

He began fidgeting with his left arm, twisting it around behind him and reaching over so that they both tipped to the left. "Whatever are you doing?" Edith asked curiously.

John cleared his throat to stall for time and then he brought his left hand in front of himself. He was holding another small package, this one wrapped in shiny blue ribbon. "Well, I believe we are celebrating another very special occasion today." He handed the package to Edith.

While she was untying the ribbon with a wide smile on her face, he continued, "Happy birthday, Edie. I wanted to get you something equal to the ring...something to let you know I worship the day you were born."

Edith turned her face to look at his, now with a look of intrigue, and eagerly went back to unwrapping the gift.

When she lifted the top off the box, her expression changed to one that questioned him. "It's a key," she stated.

John smiled at her with a secretive glint. "Yes, that's very astute of you. It is indeed a key."

An hour later, they were standing outside a quaint storefront, painted with a fresh coat of blue with gold trim. The wooden sign said "McAllister's Fine Books" in fancy script.

"I was going to have the sign changed, but I thought you would want to pick out the name yourself," John said.

"What?" Edith was completely lost. "What are you talking about, John?"

He laughed. "This is your birthday gift, Edith...get out the key."

She gaped at him. "You bought me a bookstore?" she asked with astonished amazement. He had barely begun to nod yes when he had to throw up his arms to catch this woman who loved to throw herself on him.

Edith was kissing him and laughing and crying and wondering how she had ever gotten so lucky. Finally, she pulled out the key and opened the door. The shop had been impeccably cleaned and was full of all sorts of books.

When John said, a half hour later, "I'll have the carriage sent to collect you at 5:00 for dinner," she looked up. She had forgotten he was even there.

"Yes, that will be fine," she breathed before she turned back to the shelves in total immersion. John chuckled to himself with satisfaction and locked the door behind him.

Dearest Edie,

I am completely in love! We arrived in Colfork without incident last night. The train trip was tiring for May but exhilarating for me. Peter and Cate were waiting for us—it was beautiful to watch mother and daughter reunited. I think May is wondering now how she ever left. She told me this morning that her time in Boston almost seems like one of her dreams.

Their home is perfect. I've grown used to the glamour of John's home (and now yours as well), but I think I prefer the honest simplicity of a home built with love. Peter really is talented, isn't he? I see evidence of it everywhere.

We had a quiet Christmas. May and Peter's parents both came by for dinner—they are lovely people and are obviously relieved to have May home. Everyone is acting like she was on a simple holiday, but I can detect the unspoken relief. May's mother asked me to help her in the kitchen, to give May a rest supposedly, but I think she wanted to find out more about me. I played it straight and had a little fun telling her made-up stories about my past. I must remember to tell May and Peter what I've said so I don't get caught!

Cate is a sweet, but honest little child—she asked why Aunt Edith hadn't come instead of me. I sense it will take a little time to win her over. What did you do to make such fast friends with her? Even my little gifts only brought a polite smile. Peter says not to worry, of course, she's just so happy to have her mother home.

I like the Peter I found here. Interesting that he is a very different Peter from the one I met in Boston. I can see why he needs to be here; he is made for this place. He made me a clever jewelry box for Christmas, which I adore, and he made a rocking horse for Cate—she won't get off it! But his crowning glory was the sunroom he built for May.

You wouldn't believe how surprised she was. He built it on the south side of the house, off the kitchen. The room is almost all windows, and he installed a stove to keep it warm in winter. I'll be honest with you, Edith, it is very similar to the room off our kitchen (sorry, your and John's kitchen) and I find it extremely touching that he built it without knowing for certain she would come home. It's only roughed in yet, but he got a lot done in the little time he was home before we arrived. He must have been planning it since Boston.

On that note, I will tell you I think she will stay. We haven't exactly talked about it, but she seems content, settled in a way I haven't quite known her to be. I don't want to push her to make a decision, so I'll just give it time. I'm happy here and in no rush to get back on that train. Peter has promised to take me on a hike to the river tomorrow if the weather stays fair.

I was so glad to get the message from John that you are officially engaged. I have signed all the paperwork and sent it back, so you should be free to marry within the month. I hope you don't mind if I stay for a bit longer. I trust the two of you to make any necessary business decisions without me. I want to explore this place and spend more time with May. My feelings for her are tender and evolving. As she grows larger with child, I find I want to take care of her. She's radiant with beauty and I am content to be her helpmate.

Also, I want to give you and John room to become a normal married couple. When I do return, I will move into the guest house to give you both your space.

I'll end here and write again in a few days. Give John my love, and here is a kiss for you.

Lovingly yours,

Eveline

Dear Eve,

I was so happy to get your letter and hear that all is well. You're right, Colfork is a special place. I hope you got a chance to go to the river with Peter (if so, did he take you to a large rock, by chance?).

I can just imagine the sunroom he built for May. That is typical Peter—he is so considerate and capable, and he doesn't miss much! I'll send a package with some nice fabrics so you and May can add some stylish details of your own. I was thinking about the green striped linen you used for our cushions. Do you think that would look nice?

As for Cate, all I did was help nurse her father back to health, and in the meantime, we spent a lot of time in his garden. She is a sweet child and smart too; I'm sure she has already figured out that being your friend would be a good move. Give her my love and tell her I'll send a gift soon.

I've started seeing a few women at the Dupres' again. I missed my work, and I'm glad to be back at it, but the much bigger, and much more exciting news is that I've begun a whole new enterprise. John bought me a bookstore for my birthday! Can you believe it? He is the most dear, dear man. It's on Hartford Street, between 2nd and 3rd Avenues. I've decided to call it Edie's Fine and Rare Books. I could go on and on about how much fun I'm having, but there's not enough paper in Boston! I've already made my first order from an independent printer in New York City.

Eve, you'll never believe this, but I've found there is a book about my work! I found a small publication by a Dr. James Braid from Scotland. He calls the work hypnosis. I found it on a shelf in the back of my shop! Imagine that, will you? I've already read it several times. It's all so exciting, Eve! I have many new ideas to try now and I've been considering whether perhaps I should write a book about my own work. I have notebooks full of cases. What do you think? Do you think anyone would be interested in a book written by yours truly?

John received your papers in this morning's post, so I suppose you will be officially unmarried soon. I feel very lucky that John has a lovely, selfless, generous wife. You are such a good friend to us both and we have you to thank for bringing us together. Why I seem to find myself in these unusual love triangles is a mystery to me, but I count my blessings to have such good friends.

On the subject of love triangles, do you find yourself in one? Maybe we need to live like those women in the far east where one man can have multiple wives. Wouldn't that be fun; we could be sister-wives. But seriously, I don't plan to ever hog John all for myself. We shall continue to share this wonderful man as long as we all shall live. You will always have a home here, with us, Eve.

Please give my love to everyone and a special kiss for Cate.

Love, your sister-wife,

Edie

"I NEVER MEANT for the bookstore to detract from our plans," John was explaining to Edith. "You can afford to hire a manager and salesman and still make a small profit. I just thought you might enjoy it as a hobby." He smiled at her earnestly. He hadn't thought this would be a distraction from her work as a therapist, or from their plans to move forward with the retreat.

"Yes, I know I can afford them, and I do plan to hire some help, but right now, I'm enjoying it too much to turn it over to someone else. I do have Sam, remember."

Sam was a very knowledgeable clerk who had been working at the shop for ten years and he had happily agreed to stay on when John bought the store. He'd been even happier to take a bigger role, with an increased salary, when Edith had offered it. He was able to operate everything himself when Edith couldn't be there; in fact, he was actually teaching her how the business worked, but she loved being there and that's where she spent most of her days now.

John loved watching Edith work. He'd never seen her work before since therapy is not something that can be casually observed. It's true that Dr. Dupre had sat in on a few sessions to learn from her and to offer input on some tricky patients, but that was an occupational exception.

Edith's new bookstore was only a few blocks from his office, so they shared the carriage into the city most mornings and often took their tea together at the Hotel Brunswick.

He found himself visiting the shop at random times throughout the week. He loved to walk in and hear the bell jingle on the door. Usually, Sam was the one at the front of the store and John would silently wave hello while Sam inclined his head toward the back rooms where he would find Edith studying a particular book, or reorganizing shelves, or just staring into space, lost in thought.

She never heard him, partly because he didn't want her to, and partly because she was so absorbed in her tasks. He would stand quietly, watching her, and feel himself grow hard at the sight of his fiancée, deep in concentration. Her intelligence and enthusiasm were an aphrodisiac for him. The way she would absentmindedly chew on her lower lip drove him wild. Once, he came upon her sitting on a stool in front of a row of books, sucking on a strand of hair that had come loose.

He had stood where he was, watching the light fall across her cheek, until he couldn't stand the sweet agony any longer and had crossed the room and taken her mouth, almost violently, in his. He kissed her until her lips were swollen from the harsh battering.

She was just as responsive to these unexpected ravages as he was, and a few times he had even taken a room at the Brunswick because he couldn't wait to get her home.

My dear Edie,

A bookstore! I can't imagine anything more perfect for you. I know the exact shop. A grumpy old codger used to own it, so I imagine the entire neighborhood is rejoicing about the change of hands.

I'm fascinated to learn you found a book about your work. I really thought you must have been the original discoverer of trance work, but I'm glad you're happy to find others have been doing it before you. I don't believe you could possibly have the time to write a book of your own now—but I think it's a worthwhile idea to consider in the future.

See if you can dig up a nice children's book of verse; something with lovely pictures. I want a gift for my new best friend. Cate and I are thick as thieves now. She is such a darling. We spend most afternoons together lately since May is often napping then and Peter is busy in his shop. She's showing me everything there is to see (within the quarter mile of home she's allowed to roam). Did you know there is a very large anthill fifty-eight (child) steps due west of the large apple tree on the north side of the house?

We've had to let out several of May's dresses to accommodate her growing belly; she is ravishingly, deliciously beautiful in pregnancy. Peter can't stop staring at her, and neither can I.

Your brother and sister-in-law came for dinner last night. Your family is so proud of you, Edie. They wanted to hear all about your life in the city and all about John. I highlighted some of your more colorful successes and described the grand manner in which you now live. They were properly impressed and awed. I've decided I better tell you my "story" in case you ever need to corroborate it.

My parents died when I was eighteen and I went to work for John. I never married, but I had a good friend named Margaret who took me in when my parents died. Unfortunately, she died when I was twenty-two (you can see I stuck to the truth for the most part) and John allowed me to live in his guest house. I was still working for John when I met you at the Dupres' home (where I was a regular dinner guest). I introduced you and John and the three of us have been friends ever since.

And now I want to tell you about Peter. We did get to the river, though not until this past week, and he did show me a large rock. I think you'll be surprised to learn that he told me stories about your young, somewhat unusual, love affair. Now I know why I took to you immediately! I think you believe that Peter never cared as much for you, but he speaks so highly of you. To be honest, I think you intimidated him. He also told me about what happened when you came to nurse him back to health. He said he was a hungry man, and you were a beautiful angel. His nose has a new bump which he said is a good reminder for him that he's alive; that he matters!

Edie, I think he was telling me he would be willing to become part of a new triangle. He is an uncommon man for sure, but I think he's willing to do what is necessary to not lose May, which could seem sad, but in reality, Peter seems anything but sad. He is energetic and robust; funny and flirtatious. I think you may have reawakened him! He acts like a man who has learned a lesson or two in life.

Fortunately, May is turning inward during this last phase of pregnancy and I don't need to confront any of this at the moment. I was under the illusion that country life would be simple, hah! I will stick with Cate and her less turbulent excitements!

I am happy to hear you are thoroughly absorbed. I would like to stay until the baby is born. I think I am helpful here, and it's a nice feeling. I think in Boston I would just feel in the way for now. In the meantime, Peter is teaching me about herbals. I didn't realize what a very smart man he is. I'm sure some of this knowledge will be useful with our future patients. I'm keeping a neat notebook which is rapidly filling with all sorts of antidotes and potions.

Give my love to John.

Your loving sister-wife,

Eveline

EDITH HAD FINISHED reading Eve's letter for the third time. She was in her old office at the Dupre Institute and had recently finished working with a young, very treatable, new patient.

The techniques she had learned from her new book on hypnosis had been quite effective, but she had decided to stick with her own methods which were equally effective and more natural for her. Maybe she really should write about her own work. She'd never considered it before, naively unaware of the others who had been doing this same sort of work for years in different parts of the world, but it was possible that they might find her knowledge helpful as well.

She went downstairs to the room where Mr. Han did his acupuncture. John had an appointment with him today. When he had started riding again regularly, he had experienced pain in his lower back. When the pain began shooting down his left leg, Edith had suggested he try the needles. Although he had initially balked at the idea, he was now Mr. Han's biggest supporter. The pain had left him almost immediately and he had arranged to come every Sunday morning since, not wanting to interfere with Mr. Han's Saturday clients.

He claimed he'd never felt better. Today, though, instead of having the needles, he was making Mr. Han a business proposal. His idea was to rent office space in his accounting building to Mr. Han. For a very reasonable rent, Mr. Han would provide weekly treatments for John (which would be quite convenient), and also be available for Edith when she opened her own Institute. Mr. Han would be able to continue his Saturday appointments at the Dupre Institute and build his own practice in the city. John already had a few colleagues who were interested in giving it a try.

She sat on a bench outside the door, not wanting to interrupt. She had the letter from Eve in her pocket. She liked the peacefulness in this hall. Mr. Han radiated a sort of penetrating deep quiet that she had found very conducive to her own trancing. She came here sometimes on Saturdays, just to sit quietly in the midst of it. She leaned her head back onto the wall and closed her eyes and allowed the trance to take her.

Her head was lolling slightly to the side when John opened the door and found her there some time later. He had concluded his business quickly, Mr. Han being very keen to see the office. He said if the energy of the space was good, he would take it. John had no idea what that meant but made arrangements to show it to him on Monday morning. Mr. Han had suggested that John might like a treatment then and John had readily lain down on the table.

When he saw Edith, he bowed his head toward Mr. Han and quietly closed the door. Her cheeks had a beautiful flush and the skin of her face was smooth as though free from all worry. He'd never seen her like this but knew instinctively that she was in one of her trances. His own body was still humming with the balance of the needles and an overwhelming wave of something immeasurably profound swept over and through him. He stood perfectly still; tears sliding down his face.

Edith was running down a river valley, effortlessly, as though she had wings on her feet that were carrying her along with speed. She saw everything as she sped along, bounding for long stretches of distance with each footstep. She saw familiar trees and bends in the river. It was her river. She came to the large rock and time slowed as she hovered over it. She was looking down on it from a height but was slowly descending toward it. Eventually, she was lying, naked, spread out in the warm sunshine, her body melting into the rock, becoming as ancient as the rock. All the wisdom of the ages seeping into her core. Becoming as solid and smooth and river-worn as the rock. Absorbing and radiating the warmth of the sun herself. Becoming aware of three young bodies lying on her as she absorbed their very pleasure becoming pure love. Recognizing innocence and passion...recognizing this timeless and eternal innocence. And she began to expand...to break apart into a million, and a million more particles...until she became aware that she was the very sun warming these lovers. She had the capacity to hold the immeasurable and indescribable all.

For some reason, waking to find John standing before her with tears streaming down his face was not at all surprising or alarming. They were one and the same. She patted the seat next to her and he sat, laying his head on her lap, and nobody knows how long they stayed there, lost in time and space and knowing.

Dear Edith,

This is my third attempt at writing the same letter. Be warned: I'm sending this one, no matter how it turns out! What has been causing me trouble is trying to find the right words to tell you about a vision I had. It's left me with a feeling, but I'm having a hard time deciphering what it is exactly.

Before I tell you the vision, I'll tell you all my other news. I'm glad I came home. Things are so different here than when I left. It's like all the gloom and cobwebs of the miscarriages and Peter's deepening madness have been swept clean away and everything is shiny and new again. I know Eve told you about the special gift Peter built for me. He's like a new man, or maybe like the old one. He's fun and creative and full of passion for life again. You'll just have to see the amazing work he's producing in his shop for yourself. It's brilliant and inspired! In fact, his enthusiasm is contagious—I've begun painting! I need to find a way to express these visions I'm having. Needless to say, home is a happy place again, and I think somehow I have you (at least partially) to thank for that?

I can't believe how grown up Cate is now. She takes very good care of me and "baby brudder." She wants to name the baby Jack (I can't tell you how many times we've read the book of fairy tales you sent, especially Jack and the Beanstalk). Incidentally, she had Eve borrow seven beans from the larder last week and they planted them outside her bedroom window.

Eve loves it here. She's taken to country life like a natural. I know she's using my pregnancy as an excuse to stay, but I think the truth is she doesn't want to leave. She has become an avid student of Peter and his medicines. He thinks she has a natural knack for it. Apparently, she's already learned almost his entire notebook of plants and remedies by heart.

Toby and his wife have given me many hand-me-downs from their son. Thanks to them, I feel I'm stocked and ready. Your mother didn't want to tell you, but your father caught the same fever that Peter had after you left again for Boston. He is still frail, and it has aged him. As your lifelong friend, I'm going to advise you to plan another trip home this spring. You can bring John and make your parents very happy. Dr. McAdams agreed that I should tell you.

So...my vision. I'll just ramble and hope you get the nuances. This one was different from most; instead of being a part of the vision, it was more as if I was only observing it. It almost had the quality of a book—I could turn the pages back and forth, even though there weren't any pages. If I didn't like one scene, I could go backward or forward to another one. I saw some things I didn't like, Edith. I saw Peter crying in despair; I saw a fire consuming my parents' home; I saw people suffering from a devastating plague (these people were dressed in old-fashioned clothing, thank God!) and I saw a battlefield covered in misery. But I also saw some very pleasant things: I saw Cate as a young woman, wearing a wedding dress and looking radiantly happy; I saw you, and you were holding an infant girl (I have more to say about that, but not at the moment); I saw the midwife delivering my son. I saw the three of us—you, Peter and myself—that day we went swimming. It was a beautiful day and we were all so happy. I looked at that scene for a long time. I tried to become part of it...I felt such a longing to be there again...but I could only watch from a distance. That was the most elemental part of the vision. It colored everything else, even the sad things I had already seen, with a hope, a joy. No, I know what it was now, it was eternal gratefulness. That's the feeling I was left with. Gratefulness.

I'm not sure what to make of all this. I've had visions before, but they were always directly related to me. I don't know if I can trust these images, but if I'm honest, I think I do. Have you met other women who see things in your work? I don't want to be the only one. It's a little bit frightening...

A bookstore! How absolutely perfect for you. I doubt if you care whether you sell a single book—I'll bet all you do is read there all day long. I miss your reading to me. I miss you, Edith, but I am happy for you.

Your eternal friend,

May

Dear May, Peter, and Eve (in no particular order),

I am writing to inform you that I am now Mrs. John Tate, officially. John and I were married last night at home. He had a minister come here, and we said our vows to each other in our own sitting room, in front of a roaring fire, while the snow fell softly outside. It was as picturesque a scene as could be imagined. I wore a blue, floor-length gown and John looked handsome in his formal wear. The bouquet of flowers he gave me belonged to the middle of summer! I am terribly, wonderfully, impossibly happy.

I miss all of you and look forward to seeing all your smiling faces (plus one!) this summer when we come for a visit. I've written Mother (and didn't mention a thing you said May) to tell her of our marriage and impending visit.

I'm keeping very busy with my work at the Dupres' and the bookstore, and...I've begun writing a book! I won't tell you what it is, but if it turns into anything worthwhile, you'll be the first to read it. John calls me his "little authoress" now and is (jokingly) threatening to purchase a publishing company just to make certain someone will publish it.

I'm including another package of books. There is a beautifully illustrated one of plants that Peter and Eve should like, and another book of fairy tales for Cate (hopefully she won't want to name the baby Aladdin now), and I found a book of poetry for Eve that has an interesting cadence I think you will all enjoy.

Love and hugs and kisses to all of you,

Mrs. Edith Tate

Chapter Twenty-One

"WHAT IS THIS one called?" Peter quizzed Eve and Cate. They were bending over a tiny green shoot that was coming up through last year's leaves down by the river.

"Fiddleheads!" shouted Cate.

Eve and Peter shared a smile as Peter scooped Cate up and tossed her playfully into the air. "That's my smart girl." He set her back down and then said to both of them, "If you pick this one early, before it has a chance to mature, you can eat it raw and it has a wonderful, delicate flavor." He bent down and snapped it off in his fingers and popped it into Cate's mouth.

They were having a short hike because the spring air was too tempting to resist, but they didn't like to be gone too long because the baby was due soon. The smell in the air was stirring Peter's memories. Eve and Cate had scooted down the riverbank and were tossing leaves and small sticks into the water and watching them float downstream.

Peter sat down on his old, worn, wool blanket. This was the same blanket he used to bring when he and May and Edith had their outings, and as the wetness of the earth sunk into the wool, the smell brought everything rushing back. He had to close his eyes to dull the intensity of the feelings the memory aroused.

He wanted to weep, and to shout his urgency, and to tear at his hair, the sensations were so vivid and bittersweet. He stayed like that, listening to the flow of the river, smelling the damp, remembering youthful curves, soft skin, fingers entwined in brown hair. He remembered, with an agony that almost hurt, the shocking, incredible discovery of sexual awakenings.

He opened his eyes again and looked at the world, his world, in the present. He thought about May, at home and large with child, his child. She was the same person, yet different. They all were. He sat there thinking about the flow of time; the currents of change that shape us; the futility of fighting the current.

A few deep breaths brought him back to balance and he stood and called to the girls. They both turned to look at him and for a moment it was as if he was seeing them from another era, through the mists of time. Cate as a woman, Eve as a small child.

Eve was standing next to him, her hand on his arm. She had sent Cate ahead to look for more green shoots.

"Peter," she said with a concerned voice, "what is it?"

As she had walked closer to him, she'd seen tears on his cheeks and a faraway look in his eyes.

"Do you want to talk about anything?" she asked with a kind voice.

He stared into space and tried to explain what he was feeling. She nodded her head and told him how she had felt after Margaret had died when she wanted so badly to be able to physically have her back, to be able to twist time so that she could see her for just one minute more.

Peter rubbed his hands over his face, inhaling again. When he brought his hands down, with a sigh, his gaze shifted to Eve. He saw the concern on her face, and the compassion and understanding.

His fingertips were still resting over his lips and chin as he said, "I'm all right, Eve. Come on, let's get back. We've been gone a while."

He took one of Cate's hands and Eve took the other as she came to join them and the three started home.

While they walked, Eve talked easily about the Boston of her childhood and made comparisons to what it was like for Cate, growing up here. She sensed that Peter was content to just listen and let his mind wander, so she kept her stories simple.

Cate walked between them, sometimes being swung into the air, and often interrupting to ask questions or giggle at Eve's descriptions of the awful bonnets she'd been made to wear and the punishments she endured for her tomboy ways.

As they approached the house, they all sensed something was happening. Peter dropped Cate's hand and broke into a run and Eve and Cate hurried behind him. They found May laying on her side on the bed. Everything in the kitchen had been tidied up and water was boiling on the stove. A clean stack of rags sat on the dressing table. May smiled up at them before concentrating on breathing through another contraction.

Peter was at her side, stroking her hair. "When did they start?" he asked.

"I've been feeling something starting since this morning," she answered, "but they're getting stronger."

Peter asked why she hadn't said anything earlier; why she had let them go on their walk.

She put her hand on his arm. "It's okay, Peter, everything is fine. I wanted some time to myself to get ready. Remember how long Cate took? We have plenty of time."

Eve had been standing in the doorway, not wanting to interfere. Peter looked at her now and said, "You stay with May. I'll take Cate to her grandma's and bring the midwife back with me."

Eve nodded. "Yes, of course," she said. After Peter had kissed May and assured her he wouldn't be long, she followed him back into the kitchen. "Don't worry, Peter, May has been telling me about birth and what to expect. I'll stoke up the fire and make some chamomile tea for her. I have the box of supplies waiting in my room."

The midwife had given them a list of things to have on hand, clean and ready, and she and Peter had added some herbs and tonics they thought might be helpful. Before they left, she handed Peter a case with some things May had packed for Cate; it had her new book of fairy tales from Aunty Edith along with extra clothes and her soft nighty doll.

When Eve came back into their bedroom, May's eyes were closed in concentration and she was breathing slowly and deeply through her nose. She looked beautiful in a fierce way. Eve felt excitement about what was happening. Their baby was coming!

She sat gently beside May so as not to disrupt her concentration. Before long, she understood when to rub May's back, when to offer sips of water, and when to just be still and quiet.

Later, she helped May walk around the house, stopping so May could bend over when one of the pains came on. Eve could tell the contractions were growing stronger.

"This is going to be a big, strong boy, just like his father," May said, grimacing between pains.

"You're a strong, brave woman," Eve answered. She helped May back to the bed again. May was beginning to have trouble remaining calm through the contractions. She had begun moaning and searching about for something, but it was only a way out of her discomfort that she was looking for.

Eve tried to think of something to help, wondering when Peter would return with the midwife. She had been giving her sips of the calming tea, but it didn't seem to be working anymore. She thought of Edith and something she'd once told her about a patient who had wanted her to come to her home to trance her through birth. Edith had declined, feeling this was out of her scope of experience, but Eve decided to give it a try.

She distinctly remembered the tone and cadence of Edith's voice and she tried to copy it now. She began telling some of the same simple stories she had been telling Cate and Peter on the way home. Then she tried some poetry from the beautiful small book Edith had sent May last month.

It wasn't working. Eve was becoming worried. May was in too much pain. She was sure something was terribly wrong and she couldn't get May to focus or even acknowledge her. Eve grew frantic; where were they? All her composure was leaving. She seemed incapable of thinking what to do next. She left May on the bed and paced to the kitchen again, where she sorted through the box of supplies, then to the front window to look for any sign of Peter, and then back to the bedroom where May was moaning loudly.

She had lit some candles and drawn the curtains when she finally heard footsteps coming down the path. She ran to the front door and opened it for them, rushing to tell them how poorly things were going and to please hurry. The midwife stopped in the kitchen to remove her cloak and unpack her bag. Normally polite and patient, but now panicked and frantic, Eve couldn't contain her angst. "Please hurry, May is really having a very difficult time. Please...hurry..."

The midwife smiled kindly and introduced herself as Sarah. "Yes, well, let's have a look at our mama," she said as she started down the hall toward the groaning.

Eve stood in the doorway again, her panic beginning to ebb. Sarah seemed to think things were progressing nicely and had no worries. Eve marveled at how Sarah took control of the room and brought a sense of rightness and order. May continued to be racked with pains, but Sarah said this was all very normal, just the natural course of birthing.

Peter hated to see his wife in such pain and had removed himself to the kitchen, but Sarah put him to work and made him feel useful. He was boiling rags, preparing pessaries, chopping wood. Once in a while, she would call for him to come and help May walk around for a bit. When Eve asked how long this would go on, Sarah answered simply, "Only the good lord has that answer," but when she saw this was not a helpful answer for Eve she added, "There's really no way of telling for sure, but by the look of things, I would wager this babe will be born by morning."

The night wore on. To Eve's amazement, they were all able to nap between pains, even May. They took turns keeping watch and doing their best to encourage May and rally her on. Just before daybreak, there was a shift and Sarah instructed May to begin pushing. After that, things happened pretty quickly, and Eve witnessed the most incredible miracle of her life. The baby's head emerged with dark, curly hair and brown eyes open. He seemed to pause for just a moment in this position, looking around at his new environment, and then with a final effort from May, he slipped right into Eve's waiting hands.

IF MAY HAD decided to move back to Boston with Eve, or if she had decided to throw herself into her marriage and her children, we'll never know. She died two days later from a trickle hemorrhage. She had had a chance to hold little Jeremy (which was the name she chose after having a look at him) and tell him how strong he had been and how glad she was that he had finally made it.

She told him how proud she was of her little boy, and now it was her turn to sit and wait for him by the river. Although she was bleeding slowly, she knew she needed to say her goodbyes. The midwife, Peter, and Eve all tried everything they had at their disposal, but May told them it was her time. She could see her angels waiting for her.

She held Peter with her eyes and her arms and thanked him for being the man he was. She told him not to be afraid to embrace life; to recognize that he was still alive and he had much living left to do and to please not feel sad or guilty about enjoying it.

She let him know she had never had any regrets about marrying him, not ever, and her only regret was causing him suffering with her sometimes confused desires.

She told Eve to tell her best friend, Edith, that she loved her and to continue with her work, that it was very important to many people, and most importantly, that their friendship had shaped her life.

She held Cate and tried to let every ounce of her love soak into her daughter as she held the vision of Cate, smiling on her wedding day, in her mind, as her own life slipped into another realm.

Book Three

Chapter Twenty-Two

BOSTON, 1930

Jeremy was waiting for Cate at the station. Her train was running thirty minutes late, so he had some time to kill. He had tried to persuade his sister to come to Boston with him after the service last week, but she had declined, saying she wasn't ready yet.

He knew what she meant. He wasn't looking forward to seeing this solicitor either; somehow, this step was finalizing. Their mother had passed peacefully, after a short illness, but none of them had been prepared. She was a few years older than their dad, but she had always possessed energy and enthusiasm that made her seem younger than she was. When he had last seen her, at Christmas, just three months ago, she'd been making plans to travel to New York to visit one of her old friends. It had all happened too fast.

Jeremy had adored his mother. She had been a devoted mom, but also an elegantly independent and adventurous woman. She traveled to Boston often to visit Aunt Edie and Uncle John, often bringing him and Cate along, even though their father preferred to stay home, saying he wasn't much of a city man. She and Aunt Edie had both been very involved with the women's suffragist movement over the years and twelve years ago had stood in line together to vote for the first time.

Her service had been at the town hall in Colfork, and the old building hadn't been big enough to hold all the people who had come to town to pay their respects. They came from all over New England; her circle of friends was wide.

Cate had felt sorry for their dad at the funeral. She said he seemed so small and insignificant amid all their mother's friends, most of whom their father didn't really know. But Jeremy thought his dad had seemed happy to have their mom so well honored. Honestly, he had never seen his dad as small or insignificant, but he knew Cate sometimes did.

For Jeremy, his mother's beauty, intelligence, and spiritedness didn't detract from the solid, wise, and talented man his father was. His parents had an unusual marriage, true, something he hadn't noticed until he was grown up himself, but they loved and respected each other deeply. Cate thought their dad was afraid of the world, but Jeremy preferred to see him as a man who knew what he liked and had the fortitude to live within it. His mother certainly hadn't seen her husband as weak or small. She had always held him in the highest esteem and set him as an example for their children.

But there was another reason Cate hadn't wanted to come to Boston. Uncle John had had a stroke the day of their mom's funeral and had been in the hospital for a week. After their mother's unexpected death, neither of them was ready to face Uncle John's declining health too. Jeremy had been to see him a few times, and even though he was in good spirits, he suddenly looked so much older.

He walked into the tobacconist's and purchased a box of cigars to take to Uncle John's solicitor, Arnold Case, and then decided to grab another for Uncle John.

He and Cate were having dinner with Edie and John tonight. Uncle John had recently been released from the hospital and Aunt Edie had insisted he and Cate come over.

Aunt Edie had been packing to come to their mother's funeral when John had had the stroke. Once she knew he was going to be all right, Aunt Edie had wired Jeremy to let them know what happened, and how sorry she was to have to miss the services.

She intended to have her own small ceremony at their home tonight. Her invitation had said: "We shall toast the wonderful life of Mrs. Eveline Harris, mother and friend!" This wouldn't be an easy evening.

Jeremy tucked the cigars into his briefcase and went next door to order a coffee. He'd asked around about this Mr. Case, the solicitor, and discovered that he had been well known, in his prime, for working with the very wealthy Bostonian families.

Jeremy had grown up understanding that Uncle John and Aunt Edie weren't his real uncle and aunt, but they had a relationship just as close as real kin, maybe closer. Their daughter, Ella May, was Jeremy's age and they had grown up together and even been the best of friends at one time. Jeremy and his sister had spent a lot of time in Boston, and they even had their own rooms at Uncle John's house, which was more of an estate.

Jeremy hadn't seen Ella in years. She had married a French banker and moved to Montreal when she was only twenty-one and their relationship since had consisted only of annual Christmas cards and an occasional shared Thanksgiving.

He checked the station clock against his watch and decided to head over to platform three, where his sister should be arriving momentarily.

"Jeremy," she called, waving her gloved hand in the air. His sister was very pretty, even at the age of fifty-four. Elegant. Something she had inherited from their mother.

He hugged her a few moments longer than he normally would; the sadness was still palpable around them. "I booked us a cab to take us to the solicitor's office. I didn't want to get the car out today."

"I'm still not sure why I have to go to this meeting, Jeremy. Can't you handle the details?" she asked one last time. Cate was an artist, and didn't have a head for, or at least an interest in, business dealings.

"I told you, Mr. Case was very clear that we both need to be there," he answered kindly. "You can just sit there looking beautiful, and I'll do all the listening, okay?"

A MATRONLY WOMAN ushered them into Mr. Case's office and shut the door behind herself. Mr. Case was seated at a large, somewhat cluttered, desk. He welcomed them in, jovially, saying, "Well, well, Jeremy and Cate Harris...it is a pleasure to finally meet you," then sobered somewhat, realizing the reason he was meeting them was not a happy one for them.

"Please, have a seat. I'll have Mrs. Stevens bring in some coffee...or would you prefer tea, ma'am?" he asked, looking at Cate.

"Coffee is fine, thank you," she answered.

"I might just be able to find a bottle of something a bit stronger...?" he said, with raised eyebrows in Jeremy's direction.

"That would be very welcome, Mr. Case," Jeremy said appreciatively.

Drinks were served and they all got comfortable while Mr. Case found the file he was looking for and began pulling out papers.

"Well, now, I know we are only just officially meeting today, but I feel like I've known the two of you for years. Your mother made a habit of stopping in to see me every year or so, to go over things and make adjustments as circumstances changed." He refilled his and Jeremy's glasses while the siblings exchanged curious glances.

"I want to give both of you my deepest condolences," he said with sincerity. "Your mother was a one of a kind woman, she was. I was so sorry to hear about her passing."

He cleared his throat to signify that he was now moving on to the business at hand. Jeremy accepted his condolences and said that, until recently, he'd been unaware his mother had a solicitor. He had assumed his parents' business would be taken care of by their father until Uncle John had wired him from the hospital about Mr. Case.

"Yes. It was your mother's wish to keep these affairs private, until the time of her death." Mr. Case nodded his understanding. "Please don't misunderstand," he said, looking at Cate. "Your father is aware that Eveline had an estate in her own name. This was no secret from your father. Mr. Harris was in agreement that her estate would remain intact, to be passed on to the two of you."

"It would explain Daddy's comment after the services... that he wouldn't be surprised if I heard from Uncle John soon," Cate said, as though a mystery had finally been solved. She shrugged her shoulders and continued when both men looked at her. "Daddy didn't usually mention John, and it was especially odd since Uncle had just suffered his stroke," she said as a way of explanation.

Mr. Case proceeded to outline the terms of the will and the contents of the estate. "She had a very sizable bank account," he told them. Each of the siblings would be receiving over $500,000.

Cate just stared at Jeremy, open-mouthed. "Where did it come from?" she finally asked. Their father had enjoyed a successful career, and they had grown up accustomed to some bit of wealth-by-association with John and Edie, but this was completely unexpected. Their mother had never mentioned her deceased parents having had money.

Mr. Case steepled his fingers under his chin and looked at the two of them over his glasses. "Your mother had a gift for flair. I am to give you this," and he produced a small key from an envelope and handed it to Jeremy. "It's a safety deposit box at Standard Savings on Belmont Street. I don't know what you will find there, but I have been instructed to speak to you again, only after you have retrieved the contents of the box." Then he smiled at them as though he'd been looking forward to introducing this fun game for a long time.

"So," he finished loudly and with finality, "please give me a call when you have had a chance to empty the box, and we can have another, more...enlightening, conversation." He stood to indicate that their meeting had come to a conclusion.

Their dinner with John and Edie that night was fairly short. John was tired and couldn't sit up for long, but they had wanted to see the kids, share some stories about their mother, and shed some tears. When Cate had asked Uncle John about his mother's estate, he had said, disappointingly vaguely, that he believed all would be revealed in short order, and in the manner in which their mother had wished.

JEREMY WENT, ALONE, to the bank the very next morning. Curiosity hadn't made for a good sleeping partner and he had tossed and turned all night. It wasn't just the inheritance keeping him awake. He had lost a significant amount of money during last fall's Wall Street crash and this windfall would far surpass what he'd lost.

He counted his blessings every night to have survived the "nightmare" better than most, but in common with everyone he knew, he had already lost too much sleep thinking about the financial fiasco the country was in, so he had learned to shut those thoughts off before going to bed.

No, that night his sleep disruption was caused by all the suspense and intrigue. He wasn't surprised, really; his mother was known for fun and games, and it was remembering a lifetime of surprises and adventures that finally allowed him to fall asleep for the last two hours before daybreak, with a smile on his face.

The next morning, he presented the clerk with the small key, along with paperwork from Mr. Case, giving him access, and was escorted into a large vault. Together they opened the door and he removed a long, narrow box. He was shown to a private viewing booth to explore the contents discreetly.

It wasn't heavy, so he knew it contained no gold coins or family jewels. He opened the lid to the plain gray box and was instantly hit by a familiar smell. His eyes welled up with tears as he breathed in his mother's favorite perfume. He reached in and lifted out another narrow box, tied with a yellow ribbon, which he set on the small table. The box looked old fashioned, but not overly used. He became aware of a clock ticking and realized he had been sitting motionless for several moments. He told himself to stop being silly and just open it.

Letters. The small box was filled with letters. He replaced the lid and put the box in his briefcase and took it home with him.

THREE DAYS LATER, the box still sat, unopened, on his desk. Jeremy finished writing a letter to a client and looked over at it. He reached out and pulled it to the middle of the cleared space in front of him and removed the lid. He pulled out the top letter and began reading.

My Dearest Jeremy,

I'm writing this letter with a conflicted heart. Your father believes it best to let the past lie in peace, but I have an overriding feeling that the past should be honored.

Please know the things you will learn today sprang from love. True love. The kind that endures and should be held in esteem. Love, as you know, takes many forms, and the very strongest kinds led to my being your loving and grateful mother. Nothing will ever change that, Jeremy. There is nothing in this world I have done which can compare to being a mother to you and your sister.

Your father may be right, that some things are best left alone, but I have always intended to share this with you, and my only regret is not having done it from the start.

If, after reading these letters, you feel I need forgiveness, then I beg you for it in advance but know that my intentions are to serve the highest good for everyone.

I will always and forever be your loving mother,

Eveline

Peter carefully folded the letter and put it back in its envelope. He felt a knot of apprehension in his gut but ignored it as he pulled out the next letter. It had been addressed to Aunt Edith in Boston, but no postage had been affixed, so he assumed it had never been mailed.

May 17, 1879

Dear Edith,

It is with the heaviest heart that I write you. I know you will have already received the telegram about May's death, and I apologize for your having to learn about it in that way. Peter wanted you to know as quickly as possible.

Oh Edith, there is so much sadness and heaviness here, but also an indescribable joy! May wanted to call her little boy Jeremiah. She lived for two days after his birth and I believe she gave us all a lifetime of love in those days. Time really did stand still, the way she used to talk about it doing in her trances. She entered a different place while she was in labor and never really left it. She was coherent but dreamy. It seemed to me like she was standing with a foot in both worlds. She was very peaceful and not in any pain at all. She grew weaker as the bleeding continued its slow, perilous flow and you could actually see her leaving this world for the next.

She wanted me to be sure to tell you that she had no regrets. She really didn't, Edie. She loved you and Peter and her children so much.

Jeremy is the most beautiful baby boy and Cate just adores him. She doesn't really understand about her mom, and I think it's been easier than it would have for her because she's gotten used to being cared for by others.

We received the telegram that you're coming Monday. Her body will already be buried but we will have a service on Tuesday.

Peter is distraught, but he isn't falling apart. He is so tender with Jeremy, and so solid for Cate. I know I planned to come back to Boston after the baby was born so we could advance with our plans for the Institute, but would you mind too much if I stay on for a while? Peter and I have got a rhythm going and I know I am a help and comfort to him. It's extraordinary how much work such a small person is!

I look forward to seeing you soon. Give my love to John.

Always yours,

Eve

When Jeremy's wife came in a half hour later to let him know supper was waiting, she found him, sitting in the dark, staring into space, with the letter still lying open on the desk.

JEREMY DIDN'T READ any more of the letters for over a week. He understood what the first letter was telling him. His mother was a woman named May. He knew who May was. His mother, or "Eve," as he was angrily calling her in his mind now, had always had a picture of a beautiful woman with long dark hair framed on her dresser. She used to talk with fondness about her good friend May. Cate and Jeremy had grown up believing May was some sort of storybook heroine because of the stories their mom used to tell them about her.

He remembered listening to these stories about May at bedtime when he was small. Beautiful, brave, wise May.

When the shock abated, and reality settled itself again, as it will, even after the strongest earthquakes of change, he pulled out the next letter. It was addressed to a Ms. Eveline Tate. That was the surname of Uncle John and Aunt Edith. His mother was Eveline Harris. He nodded his head slightly, as though encouraging himself to go ahead and learn the truth, and proceeded to slit the letter open with his silver letter knife.

June 15, 1879,

Dearest Evie,

You really are a marvel with those children. You're a natural mother and I agree that it is best for you to stay on and help Peter for a while. I think we can agree to put our project on hold for the foreseeable future as we both have more important things to give our energy to at the moment.

Being home, knowing May would never be with us again, was so hard. I still can't believe she is gone. She was such a special friend and I miss her terribly. I'm so thankful we had our time together in Boston, and I know her life was made happier for having known you.

When I went for that walk with Peter the last day, down by the river, I told him about the visions May had written me and described. I hoped it wouldn't be too hard for him to hear about my own pregnancy, but he was very calm about it. He respects John and I know he is happy for me. We talked about May and relived some nice memories. It was helpful for both of us to talk honestly about it all and I believe he will be okay. He told me about a visceral memory he had the day of Jeremy's birth, about the three of us, together, down by the river. It was so similar to one May had shared with me and that I had myself. It helps, to know we are all so connected. May doesn't seem quite so permanently gone.

John is worried that my sorrow might harm the baby, so he is constantly doing things to make me happy. I wish he could believe he makes me happy just by being himself. We have a good husband, Eve. Please let us know any and every way we can help you and Peter. Whenever I start to feel sad, I just think of that precious new baby and it puts a smile on my face.

Missing you,

Edie

We have a good husband, Eve? What on earth did this mean? Aunt Edie knew May and her father? They used to spend time together? He had so many questions. He lifted out the next letter, and the next, and didn't stop reading now until he had read each one several times over.

June 29, 1879

Dear Peter,

Thank you for the letter. It shouldn't be a surprise to us that May knew what was coming, or that she would put her letter to you in her sunroom, knowing you wouldn't go in there until you were feeling strong enough. She knew us both so well.

I'm glad she was able to see Eve fall in love with your children—I know it must have given her peace. Don't worry about sending Eve back to Boston; there is nowhere she would rather be than with you and Cate and Jeremiah. She fell in love with Colfork before she even went there after you talked to her about it with such fierce fondness. Some things are just meant to be, and I believe us finding her, or her finding us, is one of those things. Believe her when she tells you that she has finally found her home.

I've stopped my work at the Dupres', at least for the duration of the pregnancy. I find I don't have an appetite for it right now. My own inner life is full and busy enough I guess.

I have a channel to you, Peter. I can feel your pain, but I also feel something else which I would describe as an easiness, a contentedness. Am I right? You should feel content. Don't fight that feeling as I sense you are. You deserve to feel good; that's what May was telling you in her letter. Do what you like with her note; it does not matter to me. John will be the father of my child, and he will be an excellent one. He is not a stupid man, but he is a man of conviction. If you and I created something during that long night, none of us will ever know for sure, and I am content to let that dog lie. That is the last I will ever mention of this. May had her own secret desires and she would not harbor you or me ill will. John is not so forgiving; once is all I will get from him, but it is enough.

I've had May's room here turned into a proper nursery for Cate and Jeremy, right next to Eve's, so they have a home here always. I know better than to make a room for you, but you are, of course, always welcome for a visit.

Give Cate and Jeremiah hugs and kisses from me.

Edith

September 1, 1879

Dear Eve,

I'm writing to share our wonderful news. Edie gave birth last night to our daughter. She is perfect. She has a head of dark, curly hair and the bluest of eyes. I didn't know my heart could swell this large; it is a wonder to me! Edie had already decided to name her Ella May, and it suits her.

I was so proud of our Edie—she was very strong. Of course, she was! She is resting now, with baby Ella in her arms, and they make such a beautiful sight. I want to do nothing but protect and care for them. Is this how you feel about Cate and Jeremiah? We are lucky, aren't we? We've landed well for our interesting start.

I hope you can make a visit here soon so I can show off my girl to you. Please let me know when and I will send ticket(s).

Always lovingly yours,

John

June 12, 1880,

Dear Mr. and Mrs. Peter Harris,

The warmest congratulations on your marriage. We weren't surprised to hear about it. In fact, we were wondering what was taking you both so long.

I feel as though circles within circles of love have defined and found us all.

I am looking forward to seeing you and the children for the Fourth of July celebrations, Eve. We will take the carriage to the seaside to watch the fireworks with the children.

Warmly,

Edie

September 28, 1880

Dear Eve,

I'm hoping you can be in Boston again this spring to attend the grand opening of the Tate Health Retreat Center on April 20th. Mr. Han and his (formidable) wife have been instrumental in getting it off the ground. The work you did before you left has helped shape our direction. We will have ten rooms for extended stay clients, but the Center will be open for individual treatments on an outpatient basis.

My trance work will be just one of several new and exciting treatment options we will offer. We have a Dr. Josephine Blane who will be treating women with her homeopathic medicines, and two women Mr. Han's wife is bringing over from China to perform a manual muscle release treatment, along with Mr. Han's needle treatments and the baths, of course.

Mrs. Han has a good mind for business, so you can let go of your guilt and trust that she has everything under control! She will be in charge of overseeing the Center so I have time for Ella, trance work and the bookstore.

I'm looking forward to getting back to my work. I've spent the past several weeks interviewing nannies for Ella and I think I've found the perfect girl; now she just has to meet John's (very high) standards.

Mrs. Han saw a sample of my calligraphy and has decided I just might have the aptitude to learn some Chinese symbols (or maybe she just thinks I'm disgracing the art); either way, she has taken it upon herself to give me lessons. Although I find it nearly impossible to contradict her, I really do enjoy her spirit and her knowledge.

Love, hugs, and kisses for you, Peter, and the children.

Edie (blessings)

Chapter Twenty-Three

BOSTON, 1932

Jeremy walked down the corridor, passing Elliot's room and the pink room, on his way downstairs to see Aunt Edie. He and his wife Sarah were in the blue room, two doors down from Elliot. They were all staying with her in Boston for her eightieth birthday.

Jeremy's son, Elliot, along with his wife, Julianne, and their two children, had traveled from New York for the occasion and had arrived late last night. They were still sleeping but would be joining them later this afternoon after lunch, along with his cousin Ella May and her family, who were in from Montreal. Cate hadn't been able to make it to town for Christmas but hoped to be there for the New Year's celebrations.

Jeremy was looking forward to speaking with John alone over lunch today at John's club. It had been over a year since he'd received the letters, and for some reason, he hadn't talked to his aunt or uncle about them yet.

After he shared the letters with Cate, she had cried for a long time. On and off for weeks. She said she'd always known May was their mother, but in the foggy way that fades as children grow into adolescents. She talked about how she'd had shadow memories of a different mother her entire life. Her artwork had changed since having it confirmed for her. It had grown bolder and brighter. Cate herself seemed bolder and brighter.

Jeremy hadn't questioned why John and Edie were so good to him and Cate, giving them many of the same opportunities they gave their own daughter. He had just accepted it simply in the way children do.

He and Ella were only six months apart in age, and knowing they weren't really related, and the frequency with which they found themselves alone as teenagers, played a large role in their own secretive, painful love affair. Jeremy's sister, Cate, was already married by the time Jeremy was seventeen and when he would accompany his mother to Boston, he and Ella were often left alone in the house while the three adults went out for the evening. When they were fifteen, a mutual attraction had begun, and by the time they were seventeen they had given in to their desires and begun the fated love affair.

Ella was a beautiful young woman and was courted by many eligible men, none of whom she favored. She wanted Jeremy. As he now knew, Aunt Edie had begun to understand what was happening and sent Ella to Europe for the summer where she met a French banker and was quietly married. Jeremy had pined for almost a year before his mother guessed the cause and explained to him that the end of one love affair only opened the door for others. He took her advice and began dating and met his Jane two years later. It was easy enough now to look back and realize it had been for the best, but at the time, he had been angry and hurt.

Jeremy knocked quietly on Edith's door. She answered it herself, dressed in a rich, blue dressing gown. The smile on her face was the same genuine smile he had received throughout his life. It showered him with affection and he returned it now. He had questions to ask, but they could wait until he had a chance to properly greet her and wish her happy birthday tidings.

"You look lovely, as always, Aunty," he said as he kissed her cheek.

"Oh Jeremy, it is so good to see you," she answered warmly, leading him into the room and over to the couch with her weathered hands. Even though they had installed central heating twenty years earlier, Edith liked the crackle and heat of a fire, so there was already a roaring one going.

She sat, patiently, waiting for him to ask his questions. She hadn't seen Jeremy since that short dinner last year, and she knew Eve had left him the letters. She had her own stack waiting.

When Eve had shared her plan about the safety deposit box, John's concerns were similar to Peter's; he wondered if it might be best to leave the past to itself, not stir up things that might cause a lot of pain to people he loved, but Eve had wanted to honor May. She had always felt bad that she had somehow, without intending, robbed May of her due. Edith agreed. No one had meant for the deception to happen. It hadn't been planned, but as the children grew up, they naturally called Eve their mama, and then Eve had married Peter and officially become their mother. She had been a wonderful mother too, and a good companion to Peter. They had forged a real family, an authentic family, and the notion of telling them about their birth mother hadn't seemed like a good idea until it was too late.

May's parents had enjoyed their grandchildren, but her mother had died when Jeremy was only four years old and her father had been lost in a fire eight months later.

John once commented on the strange ways of small communities that kept such secrets, but it was true. No one in the town had ever revealed the truth, if they knew it. Edie guessed everyone just came to accept that Eve was the children's mother, and Peter's wife, without question, and she had been his wife for nearly forty-six years.

But Edith had objected to the letter from herself to Peter being included. Even though it demonstrated how happy Eve was to become the children's mother, it also revealed Ella's possible alternate paternity. She wasn't sure, even now, whether Eveline had ended up including it. She didn't want Ella to know the truth. Maybe she wasn't as strong as Eve, but even after her death, she would prefer to keep the information buried in the past. Revealing her indiscretion wouldn't help anyone. She looked at Jeremy now, wondering if she could read the truth on his face.

He was handsome. So much like his father. The big difference between the two was Jeremy was a man of the world. He thrived on hustle and bustle, even though he also knew his way around a wood shop. He'd grown up helping his father in the business and although he had a knack for it, he preferred the world of finance which John had introduced him to. Edith suspected it was something Peter hadn't appreciated, but he'd kept it to himself; hadn't wanted to hold his son back, and Jeremy had made a successful career for himself, on his own merit. They were all very proud of him.

Jeremy looked at Edie. He couldn't read the question in her eyes, but he could tell she had one. It wouldn't surprise him if she knew about the letters. His mother and Edie had been the closest of friends and he doubted if they kept many secrets from each other.

"I want to talk to you about May," he said. He hadn't planned how he would broach the subject, but, as usually happened with Edie, the simple and direct truth was easiest. "My mother," he added bravely.

He had come straight to the point. He was truly Evie's son in many ways. "She was my best friend until she died young. Your father, May, and I grew up together."

Edith recounted a brief history of their friendship and growing up together, and a very brief history of their triangular love affair. She told him it was May who had helped her learn about trancing; what they called hypnosis these days. She paused for a moment, contemplating, and continued. "After Cate was born, your mother suffered a series of miscarriages. She came to Boston to stay with me and regain her strength. It was here she learned about her pregnancy with you, Jeremy—" She looked at him. "You came to her in one of her trances..."

Edith wondered how it might feel for Jeremy to hear this story. She decided against details; if May's visions had been accurate, and her baby boy had made several attempts to come through, then it was his own story to discover, or not. She stuck to the facts. "She was so excited to have another chance. Everything went well with this pregnancy and she fell in love with Boston while she was waiting for you."

This part was a bit trickier. "I was also friends with your mom...Eve, that is. We met here in Boston." Edith paused again, considering. "Jeremy, how much information do you want? I can keep it brief, but there are...entangled details."

Jeremy wasn't sure how much he wanted to know. It wasn't because he hadn't thought about it, though. Now he wondered if there might be even more to the story than he had imagined.

"Aunty, I am fifty-four years old. If I can't handle it now, I will do my best to pretend I can," he said with his wry grin.

Edith smiled. "Okay then, all the sordid details. Just promise me one thing first... If you think any of this isn't necessary for Ella to hear, just keep it to yourself, yes?" Jeremy understood what she was asking and nodded agreement.

He would be seeing Ella this afternoon. He hadn't seen her in a decade. A decade in which his hair had thinned and his middle had expanded, though not by much, if he did say so himself. He had kept himself quite fit for a man his age. His height and naturally strong build helped, he knew, but still, he had made conscious efforts to remain trim. It amazed him how just the idea of seeing Ella had him doing a self-critique.

"There is no way Ella May can be my sister!" rushed out of his mouth.

Edith felt a welcome wave of relief wash over her.

"No, no, you're right, Jeremy. Of course, you are. I told Eve to leave that letter out, but maybe she wanted you to understand why she separated the two of you all those years ago. We knew you had feelings for each other."

Jeremy looked at his aunt sharply. "You are the one who sent Ella away that summer, not my mother," he accused. "You were aware there were feelings between us and you didn't lose any time in removing her from my world," he finished angrily. He hadn't been aware that he was still harboring any resentment, but obviously he was. He had been very angry back then, and he wasn't going to let Edith lay this on his mother. Edith looked properly remorseful.

"You're right. Again. I was only with Peter once...well, at that time, I mean...but I couldn't ever be 100 percent certain..." she struggled.

Now Jeremy was really angry. "How could you be unfaithful to Uncle John? He has always adored you," he almost shouted.

Edith was unaccustomed to his anger. He was usually calm, like his father.

He continued, "And May, my mother, your 'best friend'! Who treats their loved ones like that?" He did shout this time.

Anger with his father overwhelmed him. His father had cheated on his wife, May, Jeremy's real mother. He was, of course, aware that men aren't always faithful to their wives, but he'd always thought more highly of his own dad. He remembered the photo on the dresser in his parents' bedroom. He felt protective for Princess Maybelline and had his whole life.

He let out a very big breath in a rush. His mind was swirling and he couldn't seem to pin down a clear thought, but he wasn't ready to let go of his anger. He looked away from his aunt with a set jaw.

This wasn't as easy as Edith had hoped it would be. She had thought he would come with questions about his real mother and she would answer them honestly. It would give her the opportunity to finally give May her due, and loose ends would be wrapped up neatly. Now she wondered how she could have believed she might come out of this history clean, how any of them could.

There had been so much love between them all. More than most people enjoyed, which is something she learned early and had always been grateful for. But it hadn't been tidy and neat. She still had difficulty unweaving all the strands, and as she had grown older, and her memory had grown less sharp, it had ceased to matter to her.

She had loved Peter, who had loved May, who had loved her, who had loved John, who had loved Eve, who had loved May, who had loved Peter... They had all loved each other. Well, John hadn't loved Peter, but in his own way had accepted him. He had respected him and been thankful to him for giving Eve the life he had.

"I don't expect you to understand everything, Jeremy," she said kindly. "Most of this happened before you were even born. Maybe the men were right; maybe you should never have learned about any of it."

She wasn't going to apologize for a life well lived. They had all been happy enough, and ultimately, it wasn't Jeremy's place to condemn or condone.

She stood up and went to her nightstand. She opened the second drawer and took out her own tin and carried it back to the couch.

When she was seated again, she turned to Jeremy. "Here are the other half of the letters. They don't contain anything new, anything I'm not going to tell you now, but you can take them and read them if you desire. There are a few older ones from May that I kept for you, and you might enjoy those." And then Edith let her eyes close and her mind drift back in time.

She told old stories, not always in chronological order, but in an order that told a beautiful story. She way she recounted them made them sound like characters in a romantic novel.

Jeremy could picture them in his mind's eye. May, the charming and mystic enchantress her father and Aunt Edith had loved, but also the beguiling and brave heroine who intrigued his mother. Eve, married to the hero John, in an effort to escape the cruelties of a prejudiced society. Edie, bravely stepping into always new waters, accepting love and fate and every new challenge with enthusiasm. His father, the strong, quiet man of conviction and passion, and dear Uncle John, the rock that held them all together with his generous heart.

He couldn't help but see them through the sepia lens of time; the time before automobiles, telephones, and central heating. A simpler time, when all this complication was somehow less stark. It made the situation easier to accept— it wasn't quite real. The May Aunt Edith described wasn't his mother; she was the glamorous heroine of his childhood stories.

He heard Edith implying that his mother—both his mothers—had favored women, and somewhere in his mind that made sense. He chose not to look directly at it, but he knew his parents' marriage had been different than most. That they had loved each other, he had no doubt...but there had been signs. Growing up, he hadn't known any other mothers who went away as frequently as his did. At first, it was mostly to Boston, but as the years passed, she met other women from other places who she would go visit. Some of them were fellow suffragettes, some were friends of friends.

Jeremy often went with her. They would stay at the homes of these friends; some had husbands, some didn't. He'd always been proud of his mother, that she was so worldly. She didn't seem odd, or deviant, like lesbians were made out to be. She was intelligent and strong and loving. He couldn't have picked a better mother if he'd been given the chance.

He wasn't interested in rewriting his own history. He would keep the people he loved and had known well where they were, where they belonged, in his esteem. He would ignore the slightly uncomfortable feeling he was experiencing in his gut. He had been raised to think for himself, and that is what he did now.

"Aunt Edie," he interrupted. She opened her eyes and seemed to readjust to the room, to the day. He gave her a moment to reorient.

"I'm sorry I yelled. I shouldn't have done that. I'm not sure I understand everything you're telling me." He took a deep breath. "Hell, Edie, you've given me far more than I can digest for the moment, but I do appreciate your honesty...and your effort."

He realized recounting all these memories might be difficult for his dear old aunt. He looked at her; he saw her wrinkles and her gray hair, but he also saw a radiance. She had an aura of peacefulness about her that caused him to draw another deep breath and sink back into the cushions.

He thought of Ella—the way she looked at seventeen. She had the same adventurous, brave spirit her mother and her aunts had. When he thought of those days—and he did more than he liked to admit—he preferred to think of himself as a confident young man. A man of the world. A man with suave moves. But the truth was Ella had made the moves on his terrified, awkward self. He chuckled softly to think of this, and Edie looked at him with a small question in her gaze.

He laughed again. "I was just thinking of my own history. For some reason, mine doesn't seem as glamorous as yours." He sobered. "But I did love Ella, you know. Why did you send her away?" Edith took his hand in hers. Her skin was soft as only the skin of the elderly is. It made him think of well-worn, soft leather, better with age.

"I know you did," she said, "but one night I saw the writing on the wall. I remember it well. John had taken us on a moonlight sleigh ride through the park. When we got home, I found the two of you trying to act innocent, but the facts were written right across your faces." She laughed. "It wasn't funny then, though, I can tell you. It sent a panic straight to my heart. I was afraid to talk to John about it because I didn't want to bring up old ghosts. Eve knew, though. She looked right at me and said, 'You better do something about this.'"

Edith squeezed Jeremy's hand. "We thought it was for the best. Forgive us for ever allowing things to take the course they did."

Jeremy shook his head. "That was a long time ago...water under the bridge, Edie. Things worked out well in the end, and besides, I don't think there was anything you could have done to stop us." He sat up straight. "Now. We have some birthday details to discuss."

Chapter Twenty-Four

PETER HADN'T BEEN to Boston since he'd had his nose broken. If May hadn't died, he would have returned. He'd known that when he left the last time. May had taken a strong liking to the city, and even though he hadn't, he would have done it for her. He liked to believe he had even been considering moving there, after the baby...but then May did die, and everything had changed.

And it had been a happy life. Peter wasn't one to dwell, and after he grieved for May, he had eventually become grateful for the life that had filled in around him. He was so proud of his children; Eve had done a tremendous job mothering them. He hadn't even noticed when it had happened—the way they had become parents and partners. Even if he tried to recall how the transition had occurred, he couldn't. She was there from the beginning of the ending, and the two of them had done what needed doing, falling quite easily into a rhythm which had felt good to both of them.

He'd been angry for a while. Angry at May, angry at the fates. He had wondered occasionally why he hadn't picked Edith when he'd had the chance; the woman who had wanted him. He'd spent time angry at John, just because John had been smart enough to grab her when given the chance. He'd even been angry with Eve because she couldn't love him like he wanted to be loved. But Eve had a way of soothing his anger, of helping him out of those dark pits of self-pity he occasionally found himself him. She seemed to understand what he was going through, and what he needed to get past it.

Peter couldn't imagine what his life would have been like without Eve. True enough, it hadn't been a traditional marriage; the few times she had come to his bed through pity, or kindness, had been loving, if not passionate, but that hadn't ever been a real part of their relationship. They were friends. Good friends. They understood each other and worked well together. He chuckled to himself when he remembered the men who had tried wooing Eveline when she first came to Colfork. She had practically begged Peter to marry her so they would leave her alone. Small towns were forgiving if you put up the right facade.

Eveline hadn't hidden her affairs from Peter, but she had been discreet. There had been one woman, when Eve was in her mid-forties, who had come close to ending their marriage, but even that was a distant memory now.

But here he was in Boston again. He was marveling at the changes that had taken place in the last fifty years. They were much more noticeable here than at home. There, it wasn't too unusual to still see a horse in town, and at night, you could still see the stars in the dark sky. Last night, he had taken a walk around the block of his hotel. He couldn't get over all the electric light and the traffic.

He'd bought a car ten years ago at Eve's urging. She had loved that car and was a good driver too, but he never really took to it. His shop was still next to the house, and there weren't too many places he liked to go that his two legs couldn't carry him.

He was still a fit man at the age of eighty-one. He enjoyed tinkering in his shop but had retired from paid work eight years ago when he could no longer compete with the prices of the work being mass produced. And he enjoyed having his days open to enjoy fishing, the forests, and reading.

Eveline had a room full of books that he'd never taken much notice of until after her death. When he had started the process of going through her things, he'd thought he might box up all her books and give them to the library, but before he'd filled the first box, he had gotten absorbed in a few of them and ended up only giving away one boxful, deciding to donate the rest one at a time, after he'd had a chance to read them. This was the one time he made use of his electric light. It had become his habit to come indoors at dusk and sit in his armchair with his supper and a book and read until he was tired.

Over the last eighteen months, he had read over sixty-five books. He'd come to know the librarian quite well through his weekly, or bi-weekly, trips to donate the most recently finished volumes, and sometimes, when it was slow at the library, they would spend time discussing them. Many of the books had notes written by Edith in the front sleeve. She had sent many, many packages over the years from her bookstore and, through reading her selections, Edith had become prominent in his mind once again.

Through the busy years of child-rearing and business, his old friend had faded from his thoughts, other than the occasional mentions made by his children or Eve when they would go visit or receive letters and packages from Boston. Since Eve's death, however, he'd found himself reminded of her more frequently. She was the only one left from his earlier years, which sometimes seemed more real now than the days of his busy middle age.

Eve had kept him abreast of Edith and her businesses. John and Edith had put the plans for their retreat center on hold for a while, waiting to see if Eve would come and help run it, but when their daughter, Ella, turned three, they had gone forward with the plans on their own. Peter remembered worrying that Eve might regret her decision, but she had assured him that being with him and the children was what she wanted.

He remembered hearing Edith had sold her bookstore to her clerk's daughter some years ago. Apparently, Edith had become a mentor to the girl when she was quite young, and the girl had grown into the woman who ran the shop for Edith. As far as he knew, the store still operated and hadn't changed names.

Through her book selections, he felt as if he came to know new parts of her, or somehow, know her better than he had when they were young. She was a complex woman and sometimes he wished he could sit with her and discuss things the way he did with the librarian. When he had packed his bags for Boston, he had included a few of his favorites, ones he'd kept, thinking maybe they might have that chance.

After he had lingered over a cup of particularly hearty coffee from the hotel's dining room, which he'd had the luxury of having sent to his room, Peter bathed, shaved and dressed. He hadn't seen Edith more than twice since May died. She'd come for May's memorial service and once again when her mother passed away. Her father had gone to live with their son outside New York, then, and he'd lost touch with her family.

Eve had gone to Boston often to visit, and the two women sometimes met up at various women's conventions, but he had never joined them. When Eve died, he had expected to see Edith there, but one day before the funeral, he had received a telegram. While they were packing for the trip to Colfork for the service, John had had a stroke, so, of course, they hadn't made it. In the midst of everything he hadn't really missed her, but now he realized he was filling up with anticipation at the prospect of seeing her this evening.

He wondered what she would look like. He remembered a very beautiful, young woman, but surely time would have brought her the same changes it did everyone. He went back into the bathroom to look at his own reflection. Eve had a looking glass at the house, but he rarely looked in it, and when he did, he was checking to make sure his tie was properly knotted, or his shave was clean. But now, he really studied his face. It was the face of an older man, older than he ever remembered his own father's face looking. Weathered; that was the word people used in books to describe his sort of ruggedly aged face. People had always said he was handsome, even very handsome, and he supposed he still retained some of that. He hadn't become stooped or frail looking like some of the older men he knew, and he stood up even taller now, deciding Edith would recognize the man she had known, once upon a time. He also noticed his collar was frayed. Eve had taken care of making sure his clothes were neat and tidy, and some amount of wear and tear was fine for everyday life but would not do for Edith's eightieth birthday party. He picked up his jacket and hat, locked his hotel room door, and went down to see the concierge about finding a nearby shop where he could buy a new dress shirt.

The city was bustling. At least in this prosperous part of town, you wouldn't know the country was experiencing a depression. The shop windows were full of holiday enticements, and well-dressed shoppers were carrying packages. Peter knew he was fortunate to be financially solid. Many people were struggling, and again he was grateful that his own children were not among those crippled by unemployment. He had heard John's firm had not fared well, but John was long since retired, and besides, his fortune was much deeper than his own self-made wealth, which was appreciable. While he and Eve had lived well from his earnings, he knew John had given her a very large settlement with their divorce, and now, thankfully, his own children wouldn't ever need to worry about money, even if things were to get worse for the country.

John had been completely in the right when he'd punched him in the face. Peter was glad he had because he'd felt justified in letting go of any lingering guilt after that. He'd wondered, from time to time, if Ella May might actually be his, as May had implied in the letter she had written him before she died. If that were really true, he thought he would somehow know. Either way, John was her father just as surely as Eve was the mother of his own children, and he easily left it at that.

After he had purchased his new shirt, he decided to see some of the history of this famous city. He didn't mind the cold; he was used to spending long days outside in all kinds of weather, so after walking through Faneuil Hall, buying a last-minute Christmas gift for Edith, searching out Paul Revere's home, and strolling through the Beacon Hill neighborhood, he sat for a rest in the Boston Commons and let his mind wander where it would.

He thought about Cate as a little girl, and how she used to tell Jeremy stories about May, but in the stories, May was called Princess Maybelline, and she lived in a castle deep in the forest on the other side of the river. All the stories were about how a brave knight called Jeremiah would go to the river and wait for Princess Maybelline because of a pact they had made. The stories always ended with Jeremiah getting a brief glimpse of the princess through the thick woods but being unable to follow for one reason or another. These stories always made Eve weep; she couldn't tell him why, but she said Jeremy and Cate had a spiritual connection to their mother. Always, after one of these stories, she would plan a picnic to the river, or tell them her own stories about a special friend of hers that had visions. He'd been aware that when they visited Boston, Edith had "worked" with Cate a few times but discontinued when it seemed to upset her.

Cate had begun calling Eve "Mama" within months of May's passing. She had wanted, and needed, a real, live mother, and Eve had felt the blessings of her god when she accepted the role.

Cate had grown into an artist and she made beautiful paintings that expressed a misty, timeless quality. Eve had believed this was the medium through which Cate explored her own inner life—her memories and visions—and had encouraged her in that direction. Peter had one of her paintings hanging over his hearth, and whenever he took the time to study it, he felt a pleasing nostalgia mixed with a yearning.

Peter had led a life uncomplicated by anything more spiritual than the peace and comfort he found in nature and that is what he had attempted to pass on to his children. He supposed his life of relative celibacy had given him more time to commune with nature than was typical, but it had also given a depth to his life that had helped him accept what was. Cate and Jeremy both were well acquainted with the natural world and the solace found by being within it because he had shown it to them.

But they had other influences as well. Eve showed them a world of politics and innovation and progress, and they thrived in that world as well. Peter was glad he wouldn't be living through too many more changes. The march of progress could march on without him, would march on without him. It was an okay place to be, he reflected, the place where one was comfortable with his own mortality. He'd had enough loved ones precede him through the doors of death, he didn't fear it. He had witnessed the passing to be a peaceful one on many occasions. Who knew, maybe he would find May and Eve and other lost friends at that river.

A young, hungry child stopped in front of him, hand out, effectively waking him from his reverie and bringing him back abruptly to the concerns of life. He reached into his pockets and found a dollar note which he put into the outstretched hand. He had much to be grateful for, and he stood up to continue enjoying this life and every last moment it gave him. He had a date with a dear old friend tonight!

Chapter Twenty-Five

"EDIE DEAR, WON'T you wear that lovely cerulean blue dress?" John asked from the bedroom. Edith was in her dressing room trying on a red dress she thought would be appropriate to the season and answered as much, but John persisted. "The blue would be lovely for a starry winter's evening, no matter the season...and besides...you look so beautiful in it," he finished.

John was not stingy with his compliments, so Edith was somewhat immune to things that might easily sway another woman. She knew, however, this was a special night for John as well, and she also knew he loved her in that color, so she changed her dress and pulled out her blue shoes and white wrap.

He had begun saying things recently such as, "I want to enjoy every moment I have with you," which, in and of itself, was not so different from what he had always said to her, but his look, when he said these things now, gave them a new meaning, or at least a new urgency. Naturally, they both felt their days dwindling, but as a matter of course, Edith didn't dwell on it. All her life had been lived with a feeling of anticipation for what was to come, and although she wouldn't say she was excited about the idea of leaving this body, she did have a curiosity about what was to come after. She'd heard enough stories from women in hypnosis about their other lives that she believed, at the very least, in the possibility of a next incarnation.

When she appeared in the bedroom in her blue dress, shoes in hand, she was rewarded with an appreciative whistle from John.

She laughed. "It's a good thing you've kept all your teeth, old man... I'd miss that whistle."

John stood and walked over to her, changing his whistle to a slow tune. He waltzed her slowly around the room in her stocking feet, and they both had the thought that if this was all the evening brought, it would be enough. But the evening was just beginning.

Chapter Twenty-Six

JEREMY HAD ARRANGED to pick his father up at the hotel at six that evening. He arrived at five and took a bootleg bottle of rum up to his room. Peter wasn't much of a drinker, but Jeremy enjoyed a nip before dinner. After he had set the bottle on the small table in the corner of the room, he noticed Peter had been shopping, and asked about his afternoon.

"Yes, I did do a little Christmas shopping. In fact, I got a little something for you, Jeremy," his dad said, walking over to the bureau. He opened the top drawer and pulled out a small package which he handed to his son. "Well...maybe not for you specifically...but I thought you might like to give it to Sarah." He paused for a moment too long. "It was your mother's favorite scent."

Jeremy knew very well what his mother's favorite perfume was, and it wasn't this bergamot scent.

"Mmmm..." he answered vaguely, looking at his father with interest. He thought about the framed picture that still sat in his father's bedroom at home. "I like it."

Jeremy was trying to decide what, if anything, he wanted to say to his father. He decided this wasn't a good time to open the discussion. They were supposed to be at the Statler Hotel at 6:30 and he wanted this evening to be unmarred by his own interests.

Before talking to Aunt Edie, he had decided not to ask his dad about any of this. If his father had wanted to talk to him about it, he would have done so long ago. Eve had thought it important for him to know, but she probably guessed he wouldn't disturb his father with it.

Now, though, he wasn't so sure. Some things Edie had said made him curious about his dad. Maybe there was more to Peter than he saw. He realized he still saw his dad through the lens of the child/parent relationship most of the time, but now, Jeremy was curious about this man Edie had described.

"Thank you, I'm sure she'll love it," he said, putting the bottle in the deep pocket of his coat which he had laid across the back of a chair.

The rum was beginning to relax him. Since this ridiculous prohibition, he had begun having his drink at home, usually by himself, but he didn't enjoy solitary drinking; he found it rather pathetic. Prior to prohibition, his pre-dinner drink had been more of a social occasion, taken at his club, or on the way home from work with colleagues, so tonight was the first time he'd had a drink in some time. It felt nice.

Jeremy reminded his father that Edith had no idea he would be at her party. When Jeremy had begun planning the event months ago, in order to save Uncle John the effort, he had mentioned it to his father and been very surprised to hear from him a few days later, asking if he would be invited to the party. For his entire life, he hadn't known his dad to show much interest in Edith, John, or Boston; he had assumed the connection was solely his mother's. After reading the letters, of course, he was now aware of his father's connection to Edie, but he'd assumed their friendship had ended ages ago, so it was with piqued interest that he added his father to the guest list and began to make some surprise amendments.

"Yes, yes, I know," his father responded. "Are you going to have me springing from the center of the cake?" he added, smiling. "I can still spring, you know." He bent his knees and performed an awkward little jump. Jeremy burst into a great laugh.

"Well, that's not a bad idea, but I planned something a little less exciting," he said.

John had contacted Jeremy a little over a year ago to ask his help. He wanted to have a book published of Edith's journals on trance work. He said she had toyed with the idea for a long time, intending to try to publish it decades ago, but somehow it had never happened. Edith had done most of the editing work but hadn't thought about it in at least fifteen years, and it had sat, untouched, in her office since. He wanted to send it to Jeremy to have it looked at and see what could be done about at least a special edition being made to give her for her eightieth birthday.

Jeremy had read the transcript himself and found it fascinating. He didn't think it would be difficult at all to find someone to publish it and he had been right. Sarah had an old friend who did copy editing for the Ford Motor Company in Detroit and they contacted her about giving the book a thorough going over.

She had done it quickly, saying Edith had obviously known what she was doing because the manuscript was already nearly ready for publication. She had made a few suggestions regarding layout, and modernizing it for today's market, but felt it could go to press if they could find a publisher. She had also made the very good suggestion that they find someone to write a forward for the book.

Jeremy had asked John if he would like to write it, but John had declined. Since his stroke, words weren't as easy for him as they used to be. He had then telegrammed Ella in

Montreal to ask her. Regretfully, she had responded, she didn't know enough about that part of her mother's life to do it justice. That's when Jeremy thought about his own father. He knew from the letters Eve had left him that May and Peter both had known Edith when she had begun this work. He had scoured through many letters written between May and his mother and had found a selection written by May herself that would do very nicely for an introduction to the book. He decided to contact John and ask him if he would object to Peter writing a foreword, and also attending the party.

Unsurprisingly, John had thought both ideas quite good ones, but cautioned that Peter might not be interested. He hadn't asked Jeremy where he got the idea, and Jeremy wondered how much his mother or Edith may have told him about sharing the letters, but it didn't matter to John.

John and his father shared a trait he didn't see in a lot of people, but which he admired. Neither of them held grudges or worried about what others thought of them. Or maybe it was that they both shared a healthy sense of self which gave them unordinary confidence. Either way, it was refreshing to not have to worry about offending or hurting them.

Jeremy hadn't mentioned to John that his father had already asked for an invitation to the party, and now all he needed to do was talk to him about the book. Again, he was surprised at how readily his father agreed. The fact his dad had never done much writing didn't seem to be a hurdle in his eyes.

"I've known Edith since we were young children," he had responded, looking keenly at his son. "I suppose you know a few things about that, which is why you might be asking me," he had continued, in his usual way of taking things in stride. Then he sat down on the bench in his garden where Jeremy had found him working in a patch of strawberries that spring morning.

Peter had stood up when Jeremy called to him from the gate that day, and even though his tall form showed no signs of a stoop, it did take him a bit longer to get the kinks out. He had stood there, curling and uncurling his long fingers, loosening them after the weeding. The bench was in the shade and both men sat down there and relaxed in the slight breeze blowing across their faces. It was one of those moments when each became aware that their moments together were finite, and they felt mutual gratitude in their easy companionship.

"I've brought you a copy of the manuscript," Jeremy said. "I'm sorry to put a bit of a rush on you, but if you can have the foreword written by mid-July, that will give the publisher time to do a final edit and then have it printed."

His father had nodded, "I don't think that should be a problem. I'll start the book tonight." He put his hand on his son's knee. "It shouldn't take too long to finish... I've been reading in the evenings, since your mother's gone, and I'm becoming quite the connoisseur of books," he'd added with a grin.

Jeremy had raised his eyebrows and smiled; his dad was a complex man with many interests and talents, and even at that age he could continue to surprise his son.

Jeremy poured himself another finger of rum and sat on the edge of the hotel bed to drink it.

"So, what have you got planned for Edith?" his father asked, turning more serious. He sat next to Jeremy and said, "I am so glad you have given me the opportunity to honor her. We...we had a mutual friend a long time ago. She is the woman Edith talks about in the book, the one she calls Mary.

She was the one who helped Edith discover her talent for helping people go into trance." He lowered his eyes to look at his son and then continued, "She had a unique ability to trance...she saw things...her name was May." He stopped talking as his eyes looked into the past.

Jeremy suddenly felt tired. He didn't want so many secrets between them and he was beginning to forget who knew what. The timing might be precarious, but he decided to clear the air a little.

"Yes, Dad, I know the woman in the book, I know she was May. Eve told me a few things about her and said she was a special person...that all of you were very close a long time ago...before I was born."

His father focused on him again. "Mmm, I suspected she would. Your mother was a good woman, Jeremy. They don't come any finer. She would have wanted you to know...certain things." He stood and walked over to the dresser. He poured himself a rather large rum and threw it back.

"I'm more of a whiskey man myself, but I understand the rum is easier to come by these days." He turned back to Jeremy and said brusquely, "We'll have plenty of time to talk later. Now, why don't you call down for the car and you can tell me the plans on the way."

THE VALET DROVE up the circular drive with Jeremy's new Chrysler 8. He tipped the older gentleman and then climbed in behind the wheel as his father got into the passenger seat. The sunny day had been replaced by a cold evening with some snow in the air. The hotel was decked out for Christmas and holiday music was playing in the lobby. Both men felt a surge of cheerfulness and peace.

Chapter Twenty-Seven

SARAH AND JULIANNE were dressed and waiting by the front door for Uncle John and Aunt Edie. Elliot had disappeared down the back corridor to fetch them; John and Edie had moved to the downstairs wing after John's stroke so he wouldn't have to navigate the stairs. The five of them were heading to the Statler together and had made an excuse why they would meet Jeremy there. Julianne was telling Sarah that the housekeeper had agreed to give the children their supper and put them to bed, when Elliot appeared alone and walking briskly. The look of concern on his face sent Sarah running down the hall.

"It's John," Elliot said as he caught up with her. "Edith thinks he may have suffered another stroke. I'm going to call for the doctor."

Sarah found Edie, kneeling next to the chair where John was sitting.

"It's okay, Edie," John said, "it was just a little dizziness. Now stop worrying, I'm fine."

Edie was clearly distressed. "John, it's just a silly birthday party..." she replied, but John was adamant.

"Edie, we are going to your party and that's that."

Sarah knelt on the other side of the chair and asked Edith what had happened.

"He was tying his necktie in front of the mirror and he stumbled. I made him sit, but I'm afraid he's had another stroke," she said frantically.

John spoke in a soothing tone. "I'm fine, Sarah, just a little dizzy spell. I get them sometimes since the stroke. The doctor has reassured me that it's normal and to be expected." He turned to Edith and took her hand lovingly in his. He spoke with such tender intimacy that Sarah got up and excused herself, adding that she would see if Elliot had gotten hold of the doctor.

"I'm fine, darling. I wouldn't miss this party for anything...."

THEY WERE RUNNING an hour behind schedule by the time the doctor had cleared John to go to the party. Julianne and Elliot had left early, taking a cab, to let Jeremy know about the delay. Once they were settled in John's car, with John in the front telling his driver where to go, Sarah told them not to worry, as Jeremy was very capable of entertaining everyone until they arrived. Then she lowered her voice and said to Edith, who was sitting next to her in the backseat, "And he brought in enough contraband wine that they won't even notice we're late."

The driver came around and helped John to the curb, while Edie and Sarah gathered their handbags and wrapped their stoles around themselves for warmth. By the time they had reached the entry doors to the Statler Hotel, Jeremy was waiting to escort them to the ballroom. Edith was still worried about John, but he gave her a large smile and held out his elbow in the same gentlemanly way he had over the years, and she relaxed.

JEREMY HAD COME to her rooms this morning to talk about details for the evening. They were having dinner, he'd said, in the hotel's dining room. He had brought a menu to ask if there were any special requests from the kitchens, and he'd given her the short list of guests that John had requested he invite. He had shown her his seating plan in case she wanted to make any changes, but it had all looked wonderful to her. She didn't understand why everyone was making such a fuss over her, but she was glad they were because she didn't get to see her daughter, niece and nephew, and their respective families often enough, and she was only getting older, as this day attested to.

Edith hadn't been to the Statler yet. She had heard people talk about how grand it was since being built a few years back, but she and John didn't go out very often since his stroke. That's why she didn't realize they weren't headed toward the dining room, and when Jeremy opened the doors, she gasped and froze. The doors opened onto a grand ballroom, filled with family and friends, and decorated with hundreds of flowers and ribbons in various shades of blues and greens. Everyone began cheering and clapping, and a live orchestra struck up the notes to "Happy Birthday" as Edith stood, wide-eyed and stunned.

John took her shocked face in both his hands and wiped away a single tear that had worked its way out of the corner of her eye with his thumb. "Happy Birthday to my most beloved girl," he said, simply, as everyone came forward to give Edith their best wishes.

Jeremy had outdone himself. When Uncle John had said to "spare no expense" he had known he meant it. John wanted an evening fit for a queen, his queen, and Jeremy had made it happen. Behind the large silver punch bowl, a discreet bar served champagne, wine, and spirits, and

Jeremy had tipped the waitstaff well enough to buy their discretion. The orchestra had been put together by an old colleague of John's who had ties with the Boston Pops and the food had been catered by the hotel and included every delicacy the Atlantic had to offer, along with a dessert table laden with all the best Italian pastries from the North End. After dinner, the orchestra began playing dance music and Edith and John danced their second waltz of the evening.

"Thank you, love," she whispered in his ear as they slowly circled the floor. She was still a little nervous about his health but had stopped inquiring how he felt when she realized what he wanted most was for her to enjoy her night, not worry about him. He smiled into her eyes, seeing her as the beautiful woman of twenty-three he had met and fallen head over heels for.

After the first dance, John led Edith back to their table. On it, at her place, sat a card and a flat box tied with a silk ribbon. After reading the card, which was from John, she untied the bow and removed the top of the box. Looking up at her was a book. The title was *Trance Healing: A Life's Journey*, by Edith Tate. The cover was an ivory color and the words were printed in a beautiful blue script. Edith stared at it, seemingly unable to grasp what it was she was looking at. Very slowly, a small smile began to form on her face, and in slow motion, she reached into the box and lifted the book out.

It had an extremely satisfying, solid feel to it. She caressed the cover and turned the book over to find a picture of herself, around age fifty, with a short description of herself and her life's work. She skimmed it, finding the passage, *Ms. Tate helped over two hundred women at the Dupre Institute for Women in Boston before opening her own retreat center, where she continued her forty-year career, helping countless people, men and women, enjoy renewed health and well-being.*

She forgot anyone else was in the room; for a few minutes, it was just her and the book. She wiped away some tears that were blurring her vision and opened the front cover. She turned the pages and found the introduction by May. May? Time warped, and she saw her dear friend May as clearly as though she were sitting there with her. She heard her voice as she read:

I don't know what my life would have looked like without your gift, Edith. Learning to quiet my mind and receive, with grace and gratitude, my own inner voice, my inner wisdom, has become the single, most powerful part of my self. No matter how far away from me you are, dear friend, I can always hear your soothing, gentle voice taking me to my core. The women you will help at the Dupre Institute are the luckiest of women. They can't know yet the amazing places you'll take them, but they are in for the most wonderful adventure....

May Davis, 1861-1887

She remembered this passage, but from where? Her mind was losing its footing and she looked up to try to regain her sense of equilibrium. What, or who, she saw, shifted the plates of reality just enough to cause a minor earthquake within her, and this displayed itself outwardly as a temporary loss of consciousness.

Peter caught her easily as she slid sideways off her chair toward him. Jeremy started forward from the other side of the table where he had been watching Edith discover her book, but John reached out his hand, and with surprising strength, stayed him in his tracks.

John had also been watching from the other side of the table. After she had opened her card and then found the book, he had risen from his seat and walked around the table to an empty seat next to Jeremy that was waiting for him, as planned. Peter had then walked up from behind Edith and taken John's vacant seat. All this had been arranged by Jeremy, who had wanted to give some flair to the presentation of Edith's book.

Neither of the older men had been excited about this plan, but neither had objected either. Jeremy assumed it was because they thought the dramatic gesture was brilliant, but in reality, they both had enough curiosity about Edith's reaction to agree.

Edith had been so absorbed that she hadn't noticed the movements, which is exactly what Jeremy had guessed would happen. But he had never imagined she would faint with shock. He was mortified to have caused his aunt such fright and moved again to go to her, but John gave him a look that made him take his seat again.

John probably would have been at her side himself if he could move faster, but he couldn't. Another gift the stroke had left him was a slight tremor in his gait which prevented speedy movement. But the look on Peter's face as he watched Edith read May's introduction also compelled him to stay where he was. He saw clearly, for the first time, the lines of a triangle, faint but certain, between three old and fast friends. He imagined Edith falling into that triangle, where she was caught by the steady hands of Peter. You or I might guess John felt jealousy or anger, or at least some level of discomfort, with watching this scene, but we would be wrong. John felt comforted.

Being several years older than Edith, and in undeniably declining health, John had been worrying about leaving his wife alone. Of course, she had Ella, but Ella's life was in Montreal, and she had her niece and nephew, but they were busy with their own lives. Their contemporaries consisted of a group of elderly, mostly infirm friends, and it was a dwindling pool. Even tonight, most of those in attendance were younger, and their older friends who had made it were not often seen, as they had been when they were young. Edith was still a vibrant, healthy woman with many years of good living left to her, God willing, and he hated to think of her alone.

Through Edith's many decades of trance work, and his own lifetime of experiences, John believed there was an order and a flow to the events of our lives. When Jeremy had approached him about having Peter become involved in things, he had known there was a reason. He remembered clearly the satisfaction he'd felt breaking Peter's nose, but he also remembered, with greater satisfaction, the wonderful partner Peter had been for Eve.

John wasn't a saint. He was very content that Peter had stayed out of the picture all these past years, whatever his reasons for doing so were. He would be the first to admit he preferred to appreciate him from a distance. But times change, circumstances change, and people change. Age brings wisdom, and with it a calming acceptance of what is. Maybe it was time for Peter and Edith to find their friendship again. At any rate, she was currently lying in his lap while Peter, calmly but firmly, called her back to consciousness. John wondered if it was a slight smile he saw play across Peter's face momentarily. Not a man prone to panic; he liked that as well.

PETER HAD SAT in the vacated seat, as Jeremy had instructed him to. He felt a bit foolish; he didn't possess the same flair for drama that his son did, but as he was seated next to Edith, something in him shifted. He took a deep breath, and, without realizing it, sighed out a wedge that had been sticking in him for quite some time. They didn't despise him; here was his old friend and he was welcome.

He looked down at the page Edith was reading and saw the passage from May. His eyes focused on the dates at the bottom. She'd had such a short life, May had, but she had packed her years well. He guessed that if she'd ever had the chance to have regrets about her life, they would have been very few. He caught a whiff of Edith, bending near her, and hiding under her perfume was a familiar scent. Maybe he was imagining it. He didn't have time to wonder, though, because she looked directly into his eyes. Her confusion, which was very clear in her face, startled him and he didn't think to smile reassuringly at her as he should have, he just looked back, suddenly a bit off-kilter himself.

And then he was catching her. She was more solid than he expected. She was very much real. He laid her head in his lap and smiled to himself before saying, "Edith, come on now, it's just me, your old friend Peter, in the flesh... Open your eyes now..." He continued to speak with kind authority until her eyes fluttered back open. He smiled at her then, a funny, crooked sort of smile, apologizing for startling her and joking that he didn't know he looked so bad.

He glanced at John, expecting him to come take over, but John was still seated across the round table and he gave Peter a slight nod, as if saying he should carry on. Peter put his large hand under Edith's head and helped lift her slowly back to a sitting position. Everyone who had seen her faint, and had waited to see she was all right, had now cleared away to give her some privacy in which to recover herself.

"Well, I seem to have fainted," Edith said with a little bit of satisfaction. "I never have before, you know?" She spoke to John, whom she had located across the table.

"Yes, dear, you certainly fainted dead away," he answered her with a smile. "There's something new to cross off your list," he added with a laugh.

Edith let out a small laugh herself and then squeezed her eyes open and shut a few times to clear away the fog.

"It's not as romantic as it looks... I feel a little nauseous," she said.

Jeremy was up and at her side with a glass of water in a moment. "Here, Aunty, have a small sip."

He raised his hand, gesturing for a waiter, and requested some bread be brought to the table right away.

Edith took a sip of the offered water and closed her eyes for a moment. When she opened them again, some of her color had returned and she slowly looked to her left to see if what she thought she remembered was true. Yes, Peter was really sitting there beside her. Gray and weathered, but unmistakably Peter.

"Hello there," she said simply. When he smiled his reply, apologizing for startling her so badly, she shook her head. "No, no, Peter, please don't apologize. I think I am perhaps the one who should be apologizing." Then she laughed for real. "Though for what I'm really not sure!" She reached out her hand, unselfconsciously, and touched his cheek.

"Yes, you are really here," she declared.

That's when she remembered what had been happening right before she fainted.

She closed her eyes again and took a few deep breaths. Everyone else at the table waited patiently for her to do whatever she was going to do next. Without opening her eyes, she reached her hands in front of her and found the book. She opened it and lifted it to her face and inhaled deeply. She loved the smell of books, old or new; they each had their own unique scent, and this book smelled of a satisfying achievement. When she opened her eyes again, they were focused directly on John. She didn't have to say anything; he could see happiness written all over her face. She would have gone to him and embraced him. In fact, she began to get up but then sat back down abruptly.

"Whew...fainting makes one...faint," she said, her voice weak.

John reached his hand across the table and she took it in both of hers, "Darling," he said, "you are so welcome. I didn't plan on all this excitement, but I guess it makes the launching of your new, brilliant book all that much more memorable."

Raising his glass, he toasted Edith. "To the love of my life and her outstanding new book." Everyone at the table toasted Edith while she beamed with happiness.

AFTER THE WHOLE process of the book's birth had been explained, with John emphasizing Jeremy's critical role, and Edith had had a chance to ask some questions and admire her work again, John said, "Take a look at page five." Edith dutifully turned to page five and began reading.

Edith Tate has played a revolutionary role in the realm of mind awareness. She discovered, as a young woman, her own methods for bringing about what is currently called hypnosis. Through the methods of a true, though untrained, scientist, she found paths of healing using these special methods, and then made a career of helping women in various forms of ill health regain their lives. I had the privilege of being her friend at that pivotal time in her history, when she was making her explorations, and it is with great honor that I can recommend this book to health professionals, individuals interested in their own healing, or anyone with a curious mind.

Peter Harris

August 1932

With shining eyes, she turned to her old friend again to acknowledge the praise he had given and also the things he hadn't said. "Thank you, Peter, that is a lovely tribute."

He surprised everyone by becoming flustered. "Well, I don't know, I'm not much of a writer myself," he fumbled before regaining his composure. "It's a terrific book, Edith, and I'm truly honored to be able to introduce it for you. Congratulations."

Feeling stronger, Edith rose and first gave Peter a hug, then Jeremy, and then she asked her husband for another dance.

JEREMY WAS RELIEVED to have that part of the evening over. When he'd planned it, he had imagined Edith with surprise and pleasure literally bubbling up from within her, and if he was perfectly honest, also gratitude to her nephew for doing such a fine job. He had never imagined her fainting with shock. Nowhere had that been part of his vision for the evening. He supposed, though, watching her dance with his uncle now, that it had all turned out well anyway.

And Peter was right. It was a good book. The publisher had been very optimistic about its distribution opportunities, but more importantly, it had already been reviewed quite favorably by several reputable scientific journals as adding valuable insight to the field of psychotherapy. He had collected letters from a few of these journals which John would share with Edith later.

Elliot and Julianne had gone home so the housekeeper wouldn't have to stay too late, and Sarah had excused herself and joined them. She had never been one for late nights and large social gatherings. Jeremy had enjoyed a few dances with her and then kissed her goodnight.

He looked at his watch now, wondering why Ella hadn't yet arrived. John had taken him aside early in the evening to let him know the maître d' had passed on her telephone message that she had been detained and not to hold up the unveiling of the book, but he had expected her to be here by now.

He went to get another drink from the bar, which was the main reason, he suspected, why several of the men had stayed after sending their wives home. A female hand laid itself on his arm and the voice that accompanied it asked for a gin fizz. Jeremy grinned and turned to embrace Ella.

"Well done, cous! You managed to miss all the excitement," he greeted her. "What kept you?"

When he released her and held her back for a good look, it was his turn to be shocked. Lovely Ella had grown into a middle-aged woman. Of course she had, but we all imagine our first loves as being frozen in time, and Jeremy was no different.

She was still beautiful, but in a stately way; gone was the blatant, girlish sexuality, replaced by a more womanly confidence and sensuality. She smiled, knowingly, at him. "Train delays," she said simply. "What did I miss?"

Jeremy filled her in on her father's dizzy spell earlier that evening followed by her mother's fainting turn at the book unveiling. He assured her they were both doing well when he saw a look of concern shadow her smile.

"Come on, I'll take you to them."

They took their drinks to the table, where Ella greeted her mother and father. She was introduced to Peter, whom she realized, with astonishment, she had never met before.

"Well, it's so very nice to meet Jeremy's father...finally," she said laughing.

Peter gave her a warm smile as he took her small hand in his two large ones and said, "It is a pleasure, Ella."

Edie showed her the book and Ella spent several minutes admiring it.

"It turned out lovely," she said to Jeremy. He had sent her a rough copy the month before, thinking she would like to read it before coming down for the festivities.

"I'm so proud of you, Mama," she said, giving Edith a warm hug, and then she surprised all of them by saying she had made plans to stay in Boston, with her parents, through Easter.

"After reading your book, I realized there is so much I want to know."

Ella had left home so young. She was realizing that her parents weren't getting any younger, and she wanted to know them better. She felt a longing to spend time with them...before it was too late.

Edith took her hand now, beaming at John. "I can't think of anything I would like better," she said, once again wiping at her eyes.

Ella had developed an enchanting French accent over the years and a short time later Jeremy felt himself growing pleasantly drowsy listening to her regale them all with stories about her life and her family.

Without being aware it was happening, he slipped into a trance state, while Edith watched it happen. She knew that look well and she realized with a deep pleasure that her daughter possessed her talent. Triangles intersected as her entire life shifted again into the circular.

She felt the presence of May and Eveline, her mother and father, Dr. and Mrs. Dupre, all there with her that night. The veil was stretched thin and knew her beloved would be joining them shortly, and she, herself, would follow as surely as night follows day. The incandescent shadow beckoned.

Acknowledgements

I would like to acknowledge my muse. I didn't know I had her until this book began to write itself, providing me an amazing and gratifying experience. She is a cherished enigma. I'm grateful to Gordon Boyd, my hypnotherapy teacher and mentor. I'm thankful for the characters who told me their stories, and for the space I had in my life to write them. My family has always encouraged me in all my endeavors, which has led to a rich life of trying new things and believing in myself.

About the Author

Chris Twigg lives near the shores of northern Lake Michigan. She is a healer, hypnotherapist and writer, along with being a mother, wife, and friend. She is an advocate of truth, honesty, and reason and believes in speaking her mind. Travel, good stories, nature and solitude fill her soul; feminism, politics, and equality fuel her fire.

Email: iamtwigg@yahoo.com

Website: www.christinetwigg.com

Facebook: www.facebook.com/chris.twigg.58

Twitter: @Christwigg7

Also Available from NineStar Press

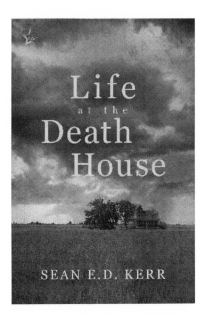

Connect with NineStar Press

Website: NineStarPress.com

Facebook: NineStarPress

Facebook Reader Group: NineStarNiche

Twitter: @ninestarpress

Tumblr: NineStarPress